"You can move in with Chad Foster tonight."

Jenna gasped. Had she heard correctly? Her mouth opened but nothing came out.

The police chief continued. "We'll let the stalker... this Rose...whoever she is, think he has a new live-in relationship. What do you think, Mr. Foster?"

"Fine with me." Chad's voice was low and Jenna was sure she saw a gleam in his eye.

"I'm not really comfortable with this, sir." Jenna finally found her voice.

The chief's eyes narrowed. "Are you turning down the assignment, Sergeant?"

"No, sir. It's just..."

"Just nothing. ███████████████████ as a nanny and m██████████████████ got a kidnapping th█████████

Jenna suppre██████████████████ally. Living with C████████ was hardly the same as spending time with a four-year-old child. Chad was dangerous—attractive, appealing and sexy. How would she reconcile her responsibilities as a police officer with her feelings as a woman? One thing she knew for sure, Chad Foster wasn't going to be any help.

ABOUT THE AUTHOR

After introducing the Foster family in *The Reluctant Hunk*
(Harlequin Temptation #523), Lorna Michaels wanted to
write a story about Chad, the oldest brother. A chance
conversation about how much of ourselves we reveal without being aware of it inspired *The Reluctant Bodyguard*.
The story is set in Houston, Texas, where Lorna lives
with her husband and four cats. She loves to hear from
readers. Write to Lorna at P.O. Box 31400, Houston,
Texas, 77231-1400.

Lorna Michaels

The Reluctant Bodyguard

Harlequin Books

TORONTO • NEW YORK • LONDON
AMSTERDAM • PARIS • SYDNEY • HAMBURG
STOCKHOLM • ATHENS • TOKYO • MILAN
MADRID • WARSAW • BUDAPEST • AUCKLAND

ISBN 0-373-70633-2

THE RELUCTANT BODYGUARD

Copyright © 1995 by Thelma Zirkelbach.

This edition published by arrangement with Harlequin Enterprises B.V.

® and TM are trademarks of the publisher. Trademarks indicated with ® are registered in the United States Patent and Trademark Office, the Canadian Trade Marks Office and in other countries.

Printed in U.S.A.

To Lucy Grijalva
And in memory of Officer Bill Grijalva
whose warmth and generosity
touched a whole community of writers

Special thanks to Lieutenant Ronnie Hill,
Nashville Police Department
and to Betsy Kaufman for technical information

CHAPTER ONE

THE ENVELOPE LAY unopened on Chad Foster's desk. He recognized the handwriting; by now it was disturbingly familiar.

He'd tried to ignore the letter throughout his busy day, but his eyes had kept returning to it. Thoughts of it hovered in his mind, distracting him, worrying him like a swarm of pesky gnats.

Now, as he sat at his desk with May-evening sunlight streaming through the window, he turned to the letter again. It seemed to lure him like an apparition lurking in shadows. He reached for the envelope, ripped it open, and drew out a single sheet of cheap drugstore stationery, flimsy white paper decorated with a garish red rose.

Dear Chad,
You didn't do what I told you. I know. I watch your news show every night. So don't pretend you did and I didn't see. I'm tired of waiting, sitting in front of the TV for nothing. You can't treat me like dirt anymore. I won't put up with it. You know what's planned for us. We were meant to be together for all time. So, do what I say and don't disappoint me again. The rules have changed. You have one last chance.

Rose, your phantom lover

He'd received the first letter a month ago, the second a week later. Since then there'd been . . . four? Five? He'd been too busy to count.

The first letter had sounded like someone's idea of a joke; a gushing fan letter in careful, schoolgirl script saying how handsome he was—his eyes the bluest, his mouth the most kissable. The thought had crossed his mind that his sister, an irrepressible prankster, might have written it. He'd left it on his desk, planning to pen a suitably effusive reply. Then, when he'd read it again, he'd decided the note wasn't quite Ariel's style, and he'd tossed it in a drawer and forgotten it. Until the second letter arrived.

In it Rose informed Chad they were destined for one another and begged for a sign that he understood.

With each note, Rose's messages grew more bizarre, her handwriting less legible. The letters no longer seemed so harmless. They began to take on the tone of a woman obsessed.

Who could be writing them, and why? Most important of all, why now?

His desk was piled with messages, memos, notes. Only five months into his new position as manager of Houston's Channel 6, he was working hard to put his personal stamp on the largest and busiest station in his family's radio-television chain.

Now, halfway through sweeps month, he had too much on his mind to deal with a bunch of crank letters written by God-knew-who. In what was becoming a too-frequent gesture, he massaged his neck, trying vainly to loosen stress-tightened muscles.

What should he do? Still working at his neck, he came to a decision. He reached for the phone and punched in the number of the Houston Police Department.

"Chief Macauley, please."

A moment later, the voice of Ed "Buster" Macauley, an old family friend, boomed across the wire.

"Buster, this is Chad Foster."

Buster's voice warmed. "Chad! What can I do for you?"

"How about meeting me for a drink this evening?"

"Something on your mind, son?"

"A small matter. I'd like to get your opinion on it."

Buster paused, then said, "Monday's my poker night, but we don't get started till nine. Meet me in half an hour at the Lancaster."

Chad pulled Rose's notes from his drawer, dropped them in his briefcase, and left his office, already feeling better. He trusted Buster's judgment. The chief would glance at these crazy letters, advise Chad to dump them in File Thirteen, and then they'd have a good laugh over them—he hoped.

Thirty minutes later, he entered the Lancaster Grille, a quiet downtown restaurant, and spotted Buster Macauley immediately. The police chief sat at an out-of-the-way table, but the man himself was anything but unobtrusive. Large and florid-faced, with a massive chest and shoulders, he still looked like the football lineman he'd once been.

He shoved a chair out when Chad reached his table. "Have a seat, son."

The waitress appeared, and Chad ordered a Scotch on the rocks. The chief grimaced at that and took a sip from a glass Chad knew held bourbon. Buster licked his lips, put his glass down and turned shrewd eyes on Chad. "What's the problem?"

"I've been getting letters. I don't know what to make of them so I'd like you to take a look at them. They're probably nothing." As he handed over the papers and watched Buster read them, Chad took a deep breath. He was a man who was rarely nervous, but the notes, especially this last one, made him uneasy, and that angered him. He detested weakness, especially in himself.

Surely any minute now, Buster would look up and let out his trademark belly laugh, and that would be the end of the letters—wouldn't it?

Instead, Buster perused the notes carefully, then stacked them neatly on the table and turned to Chad. "How long have you been getting these?"

Chad felt a flicker of alarm at the chief's sober expression and serious tone. He wasn't "good ol' Uncle Buster" at this moment; he was a cop. Chad shrugged. "Maybe a month."

"Any phone calls?"

Chad shook his head.

"Gifts?"

"No."

"Any indication someone's been in your office or your home?"

"Good Lord, no. Come on, Chief, you don't think—"

Buster tapped a stubby finger on the pile of notes. "I think you'd better treat these as a threat."

Chad realized Buster's response was what he'd expected, even as he'd hoped for a different one. He also recognized that he was furious. "Damn it, I don't have time for threats. I have Channel 9 breathing down my neck, I have an anchorman who's a prima donna, two producers baring their fangs at one another, a local businessman who wants his own show, and now you're telling me some crazy is out to get me."

"That's about the size of it," Macauley said. He signaled to the waitress and ordered another round for them both.

"I'm not finished with mine," Chad objected.

"You'll need another by the time we get through." Buster waited until the waitress left the table, then spread the notes out in front of them. "Son, these are serious. See how the style of the letters changes over time?"

"I've noticed that," Chad muttered.

"Look here in the second letter. 'We were meant to live...and *die* together.' I don't like the sound of that."

Neither did Chad.

"I guess you don't have any idea where these are coming from," Buster said.

"Not a clue."

Eyes narrowed, Buster gave Chad a thorough once-over. "Good-lookin' guy like you probably attracts a lot of fans, the kinds that get obsessed with movie stars or rock singers."

"I'm hardly a movie star or a rock singer," Chad scoffed.

"No, but you might be close enough for a person with an overactive imagination. On the other hand, this could be from someone who wants to harass you. Doesn't take too long to develop enemies, especially when you editorialize on the air like you do. I saw your piece last month on the proposal to locate a halfway house for parolees near Montrose. Lots of residents in that area wouldn't feel too neighborly toward a bunch of felons. Lots of 'em are damn angry."

Chad nodded. "I may make some people mad, but I have to speak out for what I believe in." He leaned forward. "We *have* to start rehabilitating ex-convicts, not just turning them out on the streets. They need a way to reenter society with jobs, education— Hell," he said, sitting back in his chair, "why am I telling you this? You, of all people, understand."

"I agree with you a hundred percent, son. I'm just pointing out that you've set off some fireworks, and when you do that, you take a chance of getting burned."

Chad picked up the drink he'd just set down, then realized he'd emptied the glass. Buster had been right. Chad did need another Scotch. He picked up the second glass and took a healthy gulp. "This Rose doesn't sound angry, it's more like she's loony."

"I'm inclined to agree," the older man said. "I want you to talk to one of my lieutenants, Nate Harris." He checked his watch. "Nate should be home by now." The chief pulled a cellular phone from his briefcase and dialed. He gave the lieutenant background on the situation, then said, "Nine, tomorrow morning. He'll be there. And put Wakefield on this one. Right."

He hung up, gathered the notes and put them away, along with the phone. "Harris and Wakefield are the best. Both of them have had experience with stalkers."

Chad's hand froze in midair. "Stalkers?" The word brought a menacing picture to mind: a nameless person trailing him, watching, listening. Intruding on his privacy. Taking over his life.

The chief nodded. "No use mincing words. That's what this shapes up to be. But they'll get right on it. If anyone can handle this, they can."

"Did I hear an if?"

Buster nodded. "I have to be honest with you. Stalkers aren't easy to apprehend. But let's not jump the gun until my experts have a look at this."

"All right." Chad noted Buster's surreptitious glance at his watch and signaled for the check. "You'd better get to your poker game. Look," he added as they rose and he tossed some bills on the table, "I know you'll see Dad to-

night. There's no point in worrying him about this...
situation."

"Sure," the chief replied. They left the restaurant and
waited in front for the parking attendant to bring their
cars. "I'll keep it quiet, unless it escalates."

"Escalates," Chad muttered as Buster drove off. Chad
felt a chill; the chief was obviously taking this very seriously.

His own car pulled up. He got in and drove to the town
house he was leasing while his new home was being completed. He wanted to give in to his anger and frustration,
longed to slam down the accelerator and let the Porsche
have its way, but he kept a tight rein on his emotions and
on the car.

At home, he tried to read a newsmagazine but couldn't
concentrate. With an oath, he flung it onto the floor, went
to his bedroom, and changed into shorts, T-shirt, and
running shoes. He stepped outside into the balmy May
darkness and began to run, forcing himself to focus on the
swinging of his arms, the pounding of his feet, the sound
of his breath.

When he returned, he was bathed in sweat and breathing hard, but some of his tension had dissipated. He
showered and, not bothering with clothes, went into the
living room and flipped on the big-screen TV. Yellow legal pad in hand, he settled down to watch the ten o'clock
news.

Now he had no trouble putting Rose and her letters out
of his mind. He focused, evaluated, made notes on every
aspect of the newscast. Too much time spent on a trivial
story about a traffic tie-up on Loop 610; not enough meat
in the segment about a city administrator who'd been
caught with his fingers in the till. The station had a re-

sponsibility to come down hard on public corruption. If the news media didn't act as watchdogs, who would?

Mitchell Nabors, the anchor, turned the mike over to sports commentator, Calvin "Tank" Diamond. A recently retired football star, Tank was out to make a second career in broadcasting. He'd been popular as a player; he was proving to be equally well-liked on television.

On his last item, Tank stumbled over the name of Nick Petrovich, the newest addition to the Houston Astros' baseball lineup, a rookie brought up just yesterday from the Astros' farm club. No big deal, Chad thought, but Nabors apparently thought otherwise. He looked down his nose at Tank as the camera swung back to him. "That's Pet-ro-vich, not Pee-tro-vich," he said, as if he were an instructor admonishing a bumbling student.

Chad winced. In addition to embarrassing Tank, Mitchell's behavior was the surest way Chad knew to encourage viewers to switch channels. Viewers wanted warm, avuncular newscasters. Chad had talked to Nabors before about his on-camera arrogance, but nothing had changed. Chad would have to speak to the man again and remind him that if he didn't follow Chad's recommendations this time he would be replaced. After all, there were plenty of others who'd be thrilled to step into his shoes.

Chad watched the rest of the newscast, turned off the TV and went to bed. Despite his irritation with Nabors, he felt relaxed. The run and the familiar routine of analyzing the news show had soothed him. But just before he fell asleep, he heard Buster's voice again, and the word *stalker* reverberated in his mind.

THE NEXT MORNING he rose early as was his habit. Half an hour on his NordicTrack while the 6:00 a.m. news blared from the bedroom TV; then, after a shower and shave, he was on his way to the station. Without waiting for his secretary to arrive, he turned on the coffeemaker, rescheduled a couple of meetings and began drafting a memo to Tina Parker, the evening news-show producer, about last night's broadcast.

He looked up when the door opened. His secretary, Catherine Paige, entered the office with a cup of coffee in one hand and an envelope in the other. She set the steaming mug on his desk and handed him the letter. He started to lay it aside, then glanced at it more closely. Another one.

"Catherine, where'd this come from?"

She flinched at his sharp tone. "Nancy Bayliss dropped it off. She found it in a stack on the assignments desk. It was probably there a couple of days, she said. I hope it wasn't important."

"No, not important."

He waited until Catherine left, then opened the envelope.

Dear Chad,
I watched you on the news tonight . . .

That meant the letter had been written at least five days ago, probably before the last one he'd received. He continued reading.

You smiled at Danielle Anderson when you came on. Don't you know what that does to me? I can tell by the way she looks at you that she's in love with you, but I bet you didn't know, did you? I know you don't care for her, not the way you do for me. Don't worry. We won't let Danielle or any of the others stand in our way. We'll do whatever we have to. I've been thinking maybe you should get rid of Danielle—I mean, get her off the news show, maybe even out of Houston. If she stays close to you, she might get ideas and then I'd have to make her sorry. You and I have to live out our destiny and we can't put up with any pushy news reporter interfering. We'll be happy in the house you're building. I want the kitchen painted yellow....

The letter rambled on for several more paragraphs, ending with Rose's familiar plea that he acknowledge her on television.

Chad kept flipping back to the first paragraph. How in hell did Rose know he was building a house? God, this was escalating already.

Suddenly, from the mists of childhood memory, came the recollection of a recurrent dream he'd had when he was seven or eight. Someone was following him, someone dark and menacing. He could never see his pursuer, but he could feel hot breath on the back of his neck, hear footsteps behind him coming closer and closer. He'd wake up shaking, imagining eerie figures crouched in the corner of his room. He'd never told anyone about those dreams; he'd been too ashamed. He felt the same icy terror now. And, damn it, he was awake.

Ridiculous. He was being paranoid. The police would take care of the situation. Harris and Wakefield were the best, Buster had said. And now he'd get down to the station and put matters in their capable hands. Chad stuffed the letter into his jacket pocket and told Catherine he'd be gone for a while.

AT NINE-FIFTEEN he sat drumming his fingers on the arms of an uncomfortable wooden chair outside Nate Harris's office. The lieutenant was late, and when a schedule was as crowded as Chad's, fifteen minutes was precious. If he hadn't received this morning's letter, he'd have seriously considered walking out.

At last the office door opened and the lieutenant came out. A large, balding man, he surpassed Chad's six feet by several inches, and probably outweighed him by thirty pounds. He shook hands with Chad and gestured him inside a small office, furnished in bureaucratic drab—a cluttered gray metal desk, brown vinyl chairs. The only spot of color was a map of the city stapled to the grimy, finger-marked wall with pushpins stuck in various locations.

The phone rang and Harris took the call. Chad clenched his jaw. Damn, this was going to take all morning. He tried to distract himself by studying a photograph of the lieutenant's family displayed on a battered metal file cabinet—a slender, dark-eyed wife, two strapping sons, and a ferocious-looking German shepherd. Behind the photograph were several bowling trophies and another picture, this one of a Little League team in full regalia. His survey of Harris's office did nothing to curb his impatience.

Harris hung up the phone. "Sorry," he said. "Busy day." He nodded to the notes on his desk. "Chief Macauley showed me your letters. Any idea who sent them?"

Chad shook his head. "My secretary gave me another one this morning. It apparently came several days ago but got lost in interoffice mail." He handed over the envelope and watched closely as Harris read it.

The lieutenant set the letter down and looked up, but before he could comment, a brisk knock sounded on the door. "That'll be Sergeant Wakefield. Come in," Harris called, and the door opened.

Chad turned and met the eyes of the woman framed in the doorway.

Automatically, he rose and smiled at her. Dressed in standard police-blue, she was tall and trim, with mahogany brown hair pulled back in a thick braid. She stepped forward and he caught a whiff of an enticing floral perfume.

"This is Chad Foster," Harris said. "Mr. Foster, Sergeant Jenna Wakefield."

"Hello," he murmured.

"Hello," she responded and put out her hand.

He took it and looked into her eyes. Thickly lashed, wide and velvet brown, they focused on him, captured and held him. For a moment he stood transfixed, unable to tear his gaze away. Even in his present state of agitation, he couldn't help responding to this woman with the bewitching eyes and a scent like heaven. Finally, he dragged his gaze from her, resumed his seat and focused on Harris.

"I want you to take a look at some letters Mr. Foster has received," Harris told the sergeant as she sat down. He handed her the stack of notes, and she read them, seeming to shut out everything else as she studied each one.

Chad watched her as she examined Rose's notes. Her features were ordinary. If he passed her on the street, he doubted he'd notice her...unless he looked into those incredible eyes.

Her intensity and concentration as she read the letters appealed to him. She seemed to read between the lines, as if she could ferret out Rose's every secret. Chad was used to sizing up people quickly. Instinctively, he felt he could count on Jenna Wakefield. Then, as she absentmindedly toyed with her braid, he found his thoughts veering in a different direction. Found himself wondering how her hair would look unbound, how it would feel.

"Your correspondent talks about seeing you on television. Are you a news reporter?" she asked. Her voice was low-pitched, throaty. A midnight voice.

"Mr. Foster is the manager of Channel 6," Harris said.

She scrutinized Chad thoroughly. He saw curiosity, then faint disapproval. "I didn't think station managers went on the air," she said.

"I do occasional editorials."

"Mmm."

She obviously didn't recognize him from his television appearances. Chad felt a twinge of disappointment. "Don't you watch Channel 6?" he asked.

She shrugged. "Sometimes."

"It's the best station in town. I'll send you a program guide."

The sergeant ignored his teasing tone. She nodded toward Rose's letters. "I don't like the looks of these. Either a fan has fixated on you or someone wants to scare you to death."

"I've asked Mr. Foster if he has any thoughts about who the letter writer might be," Harris said, "but he doesn't."

"This comment about the house you're building," the sergeant said, "indicates it's someone who knows you personally." She leaned toward him to point out the sentence. "Who've you talked to about your house?"

He shrugged, a rush of frustration tightening his muscles. "I've mentioned the house to at least a hundred people. Look," he continued, disappointed that these working police officers hadn't disagreed with Buster's assessment of the letters and assured him the notes weren't significant, "how serious do you think this situation is?"

"Extremely serious," Jenna Wakefield answered without hesitation. "People who write these kinds of notes are mentally unbalanced. They can turn violent—attack, even kill, the focus of their obsession. These letters don't sound like a joke, Mr. Foster. Rose has already begun making threats. I wouldn't advise you to disregard them."

Her businesslike voice, devoid of emotion, made her words all the more ominous. Chad felt a chill skitter down his spine and was reminded again of his childhood dream. "What do you suggest I do?" he asked.

"We'll need to investigate. Sergeant Wakefield will get started on it immediately," Harris said.

Shock registered on the sergeant's face. "But—"

"Chief Macauley wants the best on this case," Harris added, giving her a loaded glance.

Chad saw from the way she stiffened and glared at Harris that working on this case was the last thing Sergeant Wakefield wanted. But he'd already decided he wanted her. He didn't have the patience to deal with second best. Nor did he have the time, he added, thinking of the minutes that were slipping away, the work that waited for him at the station. He ignored the sergeant's obvious distaste for his case and said, "Give me an estimate as to how long it could take to wrap up this case."

"Cases like this are never quick," she replied. "Stalkers operate on their own timetables."

Chad didn't like the sound of that. "I'm counting on you to speed things up."

The sergeant opened her mouth, then snapped it shut and shot him an angry look. He waited silently.

"All right, Mr. Foster," she said at last. "I'll get started on your case, but I'm in the middle of something else now. I can see you in an hour."

Damn. He didn't have another hour to spend this morning, even with this sergeant with the mesmerizing brown eyes. "How about tomorrow?"

"Sorry, it'll have to be today. One hour, Mr. Foster." She gave him directions to her office, stood, and headed for the door.

JENNA MARCHED BACK to her office, fuming. Just what she needed—a spoiled rich boy, buddies with the chief. He'd demand more of her time than she cared to spend, time needed for serious police work. Not that the letters he'd received weren't serious. But catching stalkers wasn't her responsibility; hadn't been for some time.

She sniffed, thinking of the man she'd just met, in his tailored suit with the Rolex on his wrist. She'd known others of his class, and he was just like the rest. Too confident, too pushy, too...gorgeous.

Before she had time to reflect on that thought, she heard a voice. "Hey, Jenna."

She turned as her friend Graciela Rios, who was assigned to the Family Violence Unit, hailed her from the coffee machine.

"Hi, Gracie." Jenna crossed the room. She didn't have time for coffee and conversation, not with the way this morning was going, but suddenly she very much needed both. She'd told Foster she was busy and she was, but a five-minute break couldn't hurt. She dug in her pocket for change, shoved it in the slot and waited for the cup to fill.

"Guess what?" Graciela said, her brown eyes sparkling with excitement.

"Hmm?"

"Remember my friend Maria? I went with her to her parents' house for dinner last night, and who should be there but her long-lost brother, Jorge. He's moved back to Houston."

"Is that important?" Jenna asked, as they headed for one of three white metal tables clustered in the corner by the vending machines.

Gracie pulled out a chair, wiped off the tabletop with a napkin and said, "I was crazy about him in high school, sorta worshiped him from afar. Well, he's still single, still gorgeous." She fluffed her short-cropped black hair with a slender hand. "And I am currently unattached."

"And that's unusual," Jenna said, chuckling. Gracie, sharp, pretty and full of life, attracted men like a flame did moths. No one seemed to hold her attention for long. She'd ease herself out of a relationship, remaining on friendly terms, then flit to the next. Jorge was probably in for the standard treatment. "Is he interested?" Jenna asked.

Gracie grinned. "Not yet, but I'm working on it."

"More to the point, how interested are you?"

Gracie's smile was dreamy. "Very." She watched as Jenna stirred her coffee aimlessly. "What's going on with you? You look like the queen of gloom this morning."

"I've just had extra work dumped on me."

"Yeah? So what's new?"

Jenna shrugged. "Nothing. But I'm not happy."

"I can see that," her friend said. "Want to get it off your chest?"

Jenna glanced at her watch. "Yeah." She grabbed an extra packet of sugar and dumped it in her cup. "Macauley tossed a case in my lap. Local celebrity's been getting love notes and I'm supposed to track down the alleged fanatic who's writing them." She took a sip of coffee, wrinkled her nose, and continued. "Can you believe it? I've been on Juvenile for over a year, and the chief just up and decides he needs me on this. And of course, when the chief speaks, we listen."

Gracie frowned. "You ought to be flattered. Macauley probably remembered what a good job you did on the cases you handled in the past."

"Yeah, I suppose. Maybe I'd appreciate the honor if I weren't up against a stone wall in the Morales case. The kid's still missing after two weeks and we're out of leads."

Gracie put a comforting hand on Jenna's arm. "Tough."

"Yeah. I'm afraid if we do find him, the news won't be good." She swallowed the lump that welled up in her throat. She'd been involved with police work all her life, first as the daughter of a cop, then as an officer herself; but no matter how experienced you were, you never became inured to cases like the Morales one. A ten-year-old kid on his way to the mailbox around the corner had just ... disappeared.

Jenna took a deep breath. "How can I concentrate on baby-sitting some celebrity? I *have* to find Nicolas Morales before time runs out."

"You're doing your best," Graciela said.

"My best isn't always good enough."

"I know what you're thinking," her friend said, "but no one's ever faulted you for the Sullivan case."

Jenna took a last swallow of coffee and crushed the cup. "*I* have."

"You shouldn't." Graciela sat quietly for a moment, then said, "Tell me about the celebrity."

Grateful to her friend for the change of subject, Jenna shoved the letters across the table.

Gracie scanned them. "So who's Chad?"

"Chad Foster. Television bigwig. Manager of Channel 6."

Graciela considered for a moment. "Is he the kind of guy who'd attract one of those crazies?"

"I suppose. He's in his thirties, I guess. About six feet tall, tanned, well-built. You know the type—probably has a gym at the house. Blond hair—kinda sun-streaked— dark blue eyes, almost indigo. Expensive clothes, the kind that look like they were made for him."

"You noticed all that, huh?"

"Of course," Jenna said. "Being observant's my job."

"Mmm, this is a lot more detailed than 'white male, no distinguishing marks.'"

With a grimace of disgust, Jenna pushed her crushed coffee cup aside. "What does that mean?"

"Nothing," Gracie said airily. "Just that this case must've made an impression."

"Oh, he did. He impressed me as a guy who's used to giving orders and having people jump. He actually had the nerve to tell me he wanted this situation handled quickly. He's already used his connections with the chief to cut in at the head of the line." She jerked a napkin out of the holder in the center of the table and swiped at her mouth. "I know those kinds of people with their money and their charm," she muttered. "I could tell you stories...." She thought of Ken, her first serious boyfriend, a perfect example of rich and charming. She remembered the day someone had backed into his Mustang. He'd been furious as he examined the crushed fender, and Jenna had tried to calm him. "The damage isn't too bad. You can take it to a body shop and it'll be good as new."

"But it won't be the same," he insisted, then turned away. "I'll talk to my dad." He did, and within a week a brand-new Mustang replaced the dented car.

He'd replaced her just as easily when she failed to meet his standards.

Gracie cleared her throat. "Sounds to me like your gripe is with Chief Macauley. But you know how he is. He's always handing out favors to his cronies."

"Favors that'll take hours of *my* time to handle, not his."

"But you'll spend them."

"Yes, I will. I'll go over everything on Chad Foster, down to the last detail."

"Because you're a conscientious person," Graciela agreed, getting up. She removed the remains of Jenna's cup and her own and headed for the trash can. "Gotta get back to work. Feel like going to the movies this weekend?"

"Sure. We can pig out on popcorn with lots of butter and have a pizza afterward."

Gracie made a face. "And then run five miles. I'll call you and we'll get together, *if* you have time between Morales and Foster." She paused for a moment, then grinned. "And if Jorge doesn't come through with a better offer."

Jenna watched her friend saunter off, then crossed the room to the cubicle she referred to as her office. With barely enough space for a desk, a file cabinet, and a couple of straight chairs, it could pass for a closet. She reached behind her and flipped on her tape player—background music helped her concentrate.

She picked up a thick manila folder on her desk and opened it. A school picture of Nicolas Morales was stapled to the inside cover. A bright-eyed kid in a Houston Astros T-shirt, with a gap-toothed little-boy grin and tousled black hair. His face haunted her, waking her in the darkest hours of the night. His mother's voice rang in her ears. "Please, Sergeant, find my boy."

I'm trying, Jenna thought. *I'm just not making any headway.* No, she was running around like a hamster on a wheel, going over the same territory again and again. A groan escaped her lips. She was losing her objectivity, losing her confidence. Stop it, she ordered herself. She took a long breath and got to work.

A neighbor, the last person known to have seen Nicolas Morales, had come in yesterday. She'd been questioned extensively before, but Jenna had called her in again in hopes that some additional small fact, some telling detail, might surface. Nothing had. All the woman could remember was that Nicolas had waved at her as he'd turned the corner toward the mailbox. "Such a friendly boy," she'd said. "Everyone in the neighborhood liked him." Had Nicolas proved too friendly for his own good that fateful afternoon?

Jenna put her elbows on the desk and covered her face with her hands. Was there anything she hadn't done? Any stone she'd left unturned? She and the other officers assigned to this case had questioned scores of people—Nick's family, schoolmates, neighbors. They'd searched the area between the Morales home and the mailbox and found nothing—no sign of a struggle, no shreds of clothing, not even a button. They'd been forced to conclude that the youngster must have been abducted by someone he knew.

Maybe she'd try another neighbor; maybe she'd find a classmate who'd heard the boy talking about his after-school plans. She prayed she wasn't grasping at straws.

Time passed as she made more calls, asking questions and taking notes. This afternoon she'd drive by the scene again, even though she felt she knew every blade of grass, every crack in the sidewalk.

She looked up and saw Chad Foster outside her office, waiting. One of the technicians from the crime lab was out there, too, and they were talking to one another. Foster smiled at the young woman; her cheeks flushed. He was flirting with her, Jenna thought, and she was loving every minute of it.

Jenna got up and opened the door. "Yes, Pat?"

Reluctantly, the technician turned from Foster. "I have information for you on the O'Rourke case."

"Okay, come in." Jenna glanced at Foster. "I'll be with you in a few minutes."

The two women went into Jenna's office. While Jenna opened the folder she'd brought, Pat stared through the glass, her eyes fixed on Chad Foster. "Cute," she murmured.

Jenna ignored the comment. *Too cute,* she thought. She looked up and saw Foster check his watch and frown. The man had a serious problem, so she guessed he had a right to be edgy. But his attitude riled her, and she couldn't stop the thought that lodged in her mind: *Impatient, Foster? Try looking for a missing kid, then see how impatient you'd get.*

SERGEANT WAKEFIELD had left him cooling his heels for a good hour and a half. He'd already rescheduled two appointments and postponed a production meeting. His day was melting away like ice cubes in a Houston heat wave. Chad cursed Rose, the chief of police, and Lieutenant Harris, not to mention the sergeant herself.

It was obvious she hadn't liked the idea of working on his case, hadn't liked *him* for some reason; but if they were going to work together, they'd have to get along. He was skilled in dealing with people. Surely he could establish an amicable relationship with Jenna Wakefield.

Feeling someone's gaze, he looked up to see her standing in the doorway of her office. He masked his irritation with a smile. "I was beginning to think you'd vanished."

Sergeant Wakefield didn't return his smile. "I was busy. Come in," she said coolly, and motioned him inside.

This was an office? If he stretched both arms, he could touch the walls, Chad thought, as he sat and tried to find a spot between the chair and her desk for his long legs. Maybe that explained the sergeant's short fuse. Being cooped up in a space this cramped couldn't be good for her disposition.

She straightened the yellow legal pad on her desk. As she leaned forward to pick up a pencil, Chad got another whiff of her perfume, stronger this time. He couldn't identify the fragrance, but it was lush, seductive. A woman with a gun at her waist, who smelled like a spring garden. Intriguing.

"I need some information," she said. "Full name first." No preamble, no pleasantries, just business.

Chad provided the personal information she requested and watched her hands as she wrote. They didn't fit his image of a cop's hands—broad with stubby fingers. Instead, hers were surprisingly delicate, with long, slender fingers of a kind most of the women he knew would have adorned with jewelry. Jenna Wakefield's fingers were bare, her unpainted nails short and neatly rounded. He supposed police officers didn't go in for ornamentation.

On the other hand, she'd added a few decorative touches to her office. A crystal paperweight provided a decided contrast to her scarred-metal desktop. Pots of African violets on the windowsill softened the stark room with their lavenders and purples. Classical music played in the background. Ravel, he noted. *Daphnis et Chloé.*

He wondered what kind of woman adorned a closet of an office with crystal and African violets; what kind of woman listened to classical music and caught crooks for a living, wore tailored police uniforms and sexy perfume that had him wondering what she had on underneath.

"Any idea who might have written these notes?" she asked.

"No." He sighed. "Harris already told you that."

If she noticed his irritation, she didn't let it show. "Anyone have it in for you? An ex-wife, maybe?"

She said it as if he had a dozen former Mrs. Fosters to his credit. "No." Marina, his one and only ex, was happily married to an up-and-coming actor and the last he'd heard, was enjoying the Hollywood scene.

"Ex-lovers?"

Was that a note of sarcasm in her voice? Forgetting his intent to pacify her, he shook his head and said, "I leave them . . . well-satisfied."

She muttered something under her breath, then asked, "How about the handwriting? Ever seen it before?"

He'd asked himself that question many times; nevertheless, he squinted at the letter she thrust across the desk. "The handwriting's not familiar."

"What about the rose? Does it mean something to you?" He shook his head, but she persisted. "Know anyone named Rose?"

"No."

"Give anyone roses?"

"On occasion. Not recently."

"Think back," she said. "When was the last time?"

"Two months ago. March fourteenth. I sent a dozen red roses . . . to my mother on her birthday."

The sergeant's eyes, which had brightened expectantly, turned cool again. "Great. Well, I'm sure your mother hasn't been writing these notes. Try the next-to-last time."

"I honestly can't remember," Chad said. "Look, Miss Wakefield—"

"*Sergeant* Wakefield."

"Look, Sergeant, I don't have a clue who might have written these notes," he said, trying to curb his irritation. The clock on the wall behind Sergeant Wakefield told him another ten minutes had passed. "How much more do you need to know? I'm on a tight schedule."

She slapped her pencil on the desk. "So am I," she said, her voice betraying her own frustration. She took a breath, then said, "If we're going to find Rose and stop her, I need to know everything about you—who you see, who you talk to, where you go. Otherwise, we're both wasting our time."

He supposed that was true. "All right."

"Get me a list of new employees, new neighbors, anyone you've met in the last couple of months."

"I moved to Houston five months ago," he said, "so I've met a lot of new people lately. The list will be long."

"Female only. The stationery and the handwriting on these notes are feminine. So's the style. We'll start there."

"It'll still be a long list."

He saw her lip start to curl and waited for a sarcastic comeback, but she said nothing except, "I'll run records checks on everyone and get back to you." She stood, dismissing him.

He was annoyed—no, he was angry. From the first minute he'd seen her, he'd responded to Sergeant Wakefield on a basic male-to-female level. He hadn't gotten any vibes back, but he could deal with that. But, hell, he was virtually putting his life in her hands. And she'd simply looked right through him as if he didn't exist. He didn't like feeling that he was just an annoyance to her, another folder to fill. He was irate enough that he felt compelled to take her down a few notches, make her respond to him as a person, not a number.

He took his time unfolding his legs from beneath the chair, and got to his feet slowly. He walked around the desk and blocked her path to the door. "I'll fax you the list this afternoon."

Deliberately, he put out his hand so she'd have to take it or appear rude. She hesitated an instant, then gave him hers. He held it longer than necessary. Though her expression didn't change, he felt the telltale jump of her pulse. Satisfied, he let her go.

He walked to the door and turned, giving her a lazy smile. "I'll wait to hear from you...Sarge." He went out and shut the door behind him.

Jenna stared at him through the glass as he strode away. She picked up the legal pad with the information he'd given her and restrained herself from hurling it after him. Instead, she tossed it in the desk and slammed the drawer shut—on her fingertip. She cursed and put the finger in her mouth.

Arrogant, she thought, watching Foster's retreating figure. He thought he could snap his fingers, order her to hurry up and find this nutty fan, and she'd have it taken care of by tomorrow. He seemed to think the whole situation was an infringement on his time. Well, what about hers?

Maybe Chad Foster was a pal of Chief Macauley, but he sure didn't know much about police work. But why should he? He was part of the media. His role was to criticize the police, not understand them. She took her finger out of her mouth and examined the nail. The way her luck was going today, it would probably turn black.

Foster had given her virtually no useful information this morning, and she was certain his list wouldn't be much help, either. Heck, anyone who watched "Headline News" on Channel 6 could be a suspect. Wonderful.

Come to think of it, she didn't like the look Foster had given her. She disliked even more the way her pulse had sped up when he'd taken her hand. Years ago she'd sworn off men like Chad Foster—rich, handsome, charming— yet something about him had gotten under her skin. She'd have to watch herself around him. Very carefully.

CHAPTER TWO

JENNA PARKED IN FRONT of the white frame house and sat for a moment, studying her surroundings, hoping this time she'd notice something significant. But she saw nothing new. The house was typical of the neighborhood—modest but well cared-for. The exterior was freshly painted, the tiny yard nicely tended. A three-year-old Chevy was parked in the drive.

This was the sort of community that was the bedrock of America, the kind of neighborhood immortalized on fifties TV shows. June and Ward Cleaver would be at home here. This wasn't the inner city; these weren't the mean streets. Children weren't supposed to disappear from here, she thought, tightening her fingers around the steering wheel.

Someone had tied a yellow ribbon to the chain-link fence. Glancing down the street, she saw other ribbons tied around tree trunks and fence posts. The neighbors wanted Nicolas home. *So do I, people,* Jenna thought. *So do I.*

A woman driving by slowed, rolled down her window and leaned out. "Any news, officer?"

"No, nothing new."

"You'll find Nick. We're counting on you."

Could they count on her? she wondered, as she nodded. She prayed their confidence wasn't misplaced.

She took a cardboard box from the front seat, got out of her car and crossed the yard. In a corner of the porch, a baseball bat sat propped against the side of the house; a catcher's mitt lay beside it. Nick's mother hadn't had the heart to move them. As long as the bat and glove were there, she'd told Jenna, she could believe Nick was coming home, pretend he was just around the corner playing at the park. But Jenna knew Mrs. Morales was losing hope, and so was she. There'd been no new leads in the past few days. Nothing.

She rang the bell and Anita Morales opened the door. In her thirties, she was a dark-eyed woman who should have been pretty. Jenna remembered the first time she'd seen Anita. She *had* been pretty then, before distress and sleeplessness had dulled her eyes and etched lines in her face.

Anita smiled faintly at Jenna. "Officer Wakefield. Any news?" Jenna shook her head and saw Anita's shoulders slump. "Come in," she said.

Jenna went into the small living room scattered with toys belonging to the two youngest Morales children. Both girls, a two-year-old and a baby, were playing on the floor. Concepción, the older child, glanced at Jenna and smiled. "Hi." By now, Jenna had been here so often, the little girl considered her a friend.

Jenna greeted the child, then turned to Anita. "We had some flyers printed. You can give them out around the neighborhood, put them up in stores." She didn't mention that she'd paid for the flyers herself.

"Will they help?" Anita asked.

"Maybe," Jenna answered, torn between wanting to offer hope and not wanting to set up false expectations. "If just one person saw Nick or has any kind of information, it could make a difference."

"I don't know." Anita sighed. "He's been gone so long. If we find him, he could be—"

"Hush," Jenna said. "Don't think it."

But Anita's face crumpled, and a sob escaped her. Jenna put an arm around the woman's thin shoulders and led her to the couch. As she held Anita, her eyes fastened on the family picture on the mantel. Five kids, Nicolas right in the middle. Slender, with curly black hair, and dark eyes alert with intelligence. *Why?* she thought, and an uncontrollable wave of anger surged through her.

Anita's shoulders shook, and Jenna pulled her closer. Anita had told her during one of their conversations that her children were her life. Though Jenna had no children of her own, she could imagine how Anita must feel. Part of that life had been cruelly snatched away. She blinked to keep from crying herself. She couldn't let her emotions show. When Anita had exhausted her supply of tears, Jenna eased away from her. "I'm going to talk to some of the kids in Nicolas's class again, the ones he was closest to."

"Sure," Anita said without conviction. "Do...do you want some coffee before you go?"

"No, thanks." Jenna stood. "Get those posters out. I'll let you know if anything turns up."

Anita nodded. She followed Jenna to the door and stood with the screen half open as Jenna walked to her car.

Jenna drove around the corner and cruised slowly past Sally Ride Park, where the neighborhood children played. Playground equipment on one side—swings, a slide, two seesaws, a jungle gym. Playing field, picnic tables on the other. All open space. No trees to conceal a kidnapper or child molester. Typical American city park—well tended, safe.

Jenna snorted. Was any place safe nowadays? Was anyone safe? This park was surrounded by homes with crisply curtained windows, bicycles in the yards, barbecue grills on the patios. No gangs here, no drug pushers. Still, a child had disappeared fifty yards from his home.

For a moment, her thoughts returned to Chad Foster. Not even a man like that could be entirely secure. No amount of power, money, or family connections could shield Foster if someone was really out to get him. But she couldn't be as concerned about him as she was about Nicolas. Foster, at least, had been warned. And he was an adult, better able to protect himself. He could even hire protection—get a bodyguard or whatever people of his class did.

People of his class, she thought crossly. The kind of people who knew the police chief personally. People who got red-carpet treatment. Chad Foster probably resented having his case given to a lowly sergeant. Maybe he'd been anxious to get out of her office so he could go back to the chief and ask for someone else. Fine. Let him. Then he'd be out of her hair—lazy smile, mesmerizing blue eyes and all.

She parked her car and walked through the park, staring at the ground. She doubted she'd find anything, didn't even know what she was looking for. All she saw were gum wrappers, tissues, an empty cigarette pack. She picked it up and turned it over in her hand. Marlboro. No clue there. The cigarette of millions of Americans. She dropped the pack and walked on.

The May afternoon was hot, still. Almost summer. *School vacation,* Jenna thought. *More kids wanting to be in the park. And if I don't crack this case soon, none of them will get to enjoy their summer.* They'd be imprisoned in their homes by their frightened parents. Damn it, she had to find Nicolas. She couldn't let people down. Not this time.

Giving up her fruitless search, she went back to her car and drove to Nicolas's school. Taking a second box from the front seat, she went inside. In the office, she signed her name on a log. Gone were the days when someone could visit a school without leaving a record. It was a sign of the times.

The secretary looked up, recognized her, and without being asked, rose to knock on the principal's door. Principal Lila Sterling, trim, gray-haired, with a pleasant smile, came out to greet Jenna. "Any news, Sergeant?"

"I'm afraid not." She shifted the box in her arms. "I brought some posters with Nicolas's picture. Maybe some of your teachers could distribute them."

"I'll see to it."

Jenna followed Mrs. Sterling into her office and said, "I'd like to talk to some of Nick's friends, see them together this time."

The principal nodded. "A good idea. Often things surface in a group, thoughts that wouldn't come up when a child is alone with an authority figure. Knowing you're with a police officer can be intimidating. Like going to the principal's office."

Jenna smiled. She liked Lila Sterling. "Here's a list of kids I'd like to see."

"I'll send for them." She went out and handed the list to the secretary with instructions to assemble the children. "Now, you'll need a room," she said to Jenna. "We'll give you the clinic. We've had a slow day—no chicken pox, no broken bones. Come with me." She showed Jenna to a small room. "I'll have the custodian bring in some chairs from the cafeteria. Good luck, Sergeant Wakefield. Let me know if anything turns up."

Jenna sat down at the desk and thought about how she would handle the session. She'd had training in dealing with children in traumatic situations but she wasn't a psychologist. God knows, she didn't want to upset them any more than she had to.

The custodian arrived with chairs and Jenna helped him arrange them in a circle in the center of the room. She imagined the children would be nervous. What they wouldn't know was that she felt the same way.

A few minutes later five youngsters filed in. Average fourth graders in scruffy sneakers, faded jeans, and T-shirts adorned with pictures of the latest superheroes, they took their seats. They shouldn't be having to meet with a police officer, Jenna thought bitterly. They should be out on the baseball field, enjoying the spring sunshine.

When they were grouped around her, she looked at the solemn faces and saw sadness and fear in every one. One little boy chewed on fingernails that were already gnawed to the quick, another shuffled his feet and refused to meet her eyes, a third tried to stifle sobs. Jenna put her hand on his shoulder. "You're Steven, aren't you? I talked to you before."

The child took a hiccuping breath and raised teary brown eyes to hers. "Is Nick dead? Is that why you called us?"

"Oh, no, honey." Jenna tightened her arm around him, praying she was telling the truth. "I asked to see you because I hoped you all could remember something Nick said or someone he talked about that would help us find him."

Steven swiped at a tear that ran down his cheek. "O-okay."

Jenna handed him a tissue and glanced around the circle. Tears shone in several pairs of eyes.

Andy Hughes, a chubby ten-year-old, fingered the Saint Christopher medal that hung around his neck. "Are...are you gonna find him, do you think?" Jenna knew he and Nicolas had been best buddies.

"I hope so," she said, giving as much reassurance as she dared. "We're trying very hard."

Ian, a blond freckle-faced boy, the one who'd sat shuffling his feet until now, took a breath. He didn't meet Jenna's eyes but stared at a grimy bandage on his finger. "My...my dad told my mom that the man who got Nick is still out there. H-he might come back."

Steven's face paled. All the boys looked at Jenna, their eyes begging for reassurance that what had befallen Nicolas wouldn't happen to them.

Let me handle this right, Jenna thought. "The best thing we can do," she told the boys, "is try to think about the afternoon Nick disappeared. Maybe you can help each other remember something important."

Her quiet tone seemed to calm the children, and they looked at her expectantly. "Tell me what you usually do after school."

The boys seemed relieved to be asked to concentrate on normal daily activities, and Jenny could see them relax. She got the expected answers: "Play" and "Do homework."

"What about the day before Nick disappeared? Anyone remember what happened then?"

"We went to baseball practice."

"We were on the same team."

"Nick played first base, but we didn't have practice the day he...he—" The boy choked and Jenna put a comforting hand on his shoulder.

She turned to a boy in a Michael Jordan T-shirt. "David, what do you kids do after practice?"

"Hang around the park awhile, then go home."

"What about the last practice Nick went to?"

The boys frowned, then Andy spoke up. "Mr. Morales came and watched the end of practice. He took Nick and me out for a hamburger afterward. He said...he said—" Andy's voice cracked. "He was gonna take us out for a pizza if we won the next game."

There'd been no pizza, no next game for Nick. Five pairs of eyes revealed what the children were thinking.

"Have you seen anyone new in the park after practice? Any strangers?" Jenna asked.

As she expected, the kids said no.

"Can you think of anyone who just moved into the neighborhood, any new people at all—maybe someone working at the service station around the corner or at the Stop and Go?"

The kids sat thinking for a few minutes, then the freckle-faced boy said, "There's a new ice-cream man." A couple of other youngsters agreed.

Jenna's heart leaped. Maybe, just maybe, this could be a lead. With luck, the driver might have seen someone suspicious when he made his rounds in the neighborhood. Then her thoughts shifted in a more sinister direction. An ice-cream truck driver had lots of opportunity to meet every youngster in the neighborhood; he was everyone's friend. Kids came right up to the truck, which was large enough to conceal a child. "What's the name of the ice-cream company?" she asked.

No one knew. Maybe the principal could help her out, Jenna decided. "Is the same driver still around?"

"Yeah, I saw him yesterday," Ian said. When Jenna asked for a description, the boy said, "Do...do you think he's the one that got Nick?"

"No, Ian. I'm not saying that at all. I just want to ask him some questions. Maybe he can help us. Maybe he saw something. But I want you kids to be careful." A collective shiver ran through the group. Jenna continued, "Don't go up to any cars, and don't roam around the neighborhood alone."

The boys nodded.

"Tell me about the ice-cream man," Jenna said. "What does he look like?"

"He's tall."

"He's kinda skinny."

"He's old."

That could mean anything from twenty-five to seventy, Jenna thought. "Anyone else?" she asked.

None of the boys could think of anyone.

"Did any of you hear Nicolas say anything the day he disappeared, anything about plans for after school?"

"Just that he had to go home. We had a science test the next day and he had to study," Andy said. "He told me maybe we could bat a few balls later, before dinner, but... but I never heard from him."

Jenna nodded. By that time, Nicolas had disappeared. And he obviously hadn't planned on getting together with his friend right after mailing his mother's letter, or he'd have taken his bat along. Maybe the fact that he had a test—something she hadn't known before—was significant. "Could he have stopped somewhere on the way home, maybe to get help with the science test?"

The boys considered this. Finally one of them, a quiet youngster who hadn't said much, spoke up. "Mr. Chu on the next street is a scientist. He helped me with a project once. Maybe Nick went over there."

Pleased with this bit of information, Jenna asked if the boys knew Mr. Chu's first name and if he was likely to be home in the afternoon.

"His name's Huang," Andy told her.

"Sometimes he comes home early," another boy said. "I've seen him in the yard on my way home from school."

She'd look into that, Jenna decided. In fact, she'd stop by Mr. Chu's as soon as she finished here. "Was science a hard subject for Nick?" she asked the boys. "Did he go over to Mr. Chu's a lot?"

"No," Andy said. "Nick was okay in science, but we had a substitute teacher the week before and he didn't explain things too good."

No other relevant information came out, so Jenna thanked the boys and promised she'd let them know as soon as Nick was found. The youngsters filed out, talking among themselves about Nick, but Steven hung back. He said nothing, just looked nervously at Jenna. "What is it, Steven?" she asked gently.

"Do you think that man might, uh, come after somebody else?"

Jenna saw the fear in the child's eyes and wished she could answer with an adamant no. But she couldn't. "I hope not. We're trying our best to find whoever took Nick very soon."

"Okay." She saw a small gleam of hope in the boy's eyes before he turned and hurried to catch up with his friends.

Jenna stood and realized she was exhausted. The afternoon had drained her, and it wasn't over yet. On her way out, she stopped at Lila Sterling's office. She found the principal engrossed in reading from a manila folder.

"How did your session go?" the principal asked.

"I'm concerned about the children," Jenna replied. "They're afraid. It's realistic, of course, but—"

"But they're suffering," Mrs. Sterling agreed with a sigh. "We've had reports of nightmares, stomachaches, fear of going to school. I've had a psychologist out several times."

"Good. By the way, one of the boys mentioned a substitute teacher in Nick's class."

"That would be Franklin Reeves," Mrs. Sterling said. "But he wasn't here the day Nicolas disappeared."

"Had he substituted here before?"

"Several times over the last year or so. We don't always get the same people. I always cross my fingers that we'll get anyone at all."

"What do you know about him?"

The principal thought for a moment, then admitted, "Not much. Subs are in and out so quickly I don't learn much more than their names."

Jenna made a note to check out Mr. Reeves, then said, "The boys spoke about a new ice-cream man. Do you happen to know the name of the company?"

"As a matter of fact, I do." Mrs. Sterling smiled. "It's Sendak's. I'm a patron," she confided. "I can't pass up a Popsicle."

"Neither can I." Jenna smiled back, feeling better. She thanked the principal for her help, then borrowed the telephone directory from the secretary and looked up Chu's address. At least she had a couple of new leads, she thought with satisfaction as she signed out. They were slim, but she'd tried everything else she or anyone else at the department could think of. She had to check out even the most remote possibility. It could turn out to be the clue that would lead her to Nicolas.

THE CHU HOUSE WAS yellow, with rosebushes in the front yard. No one answered the doorbell, but Jenna resolved to return the next day.

She drove back to headquarters where she found a three-page fax on her desk from Chad Foster and a message that Lieutenant Harris wanted to see her in his office. *Probably about Foster,* she decided, picking up the papers he'd faxed.

As she'd anticipated, as soon as she was seated across from Harris, he asked, "How'd your meeting with Chad Foster go?"

"Predictably. He couldn't think of anyone who might have written the letters. I had him send me a list of women employees, women he's met socially in the last few months. It's—" she eyeballed the papers in her hand "—a long one, about eighty names. I can run this through the computer, but the chances are a hundred to one I won't learn a thing. Police records are unlikely, and we won't find any psychiatric problems unless the person was involved in criminal activity. But I don't have to tell you that." Slapping the papers on the desk, she said, "The writer could be anyone—a clerk in a florist's shop, a teenager who saw him on television, someone who got a deal on stationery with roses and went on a letter-writing spree."

"So what are your plans?" Harris asked.

"My plans? My plans are to interview a neighbor who might have helped Nick Morales with a science test, to call Sendak's Dairy about a new ice-cream truck driver in the Morales neighborhood, and to check on a substitute teacher. Damn it, Nate. I have work to do."

"The chief's real interested in this case," the lieutenant said mildly.

"Yeah, I got that message loud and clear. I also hear ol' Buster's stock with the mayor's gone down lately. If we solve a celebrity case, that'd bolster his image, wouldn't it?"

Harris nodded. "That's about the size of it."

"So why doesn't Buster take care of it himself?" she muttered, then held up a hand. "Never mind, don't answer that. Anything else before I run these names?"

"You might take a tour of the TV station—in plain clothes, of course—and see if you can sniff out any crazies on staff."

"You mean someone who salivates as Foster walks by? They probably all do that."

Harris raised a brow at that but didn't comment.

"If I do turn up anyone suspicious, you'll have to get someone to do the legwork. I'm up to my ears in work *besides* Morales. I won't have time to ask questions, do interviews. I need help on this, Nate."

"You've got it." He cleared his throat. "You could check out some of Foster's regular haunts, too."

"In plain clothes, of course. I'm afraid I'm not the type for this job. I'd stand out like a sore thumb at the River Oaks Country Club or at one of those posh parties where everyone wears dresses that cost more than my month's pay. Maybe I could put a designer wardrobe on my expense account. Think Macauley would okay it, as long as I'm helping out a friend of his?"

Harris's eyes narrowed. "What's eating you, Jenna?"

She sighed. "The contrast between Chad Foster and Nick Morales, I guess. Anita Morales cried in my arms this afternoon. I—" She swallowed.

"The Morales case is a tough one," Harris said.

"It's heart-wrenching."

Harris glanced at the picture of his two sons that sat on his file cabinet. "I know," he said grimly. "Cases like this, I..." He cleared his throat. "I heard about the flyers you had printed." He reached into his pocket, pulled out his wallet and took out a bill. "This'll help cover it."

"Thanks, Nate." She started to rise, but Nate put out a hand to detain her. "Hold on. There's more to this than what you've told me."

Nate had always been perceptive. That was one reason she liked working for him. She'd learned from him, considered him her mentor, but now she hesitated. How much did she want to reveal?

"Talk to me, Jenna," Nate urged.

She took a breath, wondering if she was about to make a serious mistake. "It *is* the Morales case, Nate. What if I'm not up to solving it?"

"That doesn't sound like you. Lack of self-confidence has never been a problem for you. I remember when you were just out of the police academy, working a beat. You could interrogate a suspect and judge whether he was being straight with you or feeding you a line."

Jenna stared at her hands. "Maybe that instinct's gone."

"Because you haven't found Nick Morales?"

"Partly."

"What's the rest?" Nate asked.

"Avery Sullivan."

He stared at her. "The kid whose body turned up in a field a couple of months ago? You can't feel responsible for him."

"Can't I? He was my case, and I let it go."

Nate leaned forward. "Avery Sullivan was a fifteen-year-old boy with a history of running away from home. How many times had he taken off? Five? Ten?"

"A lot," Jenna admitted, "except for the last time."

"I said you have a good instinct for police work. I didn't say you were a mind reader. With a history like his, no one would have suspected anything but another runaway."

"*I* should have suspected." She clenched her fingers. "Damn it, I should have looked harder."

"Jenna, your father didn't solve every crime. No one can be a hundred percent, not even the best of us. Put Avery Sullivan to rest."

"I can't. I keep seeing his body. I hear his mother's screams in my sleep." She looked up miserably. "Have you ever felt like that about a case?"

Nate hesitated, glanced down at his hands, then said gruffly, "Yeah, I remember a woman who got shot. I had a list of suspects, but I overlooked her next-door neighbor. Why, I don't know. He was clearly a nut case. A month later he shot her roommate." Nate stared into space, his eyes focused somewhere on the distant past, then said firmly, "But I got through it. And you will, too." Gently, he unfolded Jenna's fingers. "Maybe you need to talk to someone."

She gave him a shaky smile. "I'm talking to you."

"Someone professional."

"A shrink? No! No, I'll work it out on my own. If I can find Nick Morales, I'll be okay."

"And if you can't?" he asked softly.

"Then I'll deal with it." She felt tears coming and didn't want to break down in front of Nate. She stood. "I'll get to work on the Foster case. Don't worry, I'll take care of Chief Macauley's pal."

Nate started to say something more, then stopped. "Keep me posted."

CHAD LEANED BACK. He was glad to be on his own turf, seated at the head of the marble conference table he'd kept as a relic of his father's days at the station. The weekly planning meeting, already delayed because of his appointment at the police station, had begun thirty minutes late but was moving along briskly now. They'd covered projected ratings, then community service. Bryan Carriker, Chad's up-and-coming assistant station manager, had, as usual, anticipated Chad's thoughts and suggested a collaboration with the American Cancer Society on a fund-raiser. It was something they'd done regularly when both he and Chad were at the San Antonio station.

Now Tina Parker, evening-news producer, took over the discussion. "Planning any editorials this week?" she asked Chad.

"Yeah, another one on that halfway house for parolees in the Montrose area."

Surprise registered on Bryan's face. He frowned at Chad. "Why?"

"Nothing's happening," Chad replied, tapping a pencil on the table. "The city council keeps tabling the motion, and the mayor's dragging his feet. They need a push."

"You've already spoken out," Bryan said, pushing his horn-rimmed glasses up on his nose.

"Once wasn't enough on this one."

Tina said, "Chad, there's a lot of opposition to building that facility in Montrose."

"*Near* Montrose."

Tina shrugged. "Semantics. People who live and work there figure it's too close."

"And you?"

She took a breath, brushed a strand of honey blond hair back from her cheek and said, "I agree with them."

Chad had to give Tina credit. She was only three years into a television career, but she wasn't afraid to voice her opinions, even if they conflicted with the station manager's. He respected her for that, but in this case, he felt she was wrong. On the other hand... "You're entitled," he said. "My understanding is that the people to be housed there will be chosen carefully. We need to reassure the community that they won't be living next to murderers and rapists."

"They still won't like it," Tina said.

Chad sighed. "You know, it's frustrating. Those who talk the loudest about the importance of fighting crime don't want to do it in their own neighborhoods. There should be a way to convince them...." He stared into space.

"So?" Tina prodded. "What are you going to do?"

Chad turned to her. "Go on the air. Soften my approach. Work to educate the community, push to have the facility built and get parolees with half a chance reintegrated into society."

"You're the boss," Tina said.

"Yeah, and I won't risk compromising my principles. Which is exactly what I'd do if I let this go by without additional comment," Chad said, then grinned at her. "Besides, viewers are attracted to controversy, no matter which side they're on."

Bryan had been uncharacteristically quiet about his own views, Chad noticed. Wanting to have everyone's opinion out in the open, he turned to his second-in-command. "What about you?"

"Personally, I agree with you on building the facility," Bryan said, "but your last editorial stirred up a lot of flak. Even some hate mail."

"What mail?" Chad's heart began to thud. Not another letter from Rose!

Bryan handed him two envelopes. The first contained a typewritten letter filled with biblical quotes and promising that the wrath of Jehovah would rain down on the city and especially on Channel 6 if the halfway house for the godless was built anywhere in Houston.

The second envelope held a single sheet on which letters cut from the newspaper had been glued to spell a message unfit for polite company.

He'd have to turn these over to the police, Chad knew, but at least they didn't appear to be from Rose. "Someone else," he muttered, earning puzzled looks from his staff. He cleared his throat. "We can't let a couple of crank letters concern us."

Bryan nodded. "I was pretty sure you'd say that. When are you going on the air?"

"Tomorrow night. At the end of the ten o'clock newscast. Give me two minutes, Tina."

She nodded, made a note and rose.

Bryan made a similar note. "One piece of advice, boss. I'd order a bulletproof vest and wear it home, if I were you."

Not such a bad idea, Chad thought sourly. From what Sergeant Wakefield had said, he might need one to protect him from his friend Rose.

As soon as everyone left, Chad went to his desk and turned on his computer. He was behind schedule, tired as hell, and he still had to write the script for the Montrose editorial. He was only half finished when the phone interrupted. With a sigh of disgust, he answered. "Yeah."

"Mr. Foster, you have a call from a Sergeant Wakefield. Are you in?"

Well, that was quick. To his surprise, his annoyance faded instantly. "I'm in."

"Sarge," he said when the operator put her through. "I didn't expect to hear from you this soon." He glanced at his watch. "Eight o'clock. Have you solved the case in less than ten hours?"

"We're checking the names on your list," she said, her voice businesslike. "So far, nothing's turned up."

"And?"

"The computer's not likely to tell us much," she continued. "It'd be better if I could meet your staff face-to-face. I'd like to come out to your office tomorrow and spend an hour or so."

Good. He wanted this matter put to rest with all possible speed. He also realized he'd enjoy sparring with the sergeant again. "You're welcome any time."

"I have a stop to make on the way," she said. "I'll be there around nine."

"Fine," he said. "I have a breakfast meeting, but I should be in by nine. Plan to stay through lunch."

"No, I—"

"Mario's Restaurant is nearby. I run into a lot of people there. I'm sure you'll want to check them out, too." He imagined her brown eyes sparking with irritation and suddenly wondered how they'd look heating with a different emotion.

"All right," she said, sounding none too thrilled. "I'll see you in the morning."

"I'm looking forward to it, Sarge."

He heard the decisive click as she severed the connection and pictured her in her cramped office, sitting militarily straight at her desk, not a wrinkle in her starched, pressed uniform. He was sure she'd like to slam the phone across the room.

JENNA GLARED AT THE receiver in her hand. She felt like flinging it across her bedroom. Instead, she forced herself to replace it slowly. What was it about this man that nettled her like a burr rubbing against bare skin? She'd better learn to contain her irritation fast—by tomorrow morning.

She needed to calm down. She went into her bathroom and filled the tub, pouring in a generous helping of bath oil. She brought a glass of wine from the kitchen, then undressed.

Enjoying the feel of warm water and the gardenia scent of the bath oil, she lowered herself into the tub and leaned back against the bath pillow. Water lapped at her breasts; her hair, unbound now, floated around her shoulders. She reached for the glass of wine she'd set on the side of the tub, took a sip and savored it as she listened to the *Moonlight Sonata* flowing from the bedroom stereo.

She shut her eyes and took a long, calming breath. *Relax,* she told herself. *Blot out everything in the Morales case.* Anita's tears, the fear in the eyes of the small boys she'd spoken to this afternoon. She took another breath, let it out slowly. *Let go of the Foster case.* The long list of names, the stationery with the gaudy rose. And demanding, impatient Chad Foster with his teasing voice and taunting blue eyes.

She sighed and gave up. Her relaxation routine didn't seem to work with Foster. He'd probably keep her awake all night.

JENNA PROWLED Foster's office. Damn, he was fifteen minutes late already. Was this revenge for yesterday? His secretary had politely informed Jenna that Mr. Foster was meeting with the board of directors of the Houston Museum of Fine Arts but should be back any minute. Jenna hoped she was right.

The secretary—the nameplate on her desk identified her as Catherine Paige—had suggested that Jenna might be more comfortable waiting in Mr. Foster's office. She'd ushered Jenna inside and offered coffee, which Jenna gratefully accepted. She'd finished the coffee, which she admitted grudgingly was considerably better than the muddy stuff dealt out by the HPD vending machines, and then begun to pace.

Waiting for him made her edgy. The thought of seeing him made her edgier. There was something compelling about him, something that fascinated her as much as it annoyed. Something that made her wonder how she'd feel if he touched her, if— Damn, she'd have to cut out those inappropriate thoughts. No, wait a minute. There was nothing wrong with focusing on Chad Foster, imagining how *Rose* might feel about such a dynamic, sexy man. That was part of her job, Jenna told herself. To put herself in the suspect's shoes, to figure out what Rose would do next. Jenna had a legitimate reason for thinking about Chad Foster—a reason that had nothing to do with her personally.

She stopped pacing and glanced around the office. What could she learn about Chad from his surroundings? She frowned at a Miró lithograph on the wall. Certainly not a piece she would choose. She preferred watercolors—muted tones, pastoral scenes. What did all the little curlicues mean, anyway? She liked the Lalique crystal vase on the table, though; she went over to it and ran her fingers over the smooth glass.

The office was really something—big, airy, with expensive furnishings. It fairly shouted Power, but then what did you expect of a man who spent his mornings with the board of the art museum? She thought about her own cramped quarters and cringed, then raised her chin. To heck with that. She was a working police officer, not a fancy corporate executive, and she was proud of it. She'd followed in the footsteps of her father, a man who'd made his mark as an exceptional cop, both tough and compassionate. And she was doing her best to emulate him.

She wondered what had attracted Chad Foster to the television business. Prestige? Most of the wealthy people she'd known were into status. She walked around behind his large walnut desk. The top was bare except for an executive pen set, a calendar, and an In basket with a couple of letters. The desk didn't tell her much about Chad Foster. She wandered to the large conference table that took up one side of the room and ran her finger over it. Marble. Smooth and polished, like its owner.

She noticed a family photograph on the bookshelf. She picked it up for a closer look, and zeroed in on Chad immediately. He was smiling—that infuriatingly sexy grin that she had to admit irritated and attracted her at the same time. His arm was thrown over the shoulder of a dark-haired man with a strong resemblance to him; his brother, probably. In front of them, their parents, a handsome couple, sat side by side on a love seat. On one arm of the love seat perched a petite blonde with a smile that was an exact copy of Chad's.

Jenna studied Chad's father. Even in the informal photo, the man exuded power. He—

"My family," said a voice behind her. She jumped, embarrassed to be caught holding the picture. Damn, she'd been so absorbed, she hadn't heard the door open, and the thick carpet had muffled Chad's footsteps.

Before she could set the photograph back on the shelf, he was beside her, taking it from her hand. He stood much too close, so near she could see tiny flecks of gold around his pupils. He was far more intimidating here in his own territory than he'd been yesterday in hers. She desperately wanted to back away, but she didn't. She stood her ground, keeping her eyes fastened boldly on his. The thought crossed her mind that his lashes were too thick to be wasted on a man, that—

"Sit down, Sergeant," he said, and she blinked, hoping he hadn't guessed the direction her thoughts had taken.

He sat across from her. "Sorry you had to wait. There was an accident on the freeway, and the police were routing everyone around it." He smiled at her. "Maybe I should blame them."

Jenna couldn't help but smile back. "Why not? Everyone else does." The light interchange relaxed her, and she felt more comfortable as she got down to business. "As I expected, nothing incriminating showed up for any of the names on your list."

He nodded and opened a desk drawer. "My assistant manager gave me these yesterday. I thought you'd want to take a look."

Jenna scanned the letters he handed her. She tapped her finger on the typewritten sheet. "What's this about?"

"The halfway house for parolees that's been proposed in Montrose."

"Oh, yes."

"We've been inundated with mail on the subject," Chad said. "I editorialized about it several weeks ago—"

"What date?"

"Mid-April." He thought for a moment. "Tuesday, the nineteenth."

"Does that coincide with the first letter from Rose?"

"Roughly."

"What did you say about the halfway house?"

"Sarge, don't you ever watch the news on Channel 6?" His teasing half smile caused her pulse to leap. And, damn it, she felt herself blush. Before she could answer, Chad leaned forward. "I came out in favor of it. Strongly." His expression was serious now.

"These letters are different from Rose's," Jenna said, "but I'd like to take a look at the rest of your mail on the Montrose project." He nodded, called his secretary on the intercom, and asked her to get the file.

"What next?" Chad asked.

"I'd like to meet your staff."

"Then we'll take the grand tour," he said, rising.

"If anyone asks, you can tell them I'm researching a book on careers in television."

"Sounds reasonable." He led her out of his office, and for the next hour and a half, they covered every inch of the station, from the news studio to the business office to the employees' lunchroom. Chad introduced her to the harried assignments editor, the evening sportscaster, whom Jenna recognized as an ex-Oiler, to cameramen, office staff, even to the switchboard operator. She asked questions about their jobs and made notes, all the while observing each person carefully, especially the women and their reactions to Chad.

They entered the newsroom, where several men were positioning camera equipment and a woman was fussing over the set of the noon newscast. She looked up and broke into a smile when she saw Chad. *Late twenties, blue eyes, blond hair pulled back in a ponytail.* Jenna mentally recorded the woman's description as she crossed the room toward them, her eyes on Chad. Her hips swayed enticingly and she raised her hand to brush back a few stray tendrils from her temple in an obvious gesture of invitation.

"This is Lynn O'Donnell, one of the newest members of our staff," Chad said, smiling at the young woman. "Lynn, I'd like you to meet Jenna Wakefield."

Lynn gave Jenna an appraising look and took a step closer to Chad. If she'd spoken aloud, her message couldn't have been clearer: Hands off.

"How long have you been here?" Jenna asked her.

"Three months. Are you interviewing for a job?"

Jenna shook her head. "Taking notes for a book. I'm doing a series on careers—" she continued, but Lynn had already lost interest and turned back to Chad.

When they left the newsroom, Jenna made a note on the pad she carried—"Lynn O'Donnell...possible"—and later asked about several other members of the staff. "I'd like to come back to the station tomorrow and talk to some of the women again," she told Chad.

As they headed back to his office, a bespectacled blond man approached them. "Chad," he said, waving a newspaper, "have you seen today's TV section?" When Chad shook his head, the man handed it to him and pointed to an ad circled in red.

Chad read aloud. "'Black magic behind closed doors. Could your neighbor be involved? Find out today. Channel 9's "Afternoon Talk" with Mark Traynor exposes witchcraft in Houston.'"

"Great, huh? That Geraldo copycat is pulling in the audience while the network gives *us* Barbara Hansen with ten hints on how to clean your oven."

"Take it easy, Bryan. I have a plan."

"Thank God."

"We'll discuss it later." He turned to Jenna. "Bryan's my assistant manager. Jenna Wakefield, Bryan Carriker."

Wondering how Chad planned to counter Traynor's appeal, Jenna shook hands with Bryan. Though she didn't have time for daytime TV, she'd heard Traynor was the hit of Houston, with his show that rivaled the tabloids for sensationalism.

When they left Bryan and walked on, Chad said, "I need to stop in my office and check messages. Then we'll have lunch at Mario's."

Jenna had spent far too much time with him already. She made a last stab at refusing. "No...I—"

"Yes," he said. "Remember, I told you I bump into a lot of people there. Besides, you have to eat."

She couldn't deny that, so she waited while he took care of a couple of phone calls.

On the way out, they stopped at his secretary's desk to pick up the stack of letters on the Montrose facility. Chad gestured to a vase of flowers Catherine had put on the credenza. "Shall I wear a rose to lunch? That's what Rose keeps asking for."

"No! And don't wear it on television, either. The last thing you want right now is to legitimize what she's doing."

He nodded, and she followed him out to his car. Black, low-slung, expensive—what sort of message did it send about him? *Sexy, powerful...dangerous,* she thought, fastening the seat belt in preparation for a wild ride. She wasn't disappointed. He drove as if he owned the road.

He pulled up before Mario's, an upscale restaurant done in Southwestern style in soft shades of peach and aqua and accented with abundant greenery in terra-cotta pots. Frescoes of deserts and mountains adorned the walls.

The restaurant was mentioned frequently in the society columns. Jenna knew that power brokers met here for lunch; society matrons and jet-setters showed up at night. Chad greeted the hostess, exchanged pleasantries as if they were old friends, even commented on her new hairdo. As the woman led them to a conspicuous table in the center of the dining room, Jenna wondered if her tailored summer suit looked out-of-place.

Chad seated her, then, as if reading her mind, he leaned over her shoulder and whispered, "You look great, Sarge. Smell good, too. That perfume you wear is driving me crazy. What is it?"

She felt the tickle of his breath in her ear, his brief touch on her shoulder, and swallowed. "It's called Paris."

"Mmm," he said, as if that told him something significant about her.

He wasn't supposed to be noticing her perfume, or touching her. He was a case like any other, and she'd keep him that way. She picked up the menu, ordered the first dish she saw, then forced her mind to focus on the crowded dining room.

A trio of businessmen came in. As the hostess ushered them to a table, one of the men left the group and came over to shake hands with Chad. Chad introduced him as Lucas Molino, a name Jenna saw frequently in the papers.

"I wanted to thank you for the plug you gave the Big Brothers/Big Sisters of America on 'Houston A.M.' the other day," Molino said.

"Glad to do it. They do good work. I worked with the San Antonio agency, even had a little brother of my own.

I plan to sign up for one in Houston, too, as soon as I'm settled in."

Jenna stared in astonishment as the two men continued talking. She hadn't figured Chad Foster for the kind of guy who associated with charitable organizations on anything but a superficial level. When Molino left, she said, "I'm surprised you were involved with an organization like Big Brothers."

He frowned. "Why?"

"You seem so rushed. Didn't it take a lot of your time?"

Anger sparked in his eyes. He must have heard the hint of sarcasm she couldn't mask. Then the irritation faded. "Yes, but it was time well spent. I like kids, and I've watched enough news reports to know what can happen to boys who're left on their own."

Jenna nodded. She saw plenty of that, working in Juvenile.

"You can't change the world, but you can make a start with individuals," he continued.

"Did you do that with your little brother?" she asked, really interested.

"I hope so," he said thoughtfully. "He was fifteen when I first saw him, with a smart mouth and a chip on his shoulder you couldn't miss. He comes from a single-parent household with six kids, one of whom has serious medical problems. His mother has done the best she can, but Benjamin got lost in the shuffle."

"What did you do to help him?"

"A lot of sports, camping out, shooting the rapids on the Guadalupe River. I made him carry his own weight, like my dad did with us when we were growing up. One time he told me he'd had enough and I could go to hell," he added, shaking his head. "I gave him hell right back, and that was a turning point."

"And that's all it took?" Jenna asked skeptically. It wouldn't be enough for many of the kids she was acquainted with—the juvenile gang members, drug pushers, dropouts.

"Of course not," Chad admitted, surprising her again. "It took a lot of time, and some understanding teachers who saw Benjamin's potential, believed in him and made him work like the devil. He finished high school last year and got a scholarship to Southwest Texas State University." He pulled a picture from his wallet and passed it to Jenna.

She stared at the face of a kid who could grow up to be a good citizen ... or a gang member. Thanks to Chad and the Big Brothers, he was apparently on his way to the former. "You must be proud," she murmured, handing the snapshot back and wondering if she'd misjudged Chad Foster.

He nodded, put the photo in his wallet, then said, "Back to our present concern. I saw you writing names of people you wanted to check out. Who were they?" She gave him four names. "I'll have Catherine tell them you'll be back to interview them," he said, then asked, "How did you decide on them?"

"Gut feeling. I've worked on stalking cases before. I'll know more tomorrow, though, after I've talked to them." Her eyes traveled to the restaurant's front door. "And here comes one of them now."

Lynn O'Donnell entered the dining room. Jenna watched as the hostess led her to a table behind a pillar on the other side of the room, saw Lynn shake her head and point to a spot nearer their table, directly in Chad's line of sight. Jenna leaned forward. "I wonder if she comes here often."

Chad waved to Lynn, then shrugged. "I see her here occasionally."

"Do you ever have lunch together?"

"We have once or twice."

"Did you run into one another, or did you invite her?" Jenna asked.

"She was here, I was here, so we sat together."

"Have you asked her out?"

"No," he said, "but come to think of it, she asked me once."

"And?"

"And I turned her down. I don't get involved at work. Besides, she's too young."

The waitress brought their meals. While they ate, Jenna asked, "What kind of security does the station have besides the guard and the sign-in sheet at the front door?"

"The usual. We have an alarm system, a limited-access parking lot for employees around the back, a guard in the evenings, too."

"We may need to think about putting someone outside your office if Rose starts making more threats," she said.

His eyes turned to cold steel. "No way, Sarge. I don't want this situation blown out of proportion."

She couldn't believe what he'd just said. "Mr. Foster, unless your secretary is trained in surveillance, we may have no choice." When he shook his head, she leaned forward, annoyed. "You brought the police in on this. We're the experts. If you want us to catch Rose, don't get in our way."

"You don't mince words, do you, Sergeant?" he said. "All right. You've made your point, but wait a few days before you send someone. Maybe we'll get lucky and you won't need to. And if you have to station a guard at my office, make sure he or she is unobtrusive. I don't want to make a media event out of this."

She nodded. "You've made your point, too."

He smiled at her. God, the man had a dynamite smile. She could easily see why a woman might fixate on him. "I agree that the situation's not critical enough to send someone now, but—"

She broke off to meet the eyes of a sultry, red-haired woman seated a few tables to their right. Jenna was certain she'd never seen her before, but the woman was looking daggers at her. "Friend of yours?" she asked Chad.

Chad followed Jenna's gaze, then nodded to the woman. "That's Mona Switzer."

Jenna recognized the name; it appeared regularly on the society pages of the local newspapers. "I took her out a few times when I first moved to town," Chad continued, "then broke it off."

"Why?" From the way the redhead was staring, Jenna could tell the breakup hadn't been Mona's idea.

Chad laughed. "Nosy, aren't you?"

"It's my job," Jenna insisted. "Why'd you break it off?"

He shrugged. "I lost interest, that's all."

Jenna said nothing. She continued eating, feeling the eyes of both Lynn and Mona on her as she toyed with her food. When she finished her salad, she excused herself and went to the ladies' room. She stood in front of the mirror, checking her makeup, waiting. In a few minutes the door opened, and Mona entered.

Their eyes met in the mirror. "Seeing Chad Foster?" Mona inquired.

Boy, you don't mince words, either, Jenna thought. She shrugged.

"I wouldn't get too interested if I were you," Mona advised. "He has a short attention span."

"Thanks. I'll keep that in mind." Jenna put her lipstick in her purse and walked out. Obviously, Mona was not one of the ex-girlfriends that Chad had left well-satisfied. When she returned to the table, where coffee was waiting, she took out her notepad. "We'll add Mona to the list."

"Then what?" Chad asked.

"I'll come back to the station tomorrow. And I need to get more detailed information from you—a rundown of your workday, for starters."

"My workday varies, but I can give you a general picture."

"Fine. You can fax it to me. I also need to know how you spend your weekends. Try to be as specific as possible. You can fax that, too."

He smiled. "I have a better idea. I'll show you. Spend the day with me, Saturday."

She almost choked on her coffee. "What?"

"Saturday, Sarge."

"I, uh, I have to work on Saturday."

"But, Sarge," he murmured, "I'm part of your job."

He was right. Harris had made it clear that he and Chief Macauley expected Chad Foster to get her attention. "All right," she agreed.

"I'll pick you up at ten."

"No!" she said hastily. "I'll drive myself."

"Here's my address." He scribbled it on the back of a business card. "We'll have brunch." He handed her the card and signaled the waitress. While he paid the bill,

Jenna wondered why she'd let him manipulate her into Saturday.

As they got in the car, she glanced back at the restaurant. "Do you eat at Mario's every day?"

Chad flipped on the radio to a rock station. "Once or twice a week. If I'm in a hurry, I have Catherine bring me a sandwich from the lunchroom." Jenna breathed a sigh of relief. She'd been half afraid she'd have to hit all of Houston's fashionable eateries with him, checking out the clientele.

"I like Mario's food," Chad continued. "My sister introduced me to it. She's into healthy. You Are What You Eat is one of Ariel's mottoes."

"Sounds like a good one."

"Ariel has a motto for every occasion," Chad said, smiling fondly.

"She must be the cute blonde in the family picture." How had they gotten onto personal topics? Well, it wouldn't hurt to find out more about his family.

"Yes. She manages the family television station in Corpus Christi. Does a damn good job, too. She brought it up to number one in the city."

"Really?"

He turned into the parking lot, pulled into his space and killed the motor. "You sound surprised."

"Well, I pictured her, uh—"

"Go on."

"Playing tennis at the country club," she admitted.

Anger flashed across his face. "You know, Sarge," he said, his voice low and dangerous, "you have a jaundiced view of me and my family." When she started to protest, he cut her off. "Don't deny it. I hear it in your tone." He reached across the seat and caught her wrist. "I'm going to change that."

Jenna felt her pulse shoot up. From fear? Excitement? She stared pointedly at his hand. "That sounds like a threat."

"I meant it as a promise, but have it your way. Threat or promise, it's a fact. I'll see you Saturday."

She jerked at her arm, and he let her go. Jenna shoved the door open and got out. Taking a deep breath, she forced herself not to run as she headed across the parking lot to her car.

CHAPTER THREE

JENNA STOOD AT THE DOOR of the yellow frame house belonging to the Chu family. Late afternoon sunlight sparkled on the windows. From the bushes behind her, the scent of roses wafted to her nostrils. She heard the bell chime, and a moment later the door was opened by a slight, balding man wearing a gray suit. He stared at her from behind gold-rimmed bifocals. "Yes?"

"I'm Officer Wakefield of the Houston Police Department. I'm working on the Nicolas Morales case. I'd like to ask you a few questions." She held up her ID.

Huang Chu seemed surprised, but he agreed without hesitation. "Of course. Please, come in. So sad about the little boy," he said as he showed Jenna into a small, tidy living room. "Sit down, please," he said, motioning to an overstuffed armchair upholstered in flowered damask. He sat on the matching couch. "How can I help you?" His voice was quiet, well modulated, with no hint of nervousness.

"I'd like to speak to your wife, too," Jenna said.

"I'm sorry. She is away on a business trip. She will return on Saturday."

She'd question the wife later if necessary. "Did you know Nicolas Morales?" Jenna asked.

Huang nodded. "Yes, he was . . . *is* a bright child, very likable."

Did his changing the "was" to "is" mean anything? Jenna asked herself. "What was your relationship with him?"

"I help the children in the neighborhood with science projects. Sometimes I explain subject matter they do not understand."

"You're a scientist, then?"

He nodded. "A physicist with Shell."

She'd check that out. "And did you ever help Nicolas Morales?"

"On a few occasions." Chu relaxed on the couch.

"Mr. Chu, I understand Nicolas had a science test coming up at the time he disappeared. Did you go over it with him?"

"No. I was in San Francisco when he disappeared, presenting a paper to the American Institute of Physics. In fact, I presented that very afternoon."

That would be easy enough to verify. "Was anyone at home that day?"

"My wife attended the conference with me. She is also a physicist."

"Could anyone else have been here that afternoon?"

He hesitated a moment. "Sometimes my nephew Peter studies here in the afternoons. He is a student at Rice University. A graduate student in physics."

"Does your nephew have a key to the house?" When Chu nodded, she asked, "Where can I get in touch with him?"

"He lives at the Rice graduate house. He is working on a project for the head of the physics department and spends most of his time on campus."

"Can you tell me how to find him?"

Chu nodded and carefully drew her a map with a pencil. "Here is the Physics Building," he said, drawing a small square and underlining it. "But why should you want to talk with Peter? I'm certain he had nothing to do with the child's disappearance."

"I'm talking to anyone who could have the slightest bit of information," she said. "Maybe he was here that day and knows something that could help my investigation."

Chu shook his head. "I am sure he knows nothing. He is not involved, I know." He spoke almost too earnestly. "Peter is a good boy, quiet."

She'd see about that, Jenna decided. She put the slip of paper with the map of the campus in her pocket and asked, "Can you tell me anything about Nicolas that might help in our search? Sometimes just one detail, something that seems insignificant, can lead us to a missing person."

Chu leaned back again. He thought for a moment, then said, "All I can tell you is that Nicolas is a fine little boy. He is eager to learn, curious about everything." Chu smiled. "And he likes my wife's almond cookies."

No help there. Jenna rose. "Thank you for seeing me. If I have any other questions, I'll let you know."

Instead of returning to headquarters, she drove to Rice University. Nearly deserted now that the spring semester was over, the campus was peaceful with its tree-shaded lawns, winding streets and red brick buildings.

She followed the penciled map to the Physics Building, parked and went inside. When she found the departmental office, she asked to see Peter Chu. While the secretary left to get him, Jenna sat in a straight-backed wooden chair. On the end table beside her were several physics journals, a university catalog, and an ivy plant with drooping yellowed leaves.

A few minutes later, the secretary returned, followed by Peter Chu. A slight young man, he wore thick glasses, faded jeans, and a Rice Owls T-shirt. He looked puzzled.

Jenna motioned him into the hall, then introduced herself and said she wanted to ask him some questions about Nicolas Morales.

Peter's puzzlement changed to anxiety. He glanced at the open office door. "The kid that disappeared?" he asked, his voice cracking. "Why me? I saw his picture and read about him in the paper, but I don't know him. Where'd you get my name?"

"From your uncle," she said. "Why don't we sit down somewhere and talk?"

He glanced nervously down the hall. A couple engrossed in conversation stood a few yards away. "Not here."

"Outside, then."

Peter followed her out to the lawn. "How about sitting in my car?" she suggested.

"Are you nuts, lady? You want me to sit in front of my building in a police car?"

"I'm driving an unmarked car," she explained, gesturing to the blue Ford Taurus sedan parked nearby.

"Okay, but I've just got a few minutes. I have to get back to work."

"Is that what you're doing this summer?" Jenna asked. "Working in a lab?"

"Yeah, Rice doesn't offer much in the way of summer courses. Look," he said, his voice rising, "you're not here to ask about my summer schedule, and I don't have time to sit around shooting the breeze."

"This won't take long," she said, unlocking the car. Peter got in and slouched against the passenger door. "Your uncle said you study at his house sometimes."

"Yeah, when I have a test and I need a quiet place."

"How about the afternoon of May third? Did you study at your uncle's then?"

"Maybe. I... I don't remember. Hey, am I under suspicion or something? Maybe I need a lawyer." He reached for the door handle.

"I'm conducting an investigation," Jenna said, "but if you want a lawyer present, that's your choice. Have your uncle recommend an attorney, and come down to headquarters Monday morning. Eight-thirty." She handed him her card. "You're not under suspicion, Peter, but I wouldn't leave town until we've talked."

The hand on the doorknob began to shake. "I... I have plans to go to Dallas this weekend."

"Cancel them."

She saw a look of fear in his eyes, then he shoved the door open, got out, and headed back across the lawn. "You *weren't* under suspicion, Peter," Jenna murmured, watching him hurry inside, "but now I'm not so sure."

She returned to headquarters too late to contact anyone in Personnel at the school-district office about the substitute teacher, Franklin Reeves.

She reread the information she'd gotten from Sendak's this morning on the ice-cream man. He was fifty-four, had been a factory worker in the automotive industry in Michigan, had been unemployed for some time and had moved to Houston seeking a job. Driving the truck was apparently the best he could do. He was married but had no children. Jenna decided she'd dig a little deeper. Tomorrow.

Tomorrow she'd also have to return to Channel 6 to look more closely at some of the women in Chad Foster's life. Well, not really in his life, because he seemed virtually unaware of the women she'd singled out today. But they were extremely aware of him. Not surprising. There was something feral about him; something untamed, exciting. The expression in his deep blue eyes, the lazy, sexy smile— "Oh, go away, Foster!" she muttered.

She shoved her chair back from her desk. She was too tired to do anything more today. Instead, she'd go home, put her feet up and relax with a good novel. Pure escapism, that's what she wanted. A story with no violence, no crime, and a happy ending.

At home she fixed herself a sandwich, took a bath, and read in bed until time for the ten o'clock news. Then she switched on the television, and lay back to watch Channel 6.

Another robbery-shooting at a convenience store, a high-speed chase on Interstate 10, two city councilmen hurling barbs at one another over a raise for fire fighters. Yep, another happy day in the big city. Even the weather report was depressing. Cloudy tomorrow with a sixty percent chance of rain. In Houston that translated to, "Don't forget your umbrella. Rain's a sure thing." She had her finger on the Off button when the anchor said, "And now for 'Viewpoint,' a Channel 6 editorial. Here's our station manager, Chad Foster."

Lord, she couldn't get away from the man. There he was, right in front of her.

The sensual smile was gone now, replaced by a solemn, intense expression, but even on television he'd attract a woman's attention. Those eyes seemed to look straight at you, as if they could see into your soul. The studio lights intensified the gold highlights in his hair, and his voice was deep and sexy enough to stir the most erotic fantasies. The feelings she'd had when he touched her this afternoon reasserted themselves—nerves, excitement, arousal. She imagined his mouth touching hers. She could almost feel it, almost taste him.

For a moment, she was so absorbed in her fantasy that she nearly missed what he was saying. She quickly forced herself to listen.

"Two months ago a halfway house for parolees to be located near downtown was proposed. Reasons for it are sound. With Texas prisons overcrowded, with more and more prisoners released every day, our cities are swarming with ex-offenders. Parole officers' caseloads are virtually unmanageable. Rehabilitation of ex-convicts is only minimally successful, resulting in a revolving-door system in our state—individuals moving in and out of prison at an alarming rate."

He paused for a second, and another camera zoomed in on him for a close-up. Now Jenna could see the tiny smile lines around his mouth, the way the small pattern in his tie brought out the blue of his eyes. Good grief, she was no different than the women who'd fawned over him that morning. *Welcome to the club, Sergeant.*

"The time has come," he continued, "for new, innovative approaches to dealing with the problem. The Montrose facility is such an approach. It will provide housing for ex-convicts, job training and tutoring, and it will provide authorities with a better way to keep track of these individuals.

"Yes, there is opposition to locating the facility in Montrose. But Department of Corrections officials have assured us that residents for the house will be carefully selected. Only those with the greatest potential for becoming functioning members of society will live there. And they will be well supervised.

"The Montrose-area site makes sense. The building is available. Construction costs would be minimal. Montrose is close to downtown, to transportation, to jobs. And, most important, it offers these young men a new environment outside their old crime-ridden neighborhoods. That makes it the ideal location for such a facility.

"We urge the mayor and the city council to stop dragging their feet. We urge them to act...now."

"Wow!" Jenna said, as a commercial came on. Chad's arguments were impressive, but no wonder he'd gotten hate mail. Who wanted to live next door to an ex-con?

She turned off the television and lay back in bed, thinking about Chad Foster. Yes, he was arrogant and impatient, but he wasn't afraid to spark a controversy over a good cause. And he'd willingly given his most prized asset—his time—to a kid no one else had time for. She wondered what else lay behind that sexy smile.

THE NEXT MORNING she arrived at Channel 6 and checked in with Chad's secretary, who showed her to a small conference room, bare except for a television monitor, a table and several chairs.

Lynn O'Donnell was first. She took a seat and subjected Jenna to the same thorough assessment Jenna gave her. "I saw you at lunch yesterday," she said, glancing at her coral-tipped nails. "Are you a friend of Chad's?"

"An acquaintance. I think I told you I'm writing a book."

Lynn nodded. "Oh, yes, on television careers."

"Yes. Tell me about your job." She listened as Lynn described her duties, then asked, "What made you choose television production as a career?"

Lynn shrugged. "I grew up watching TV. It seemed like an interesting field."

"In what way?"

"Watching news stories develop. There's always something happening at a TV station. And the people you associate with are interesting."

"Tell me about some of them."

She wondered if Lynn would mention Chad, but the young woman focused on Danielle Anderson, a reporter whom she evidently viewed as a role model. "Danielle has charm, looks, intelligence," she finished.

Jenna changed the subject. "Is it hard to get a job like yours?"

Lynn shook her head. "Not really. Channel 6 was my first choice and my first interview."

A perfect opening. "How did you make that choice?"

"I watched KSAN, the Foster station in San Antonio, and I was impressed."

"Why didn't you interview with them instead?" Jenna questioned.

Lynn shrugged. "I preferred Houston."

Had Lynn seen Chad on TV in San Antonio, then followed him here? "How long have you been in Houston?" Jenna asked.

"Four months. I've been working here for three."

The timetable was right. "Do you enjoy working for Mr. Foster? I got the impression that he's demanding."

Lynn laughed softly. "He gets what he asks for, and more, from everyone." She didn't elaborate, and Jenna wound up the interview. The young woman hadn't said anything that could be construed as suspicious, but Jenna decided she'd check further. Sometimes you had to go with your instincts.

She spoke to two more women—a news reporter and an assistant director. Both were straightforward in their replies, neither seemed particularly focused on Chad.

Her final interview was with Sandra Townes, who worked in the accounting department. A frail-looking, sallow young woman with lank brown hair, she walked into the room, sat down, and asked hesitantly, "Why did you want to see me?"

Jenna repeated her spiel about writing a book on television careers.

"My job isn't really television related," Sandra explained. "I'm a bookkeeper. I could do the same thing anywhere."

"Good point," Jenna replied. "but I'd like to know if there's anything distinctive about being a bookkeeper for a TV station."

"Nothing."

"Is your work interesting?"

"Yes," she said, but her tone lacked enthusiasm.

Jenna asked about the particulars of Sandra's job, and the young woman answered laconically. Then Jenna nudged Sandra toward the subject of her co-workers. "What's the atmosphere like here?"

"Okay."

"What about the people?"

"They're okay, too."

Jenna wondered if Sandra ever strung more than two or three words together. "I understand you've had a change in management. How has that affected you?"

Sandra's forehead wrinkled. "What do you mean?"

Jenna shrugged. "The new manager must have a different style, different expectations."

Sandra fiddled with a lock of her hair. "I guess."

"Are you enjoying the change?"

"I . . . yes. Mr. Foster is very nice to work for." Her cheeks flushed. Her hands continued to move, clenching and unclenching in her lap. "He takes a, um, personal interest. He talked to everyone when he first took over and said if...if we had any questions or any problems to let him know. His door is always open, he said."

"You must feel secure, having the new manager tell you that."

"Yes, I know he cares."

Jenna concluded the interview and leaned back in her chair, tapping her pencil on the table. Although she felt most strongly about Lynn and Sandra, she decided to have the rookie cop who'd been assigned to her delve more deeply into all four women's backgrounds. It wouldn't do to overlook someone. Maybe she'd be lucky and this case would be solved in record time. Sure. She might as well wish for the moon.

CHAD CHECKED HIS WATCH as the doorbell rang on Saturday morning. Sergeant Wakefield was right on time. He grabbed a shirt, sprinted downstairs, buttoning as he went, and opened the door.

She stood in the doorway, dressed in khaki slacks and a green knit shirt, looking morning-fresh and smelling morning-sweet. "Am I too early?"

He grinned. "You're right on time. Let me get my keys and we'll be on our way."

"I want to look at your security system first."

Of course. When he'd seen her in the doorway, he'd momentarily forgotten she was only here because she had to be. Trust Officer Wakefield to remind him. He led the way.

After she pronounced the system satisfactory and they returned to the living room, he went upstairs. He returned to find her standing before his wall of nature photographs.

"These are wonderful," she said, smiling at him for the first time since she'd arrived.

"Thanks. I'm pretty proud of them."

"You took them?"

"Yeah, photography's a hobby of mine. I had a darkroom in San Antonio. I miss it here, but I'm putting one in the house I'm building. For now, I have my pictures developed at a lab."

"I like this one," she said, pointing to a scene of trees decked in autumn colors.

"That's Lost Maples Park. Ever been there?"

"No, but I'd love to go. I hear the fall colors are stunning."

"They are. Every bit as brilliant as what you see in New England."

"Lovely," she murmured again.

"I have more. A whole wall of beach photographs upstairs. Wanna come up and see my etchings?"

She looked uncomfortable. "I think I'd rather go for brunch. I'm starved."

"You're a spoilsport, Sarge."

"No," she said firmly. "I'm a police officer, and I'm on duty."

He gave an elaborate sigh. "Let's take off, then. Food first."

They went to the River Café, a small, trendy restaurant in the museum district, which offered outside tables and an eclectic menu. They ordered a basket of rolls, assorted cheeses and a tray of fruit, and settled back to watch the Saturday-morning traffic. After two days of rain, the weather was sure to be Houston-muggy in a couple of hours, but for now—before the next rainfall— the air was cool and fresh. Cars crawled by, their windows open to catch the rare spring breeze. A jogger with arms pumping rhythmically and brows furrowed in concentration sprinted past.

"I saw you on TV the other night," Jenna said. "Your remarks were interesting."

"Only interesting?" he asked, disappointed.

"You laid out the issues very well," she said.

A cool response. Damn, he wanted some emotion from her, even if it was negative. "The mayor and council are knuckling under to pressure," he said, "but Houston is inundated with parolees. We have to find a way to rehabilitate them, especially the young ones." He stared into the distance for a moment. "We did some interviews with two newly released prisoners when I was in San Antonio, then decided to follow them for a year. One got accepted to a program similar to the one proposed here. The last I heard, he had a job and was studying for his Graduate Equivalency Diploma."

"And the other?"

"Six months after his release he was dead. Took a bullet to the chest during a gang shoot-out." He shook his head. "He'd gone back to the same environment that had sent him to prison. Maybe if he'd had the chance the other guy did, he'd have made it. That's why I'm so committed to this program *and* the location. Do you agree with me?"

Jenna nodded and he saw a glimmering of respect in her eyes. "You should tell that story next time you're on TV," she remarked. "You were very eloquent just then."

"Thanks," he said, pleased. "I'll do that."

"I read the rest of your mail," she said. "You're making some powerful enemies over this."

He shrugged. "Goes with the territory."

Their order arrived, and they were quiet for a while, concentrating on the food. Chad watched Jenna's hands as she buttered a roll. Again, he was taken by their delicacy. "You have beautiful hands," he said. "You should wear jewelry."

"I can't wear jewelry when I'm working," she said stiffly, "so I've never gotten into the habit." She looked away, then abruptly reached for her purse and pulled out some papers. "I've had someone check on the women I interviewed the other day."

So they were back to business. She'd shied away from his personal comment. Well, he reminded himself, they were here on business, and though she seemed to respect his stand on the halfway house, he still had something to prove to her—about himself, about his family. Nevertheless, he found the contrasts he saw in Jenna Wakefield intriguing, and he fully intended to get back to "personal." Very soon.

She spread several sheets of paper on the table.

"What did you find out?"

She brushed the first pages aside. "These two are off the list. Nothing suspicious in their backgrounds. One's been married, apparently happily, for six years. The other just got engaged."

"And?"

"Lynn O'Donnell, the production associate—that's what you called her, right?—is a recent communications graduate of Trinity University in San Antonio. She's bright, made the dean's list, and was active in campus activities. But she has a history of instability, dropped out of school one semester because of a near nervous breakdown, has been on medication in the past to alleviate depression."

"Lynn? She seems pretty together to me."

"Apparently she is at the moment. Another thing—she spent the last four-and-a-half years in San Antonio, where you were. That means she may have seen you on TV there, had time to develop an obsession with you, and then followed you here on purpose."

"I can't believe that."

Jenna gave him a wry smile. "I can. For one thing, she told me she decided to interview with your station here because she liked KSAN. Isn't that where you were?" He nodded, and she added, "When you've been involved with police work as long as I have, you learn to believe anything."

He raised a brow. "You sound as if you've been a policewoman for thirty years. You don't look it, Sarge." She remained silent and shifted in her chair. Her discomfort was obvious, so he returned to the business at hand. "What else did you find out?"

"Sandra Townes in your accounting office is a candidate. She's a loner, doesn't do much besides work and go to movies, sometimes the same movie over and over again. She fits the picture of the woman who fixates on a 'dream man,' someone out of reach. Usually these fans keep their fixation at the dream level, but occasionally something sets them off and they become consumed by the idea of making the dream come true."

"And Mona Switzer? She was on your list, too."

Jenna folded the papers. "She's apparently still angry at you for breaking off your relationship, but she's also involved with someone else now, so I don't think she's a likely suspect. I'm not even sure the information on Lynn and Sandra is significant, but we have to start somewhere." She took a sip of coffee. "By the way, one of Rose's letters mentioned the new house you're building. Give me a rundown on the people in your architect's office. Your contractor's, too."

"The contractor's staff is all male," Chad said. "There are several women in the architecture firm, including the architect herself."

"Tell me about her."

Chad laughed. "Cynthia Morrow's the last person I'd picture writing crazy letters."

"Not a good reason to discount her," Jenna said. "You know, after someone goes on a killing spree, his neighbors always say, 'But he's the last person I'd have suspected would do something like that.'"

Chad shook his head. "I still say Cynthia's not the type. Besides, she gave birth to her third child two months ago. When would she have the time...or the interest?"

"Good point," Jenna said. "But just to be on the safe side, I'll check out Cynthia and her staff." She took a pad from her purse and made a note.

"So what happens next?" Chad asked.

"Until we have a better handle on who Rose is, keep your security system operative. Don't open your door to anyone unless you know them well, and watch your back."

On that ominous note, breakfast ended.

Jenna followed Chad to the counter and waited while he paid the bill. "Errands next," he told her, as they made their way to the car.

To the accompaniment of rock music, they drove through the city. By the time he finished his chores, they'd visited a bookstore where he purchased half-a-dozen paperbacks for his parents to take on a cruise, an exclusive men's clothing store where he bought eight—*eight?*—shirts, a computer discount store, a hardware store, and the cleaner's.

At each stop, Jenna observed Chad's interaction with the clerks carefully. She felt she had pretty sensitive antennae, but she saw no one who put her on alert, no one who seemed inordinately interested in Chad, although women certainly gave him flirtatious glances. Which, she noted with disgust, he had no compunction about returning. *Thanks, mister,* she castigated him silently. *Make my job harder.*

"I have a meeting at the station now," he said as he put his cleaning in the car.

They arrived at Channel 6 a few minutes later. The meeting took place in Chad's office. The others present were his assistant, Bryan Carriker, and Tina Parker, a producer. "I've invited Ms. Wakefield to sit in on our meeting," Chad told them. "She'll be taking notes for her book."

As they took their places, Jenna wondered how Chad would interact with his staff. Autocratic, she'd bet. He was so sure of himself, he probably didn't accept, or even want, input from anyone. Probably gave orders and expected his employees to bow and scrape and carry them out. She settled back to see.

Chad leaned his elbows on the table and said, "I've been thinking. The city needs a public forum where people can discuss issues like the Montrose halfway house."

"Anyone can speak at city council meetings," Tina observed.

"Good point," Chad said, "but I'm thinking about a wider forum, where people could listen to experts, exchange views, argue things out."

"Mayor Hamilton's sure not going to provide that," Tina said.

"So we will."

Along with his two colleagues, Jenna stared at Chad in mute surprise. Finally, Bryan asked, "What do you have in mind?"

"The idea's just a vague one," Chad said. "I need your input, first to see if it's viable, and if it is, to flesh it out." Jenna was surprised at that. The autocrat she'd expected seemed nowhere to be found.

His voice eager, Chad continued, "Let's provide that forum with a weekly show. What do you think?"

"I think it's feasible," Tina replied. "In fact, I think the idea is fantastic."

"Second," Bryan said.

"Good. I'm glad you both approve," Chad said. "Question is, how do we implement it? What's the format?"

"How about..."

For the next two hours, Jenna listened as the three of them brainstormed. She watched Chad's eyes gleam with enthusiasm and found herself catching some of the excitement about the new show. "A public soapbox," she murmured.

"What'd you say?" Chad asked, and when she repeated her comment, he nodded. "The perfect name. 'The Public Soapbox.' Write that down, Bryan." Then he flashed Jenna a smile that would have turned her head— if she were the kind of woman to be charmed by a hundred-watt smile. She wasn't. Nevertheless, she found herself softening a bit more toward him. He was good at what he did. She had to respect him for that. And he wasn't dogmatic at all. He asked for everyone's input and listened to all opinions.

She was impressed, too, with his efficiency. By the time he and his colleagues had finished their discussion, plans were in place for the new program. Tina would determine when to air it, Bryan would arrange for publicizing it, and all of them were to come up with a list of possible issues for discussion, along with the names of appropriate experts.

The meeting had been so interesting, Jenna was surprised when she looked at her watch and saw that it was past five. On the way back to Chad's town house, he asked, "Did you come up with any more suspects today?"

Jenna shook her head.

"What's the next step, then?"

"I want to dig a little deeper on the women I told you about this morning and check out your architect. Monday I'll talk with Nate about the idea that someone in the television audience may be writing the notes. Then I'll get back to you."

"And in the meantime?" he asked, parking in front of his town house. They got out of the car and met on the sidewalk.

"Meanwhile," Jenna said, "sit tight, keep your eyes open, and if you get any more mail, call me immediately. You have my number." She turned and started toward her own car.

"Jenna."

He touched her arm. The contact was light, but it stopped her as surely as if he'd grabbed her. "Yes?"

He stepped closer. "Come inside."

She stared at him. "The schedule you sent me didn't mention plans for the evening."

"I don't have any," he said. "There's no one for you to check on, but I'd like your company. We can have a glass of wine and talk." His voice was soft, seductive.

"I . . . have plans," she lied.

His eyes told her he didn't buy her excuse, but he didn't press her. "Another time, then."

She didn't answer, just walked quickly to her car and got in. As she drove away, she admitted she'd been tempted to stay. Well, who wouldn't be? He was an interesting conversationalist and certainly handsome. But who knew better than she that you couldn't trust what you saw on the surface? Slick packaging could cover a multitude of sins.

ON SUNDAY Chad relaxed. Thank goodness the postal service took a day off each week, a day he didn't need to worry about hearing from Rose. In the evening, he decided to call both of his siblings to tell them his plans for "The Public Soapbox." He was sure Ariel would have some pithy comment, and Daniel, an analysis of the pros and cons of scheduling a new show.

Neither was home, but Ariel replied to his message via a fax he heard coming in just as he awakened Monday morning. "Great idea. I may try it myself. Imitation is the sincerest form of flattery." Chad chuckled as he read. How typically Ariel.

The machine began humming again. Chad pulled out two typed single-spaced sheets from Daniel. The analysis was there as expected, as well as a stern admonition to keep his life balanced. "Or," Daniel concluded, "as Ariel would say, 'All work and no play makes Chad a dull boy.'"

He laughed and dropped the two faxes on his dresser. Why should he strive for balance when work was so satisfying? He sprinted downstairs, further plans for "The Public Soapbox" percolating in his head. He couldn't wait to implement them.

In the kitchen, Chad popped a bagel in the microwave, and with a glass of orange juice in hand, went to the door to get the newspaper. It lay on the threshold, neatly folded. He bent and picked it up.

His hand froze in midair.

Beneath the paper was an envelope with one word scrawled across the front: "Chad." The same stationery, the same handwriting.

Gingerly, he picked up the envelope, then glanced up and down the street. Empty. Just his next-door neighbor's garage door opening and the sound of the car starting. He strode to the curb and peered around the corner. Nothing.

Back inside the house, he opened the letter.

Dear Chad,

Last night I dreamed about you and me. About us sitting in front of your fireplace with the lights turned low. I know I said you had one more chance to acknowledge me on television and you didn't. At first I was angry, but then I understood that the time wasn't right. You were just telling me we'll keep our love private for now. But you can't fight destiny. That's right, my darling, you can't fight me. We were meant to be together, and we will be—*soon*.

Rose, your phantom lover

Who was she?

Where was she?

Receiving the notes in the mail at his office made them a nuisance but easy to dismiss. Finding them at home, on his very doorstep, made them downright sinister. His unwanted pen pal could have peered in the window, could be lurking outside now. Watching. Waiting.

Annoyed but unable to stop himself, Chad went back to the door and turned the dead bolt. He closed the shades on the living room window, then went to the phone to call Jenna Wakefield.

CHAPTER FOUR

"SERGEANT WAKEFIELD."

The cool, businesslike voice was somehow reassurring. Damn, he didn't *like* needing reassurance. "Jenna, this is Chad Foster."

"What's wrong?"

Was his distress so apparent that she could read it in his voice? Any other time, he might have tried for flippancy, come back with something like, "Why, Sarge, couldn't I be calling just to say hello?" But not now, not with the sheet of rose-bedecked stationery glaring up at him from his coffee table. "I got another letter."

"Today? This early?"

He glanced at his watch, surprised to see it was only a few minutes past seven. "I found it under my newspaper."

"At your office?"

"At home."

"Bring it down—now. And don't handle it any more than you have to."

Irritated anew by the sense of relief that flowed through him at Jenna's words, he picked the letter up by one corner, grabbed his briefcase, and went out, bolting the front door.

He backed the Porsche out of the driveway and turned to scan the street again. Nothing suspicious. But, of course, he realized, beginning to feel paranoid, Rose might not be a stranger. She could be the redhead two doors down, the leggy blonde who jogged by his house every morning, even the gray-haired matron across the street.

In a few minutes, he turned onto the Katy Freeway and joined a line of cars that seemed to stretch endlessly ahead of him. Traffic was the bane of Houston's existence. Maybe he should do an editorial on that.

At police headquarters he hurried straight to Jenna's office. This morning she opened the door immediately and motioned him inside. "Let me see the letter."

He handed it to her, and she read it with the total concentration he'd come to expect from her. When she looked up, her face was solemn. "I don't like the idea of her coming to your home. She's getting desperate. I'll drop this off at the lab and have them do a fingerprint check. Be right back."

When she returned, she said, "I don't want to wait around for Rose to make her move. That could take days. We need to do something now." She leaned forward. "I want you to go on TV tonight and signal her. A rose in your lapel—isn't that what she wants?"

"Yes."

"Good. Let's see if that'll flush her out."

"That's it? I stick a rose in my buttonhole and hope she shows up on my doorstep? Then what?"

"We'll have someone watching you."

He hated the idea of someone patrolling his street, *baby-sitting* him.

Either his feelings were apparent or the sergeant was extremely perceptive. "If you want this woman out of your hair, you have no choice," she said firmly.

She was right, of course. He nodded.

"After the news show, go straight home," she told him. "Someone will follow you and watch the house."

"You?"

She shrugged. "Someone." She glanced past him at the glass in her door. "I'll call you later with details," she said, rising. "Don't worry. We'll wrap this up."

"I... Thanks, Jenna."

He left and drove to his office with the windows down. The odor of police headquarters lingered in his nostrils. Institutional floor cleaner, sweaty bodies, stale cigarettes ... and the reassuring scent of floral perfume.

AN HOUR LATER, Jenna shook hands first with Peter Chu, then with his attorney, Milton Babcheck, a rotund man in a suit that could have used a pressing. Peter wore typical college-student attire—jeans, T-shirt, and sneakers.

Babcheck took the chair Jenna indicated and leaned back, steepling his fingers. Peter sat on the edge of his chair, hands knotted in his lap, one foot tapping a nervous rhythm on the vinyl-covered floor.

Jenna repeated what she'd told Peter a few days before and began her questions. "Peter, your uncle indicated you study at his house occasionally and that you have a key."

"Yes."

"Did you study there on the afternoon of May third?"

"No, I didn't remember when you asked the other day, but I had a final." His voice cracked.

"In what subject?"

"Molecular physics."

"I assume you have a grade report to confirm that you were enrolled in that course?"

He pulled a sheet from his pocket and handed it to Jenna. She'd check with the department and verify the date of the exam, too. She noted his four-point average and looked up at him. "You're a good student, Peter. Finals must be a breeze for you."

"Yeah."

"So, did you finish this one quickly and leave early, maybe?"

A muscle in Peter's cheek twitched. He glanced at Babcheck, who nodded. "I . . . I don't know exactly what time I got through. Maybe around four."

Plenty of time for him to drive to his uncle's before Nick disappeared. "Where did you go when you finished the final?"

"B-back to the graduate house."

"Anyone see you there?"

Peter's gaze flicked to his lawyer, then back. "I don't know."

"Think about it."

"Hey, it was just an ordinary afternoon. How do you expect me to remember who I saw three weeks ago?"

Jenna narrowed her eyes. "No witnesses, Peter? You didn't see anyone on that 'ordinary' afternoon?" She kept her gaze on him, watching his Adam's apple work as he swallowed.

"W-wait, this guy on the next floor. I . . . Yeah, I saw him at the soft-drink machine."

"What's his name?"

Peter squirmed in his chair. "Larry. Larry Knowland."

"All right. I'll give Larry a call. Now, Peter, were you acquainted with Nicolas Morales?"

"No!" His voice came out in a squeak. "I never saw that kid except for his picture in the paper. I never went near that playground—"

"Never?"

"Never."

"Yet you *recognized* Nicolas from the picture in the paper."

Peter flushed, then turned pale. "Wh-what I meant was, I...I recognized the name of the subdivision he lived in. It's the same as my uncle's."

"And were you aware that your uncle knew Nicolas?"

"I know my uncle helps kids in his neighborhood. Later, he told me that boy was one of them. My uncle was upset when he heard the little boy disappeared. He talked to me about it."

"So you know he visited your uncle. Are you certain you didn't see him, even once?"

Babcheck held up his hand. "Sergeant, my client has answered the question. Peter is an exemplary young man. He's an honor student, he's working for the head of the physics department, he volunteers his time in a tutoring program for young children."

Young children. That set off Jenna's internal radar.

Babcheck continued. "Peter has an airtight alibi. He can produce a witness who saw him at the time the Morales child disappeared. What more do you want?"

"Nothing right now," Jenna said. "We're through for today. But, Peter, I still wouldn't plan on any out-of-town trips. I may want to talk to you again."

She rose, saw them out and watched, frowning, as they hurried away.

Why was Peter so antsy? Was he intimidated by the police questioning him as most people were, or did he have something to hide? Did Peter's nervousness warrant putting a tail on him? Taking up someone's time for what could well prove to be a wild-goose chase? She headed for the office of Zack Raymond, head of the Juvenile Division, and recounted her visit with Peter. "I think we should keep an eye on the boy, at least for a few days,'' she concluded.

"You're the boss on this one, Wakefield. Go for it."

She hurried back to her office and made arrangements for Corey Phillips, one of the best cops in the division, to tail Peter. "Get on it now," she told him. "I want to know what he does *this morning.*"

When Corey left, she sighed and shut her eyes. *Lord, don't let Corey find out anything terrible.* She didn't want to have to face Anita if Peter had—

Part of your job, Wakefield, she reminded herself. But it was the part she despised. The memory of Avery Sullivan's mother, her face contorted, screams tearing from her throat, played like a video in Jenna's mind. She didn't want to repeat that experience with Anita Morales. Automatically, she reached behind her to turn on the tape deck, then massaged her temples as soothing music flowed around her.

She checked her watch and groaned. Barely eleven o'clock, and she had a long day ahead. She checked on the date of Peter's final, then drove to the graduate house at Rice University in hopes of questioning potential witnesses. She was disappointed but not surprised to find only a handful of students in residence. Hadn't Peter remarked that Rice had limited summer school offerings? The couple of students she managed to locate couldn't remember seeing Peter on May third, in fact couldn't remember much about that afternoon at all. What did she expect? May third had been an ordinary day in most of their lives. Only for the Morales family was it a day to remember.

She stopped at the registrar's office next. Larry Knowland, she learned, was not enrolled this summer, so she got his home phone number in Fort Worth. Back at headquarters she placed a call to him. No answer.

Jenna leaned her elbows on her desk and dropped her head to her hands. She kneaded the taut muscles at the back of her neck, but that didn't dispel the tension. Even music didn't calm her. Why hadn't she found Peter Chu earlier, before the semester was over, before anyone who might have seen him after his final had left the city? Had she waited too long? Again?

Peter might well be telling the truth, but she couldn't rule him out as a suspect—not with his uncertain alibi and his uneasiness at being questioned. And Peter's involvement in the tutoring program made her uneasy. Was he really an exemplary young man volunteering his time to help young children, or did he have a more sinister motive? Well, at least she'd arranged for a tail. Maybe Peter would lead them to something. She hoped so. She hoped not. She couldn't face another Avery Sullivan.

She sat at her desk, eyes closed, for a long moment, then forced herself to alertness. She had work to do. Her next order of business was to arrange protection for Chad Foster this evening. And to see that her rookie assistant checked out every female in his architect's office, starting with Cynthia Morrow.

She got Nate's okay to have an unmarked car follow Chad home after his television appearance. "I'll do the stakeout," she told him.

"Okay. I'll put Monroe on with you."

"Good." She called Chad to tell him the procedure for this evening. "Have you made arrangements to go on the air?" she asked.

"Yes, I'll be on, red rose in my buttonhole."

Something in his voice revealed that he wasn't quite as cool as he tried to sound. In his own way, Jenna suspected he was as nervous as Peter Chu. That made him seem more human, more . . . approachable. Jenna cleared her throat. "Good. We'll have a car follow you home, park across from your town house, all night if necessary. And we'll put a tap on your phone in case she calls."

"Sounds like you've covered the bases."

"I think we have."

"Good. This should be a piece of cake," he said, a hopeful note in his voice.

"If all goes according to plan, it will be." She didn't add that was a very big if.

THAT AFTERNOON, JENNA rang the bell at the home of Arthur Green, ice-cream truck driver for Sendak's Dairy. He lived in a garden apartment in a section of town her college sociology text would have described as "economically challenged." His apartment complex was surrounded by body-repair shops, a used-car lot, and a pool hall.

"Garden apartment" was a misnomer. There was nothing remotely gardenlike about the property. The two-story brick units, grouped around a central courtyard, had been hastily constructed during Houston's last building boom. Clearly, they hadn't been built to last. Jenna noticed loose shingles along the edges of roofs, cracks in the walkways, peeling paint on Green's door.

A thin, disheveled man with iron gray hair answered the door. He wore a frayed bathrobe. "Yes?"

"Sergeant Wakefield, HPD." She showed her ID.

"You must have the wrong apartment."

"Arthur Green?"

"Yes." He looked puzzled, then scared. "What do you want with me?"

"I'm investigating the disappearance of Nicolas Morales. I'd like to ask a few questions. May I come in?"

He stepped aside and motioned her into a sparsely furnished living room. A TV set with the volume down was tuned to an afternoon talk show. Before it sat a lumpy armchair with sections of the day's newspaper scattered around it. A sofa in a garish mustard color completed the decor. Gingerly, Jenna sat on the couch. "I understand your route includes the Morales's neighborhood."

"Yes, but you don't think I—" He bit off his words. "Yes."

"Do you know Nicolas Morales?" She took out a photograph and handed it to him.

He didn't bother glancing at it. "I didn't know his name before, but I recognized him from the picture in the paper."

"Was he a customer of yours?"

"Sometimes when I went by the park, he'd come up to the truck."

"Alone or with a group?"

"Usually with a bunch of kids...a Little League team, I guess. They had baseball equipment."

"Did you ever see him alone?"

Green stared at the bare walls of his living room as if they might provide an answer. Finally he said, "Maybe once or twice."

"Did you ever have a conversation with him?"

"Sure. I talk to all the kids, ask 'em about sports, about school. That's the best part of the job, you know?" He smiled at her tentatively, and Jenna nodded.

"How long have you been with Sendak's, Mr. Green?"

"Two months."

That checked out. "What did you do before?"

A pained expression crossed his face. "Worked in an auto plant in Michigan. I got laid off over two years ago." He lapsed into silence.

"And you moved to Texas," she prompted.

"In January."

"Did you go to work when you first got here?"

"No, but not because I didn't try. The economy's not so great anywhere nowadays. I couldn't find anything. I saw the ad from Sendak's when I'd just about given up."

She'd heard similar stories. Times were hard. "Do you like driving an ice-cream truck?" she asked.

He brightened immediately. "Yeah. There's something about working with kids, makes it worthwhile. Listening to them, it helps you remember what life's all about."

She filed away that bit of philosophy to mull over later. "Your time sheet indicates you worked on the afternoon of May third."

His face turned chalk white. "You... you went to my job and asked about me? Look, lady—" he shot out of the chair and began to pace "—don't give me any trouble, please. I need this job. I didn't have anything to do with that kid, and I don't want Sendak's getting any idea I did." He reached the window, swung back around and glared at her.

"Mr. Green, a child's life is at stake. I'm talking to anyone who can give me information."

He sighed. "Y-you're right, of course." He returned to the chair, slumped down, obviously still upset. "I worked that day. What else do you want to know?"

"Did you see Nicolas?"

"I... don't remember. I see a lot of kids."

"Try, Mr. Green. It's important."

He frowned, concentrating, squeezing his eyes to slits. "I don't believe he came by that day."

"Did you see him in the neighborhood?"

Green shook his head. "I don't think so. I told you, I see a lot of kids."

"How about anyone else? See anybody who looked suspicious, anybody who didn't belong there?"

"N-no. Well, there might have been a few cars I hadn't seen before. I notice cars, you know, being from Detroit. Kinda keep a count of how many different makes I see every day. Just a little game I play with myself." He gave her a sheepish smile.

"And on May third, did you see any unusual vehicles?"

"I keep a record. Just a minute." Green got up, disappeared into the bedroom, and returned with a small spiral notebook. Jenna's pulse sped up as he flipped through the pages. He'd just presented her with a potential treasure trove of information. "'May third,'" he read, "'1960 blue Thunderbird, mint condition.' But I saw that one on the main street outside the subdivision. And, let me see, a van I hadn't seen before, a Toyota. I noticed it because the right rear tire was low and the back bumper was nicked, like someone had run into it at a slow speed."

"What color was the van?"

"Gray."

Jenna made some notes. "That information could be helpful." Green relaxed and smiled at her. "I don't suppose you noticed the license numbers on those vehicles?"

"No."

"May I take the notebook and make a copy?" she asked. "I'll get it back to you."

"Sure," he answered. "Glad to help."

"Mr. Green, did you work today?"

He nodded. "Yes, I have the morning route this week. I get up real early, come home afterward and take a nap." He glanced down at his robe.

Jenna stood. "I'd like to look at your truck."

Instantly, his tension returned. "Why?"

"Part of my investigation." He knew. He was well aware she'd go over every inch of that vehicle, searching for a trace of Nicolas Morales.

"It's not here."

As if that would stop her. "Is it at the dairy?" Though obviously reluctant to answer, he nodded and she said briskly, "I'll stop by."

He opened his mouth to protest, then apparently thought better of it. "Do you want me to come with you?"

"No. Thank you, Mr. Green. I'll be in touch. And from now on, when you list the cars you see, write down the license numbers. It'd help us a lot." He followed her to the door, and she heard the chain fall into place after he shut it.

She stopped by Sendak's and got their permission to check the truck. There was no barrier between the driver's seat and the rear of the truck, allowing easy access to the large freezers on either side. She'd never seen the inside of an ice-cream truck before, she realized, although the summer she was eight she'd fantasized about sneaking into the truck that roamed her neighborhood and binging on Popsicles to her heart's content.

Her inspection turned up nothing. No suspicious stains on the walls or vinyl floor, no bits of cloth or hair—at least none she could spot. She radioed the lab and put in a rush request for an investigator to comb the truck more thoroughly than she could.

Next, she contacted Corey Phillips. "Got anything on Peter?"

She could hear him yawn over the radio. "Nothing. I've been sitting here in front of the Physics Building for hours. Haven't caught sight of him since he went inside this morning."

"Stay with him," Jenna said. "I'll get someone to relieve you." Back at headquarters she made the necessary arrangements, then left.

She went home, took a bath, thawed out a package of frozen enchiladas, and lay down for a nap. She'd be up all night so she'd better get some rest while she had the chance.

EYES, CHAD THOUGHT as he entered the news studio. Thousands of pairs of eyes staring at him on their television sets. Did one pair belong to Rose?

He'd never given a thought to the viewers, at least not in this personal sense. He'd thought of the audience in collective terms. Now he was eerily aware of individuals, one in particular. What did she see when she looked at him? And more important, what did she *want?*

Distracted, he took his place at the anchor desk and began his editorial on Houston's traffic problems. He hoped Rose noticed the flower he wore. Tina Parker certainly had. "A rose in your lapel?" she'd teased. "Why not in your teeth?"

"Interferes with my speaking style."

He'd checked his reflection in the dressing-room mirror before he'd entered the newsroom. The perfect blood-red rosebud protruded from his buttonhole like a sinister red eye. Its too-sweet perfume drifted to his nostrils. He'd never send anyone roses again.

Now, as he concluded his editorial, he realized he had no idea what he'd said. He'd read his script automatically. For all he knew, he could have delivered it backward.

Apparently not. When he walked out of the studio, Tina, who stood in the hall, gave him a thumbs-up sign. "Sounded good."

"Thanks." Forgoing the usual after-broadcast chatter with the news team, he hurried to his office, picked up his briefcase, and headed out.

The parking lot was silent, almost deserted. A saffron moon rode high, centered in the dark sky. Chad approached his car. The Porsche cast a black shadow on the concrete, and Chad glanced at it warily, half expecting someone to be lurking beside it.

Of course not. There hadn't been time. Unless Rose was at the station already, a member of the staff. He turned to check the door to the building behind him. Nothing. Two steps more, and he reached his car. He peered into the shadows surrounding it. No one was there.

On the way home, he glanced repeatedly in his rearview mirror. Whatever cop was following him home was as invisible as a ghost. By the time he reached his street, he'd begun to wonder if anyone was really behind him. Then he saw a nondescript blue Ford Taurus pull up and park diagonally across from his town house. He caught sight of the long braid on one of the figures in the front seat and knew a feeling of relief. Jenna.

He pulled into his garage and went inside, wondering what to do next. After wandering through the house and suppressing the urge to look under his bed, he poured himself a glass of Scotch, grabbed the latest issue of *Time*, and sat down in the living room to wait. He remained there while his neck muscles screamed with tension, then dozed until the magazine falling to the floor roused him. Two-thirty. Surely Rose wasn't a post-midnight prowler. He went upstairs to bed.

ACROSS THE STREET, Jenna saw the light go out in Chad's living room. What had he said when she'd spoken to him earlier? That this evening would be a piece of cake?

It wasn't. It was nerves, boredom, frustration. She and Buck Monroe had been camped here for four hours, cooped up in the car, waiting for someone to materialize out of the darkness. She'd watched until her eyeballs ached and her head throbbed. She and Buck had chatted desultorily, shared division gossip, voiced the usual gripes about too-long hours and too little community appreciation, then lapsed into silence. She'd wondered if Chad was as bored as she was. She'd wondered if he felt like a prisoner, alone in his town house.

At 2:00 a.m. she and Buck shared a snack of turkey sandwiches, soft drinks, and potato chips that had long since gone limp. Police work was a waiting game, but she detested waiting in the car. Stakeouts were the pits.

Then she saw Chad's light go on upstairs. He was going to sleep, she guessed. Now *he'd* be stretched out in a comfortable bed, while she and Monroe had the dubious pleasure of spending another four hours in the confines of a car that had begun to feel like the city jail.

She had a good idea that Rose wasn't going to show tonight. When did the woman intend to make her move?

CHAPTER FIVE

CHAD WOKE ABRUPTLY the next morning. He jerked to a sitting position, stiff and disoriented, and gazed blankly around the room. Nothing had happened. Rose hadn't shown up. Surely Jenna would have called him if she had.

He went to the window, lifted a corner of the blind and peered out at the empty street. No use calling Jenna now. She was probably home, dead to the world.

Downstairs, he opened the front door and cautiously picked up his newspaper. Nothing underneath it today. Maybe the idea of meeting him in person had given Rose cold feet and she'd decided to back off. He wished he could believe it.

He skipped his usual breakfast, settled for a cup of strong coffee, and went to the station. The day dragged interminably, broken only by a brief call from a sleepy-voiced Jenna around noon. "Last night was a bust, but sit tight. She could still show."

He sat tight and when the mail arrived at midafternoon, he found a familiar envelope in the stack.

Darling Chad,
You wore the rose! Just seeing it, hearing your voice, and knowing you were talking to *me* was heaven. It doesn't matter that you were talking about traffic. I knew what you meant: that you and I are going to get in your beautiful black car and ride down the high-

way of life together. And we will, my love. Starting tonight. Meet me at the entrance to your parking lot at ten. I'll be waiting for you. My heart's already pounding.

Rose, your phantom lover

He called Jenna immediately.

"Do what she says. I'll be there tonight, parked across the street."

Suddenly he was nervous about Jenna trying to apprehend Rose single-handedly. The woman could be crazy enough to shoot Jenna or stab her. "You won't be alone?"

"No, Buck Monroe will be with me. The same guy who was there last night."

"Good."

"Chad," she said, as he was about to hang up, "don't do anything foolish when she shows up."

"Foolish?" What did she think, he was as crazy as Rose? "What do you mean?"

"I mean, like trying to detain her yourself. Leave that to the experts."

"Sure," he said dryly, knowing she *was* the expert, but resenting it.

He continued through the afternoon on automatic pilot, his mind on Rose and who she might turn out to be. A lonely, pitiful recluse obsessed by a face on TV? A knife-wielding psychopath, the rose a symbol for blood? A man using a feminine style in a clever attempt to lure a victim into a trap? Good God, his fantasies were becoming more macabre by the minute.

At four, irritable and edgy, he wandered down the hall to the tape room. It was empty and quiet, and he immersed himself in the files.

"Chad." He turned and saw Lynn O'Donnell advancing toward him. "I saw you come in here. Can I help you find something?"

"No, thanks. I'm just browsing."

She came closer and stood beside him, resting one arm on the shelf above them, allowing him a side view of full breasts straining against her knit blouse. "It's fascinating, isn't it, looking at these old tapes? Like a history lesson."

He glanced at the tapes, most of which were less than a month old. What was Lynn doing here? Could she be Rose? He remembered Jenna's words: *Lynn O'Donnell is a possibility.* Suddenly he felt boxed in. He stepped back.

Lynn took another step toward him, her skirt brushed against the shelf, and he heard the clink of metal in her pocket. A knife?

What to do? They were in an almost-soundproof room at the far end of the building. No one would hear a scuffle...or a shout.

Lynn smiled at him. "I watched your editorial last night," she said, her voice a purr.

Would she mention the rose? "What'd you think?" he asked.

"It was good. *You* were good." She gave him a slow, seductive smile. Then the hand she'd held behind her slid forward. Toward her pocket.

Chad tensed. He remembered Jenna's words: *Don't try to detain her yourself. Leave that to the experts.* The hell with that. There were no experts here. He waited, poised to spring.

Lynn slipped her hand in her pocket, brought out a tissue...and dislodged a key ring brimming with keys. It clattered to the floor.

There was his "knife"—a bunch of keys.

The door opened, and Catherine Paige poked her head in. "Excuse me, Chad. The production meeting is starting."

"I'll be right there." He glanced at Lynn, who had stepped discreetly away. "I'd better go," he muttered and started for the door.

"I'll see you later."

At ten? he wondered, but didn't ask.

He sat through the production meeting, glad he didn't have too much to say, then returned to his office. He leaned back in his chair, thinking he'd become certifiably paranoid. Before Rose, he wouldn't have had the slightest concern about the content of Lynn's or anyone else's pockets. Now, his imagination had gone wild, conjuring up perils even in harmless situations.

At seven, a knock sounded on his door, and he jumped. "Come in."

Tina poked her head in his office. "Are you planning to go on tonight?"

"Um, no."

She waved and shut the door. Chad scowled after her, hating the startle reflex he hadn't been able to control. *Just let Rose show up,* he thought, *so I can get on with my life.*

Time passed, minute by lengthy minute. At exactly two minutes to ten he left his office and walked toward the lobby door, wondering what awaited him on the other side.

"Night, Mr. Foster," the guard said.

"Good night," he answered, and opened the door.

He drove his car across the lot and parked just outside the entrance, got out and leaned against the front fender. Down the street he saw a car—a Chevy this time, with two occupants.

He stood by the Porsche, trying to look casual, while his muscles knotted with tension. He gazed up and down the street, but saw nothing. At ten-forty, members of the news team began leaving the lot. Tank Diamond, the sportscaster, slowed and rolled down his window. "Having car trouble?"

"No, just waiting for someone."

Tank drove away, other cars followed, and Chad was alone again. He looked at the sky, overcast tonight, counted the cars left in the parking lot, the windows in the building across the street, the pebbles on the pavement in front of him. Where in hell was Rose? Was she playing cat and mouse with him, telling him she'd be in one place, waiting to spring at him in another?

At eleven he saw the door of the Chevy open. Jenna got out and started toward him. He crossed the street and met her on the other side. "I don't think Rose is coming tonight. Something must've scared her off," she said. "You might as well go home."

"What about you? Are you through for the night?"

"Yeah."

He gestured toward the Chevy. "Is that your car?"

"No, it's Buck's."

"I'll take you home, then."

"Buck will drop me off."

He reached for her arm. "Come on, Sarge. If you're not too tired, we can stop off for a drink first. I need the company." *Not just any company. Yours.*

She started to pull away, then paused and looked into his eyes. "I guess you do. Let me tell Buck. I'll be right back."

As she returned to the car, he watched, admiring her graceful stride, the enticing sway of her hips. Even his frustration with Rose couldn't dim his appreciation of this attractive woman. A few minutes later, in the close confines of his sports car, with her sweet scent wafting to his nostrils, he was very aware of her nearness. He longed to touch her, but he clamped his hands around the steering wheel.

He drove to City Lights, an intimate club located on the top floor of the Stouffer Hotel in Greenway Plaza and one of his favorite late-night spots. He parked in the garage downstairs and came around to open Jenna's door. She started to get out, then paused. "I . . . I can't go in there."

"Why?"

"I'm not dressed appropriately."

He chuckled at that. With her tall, lithe body, her dark hair and ivory skin, she was striking. She wore a skirt that showed a length of long, slim leg. In that skirt and her soft, clingy blouse, her face devoid of makeup except pale pink lip gloss, she'd look better than the roomful of overdressed, ultra-aggressive females upstairs. She could wear a sack and still outshine most other women. "Come on, Sarge." He took her hand. "You look fine."

Instead of letting her go, he tucked her hand under his arm and kept her close as they walked into the lobby. They rode up in a glass-enclosed elevator that provided a view of lighted fountains in the atrium. Upstairs, they took a table by the window and ordered—mineral water for Jenna, Scotch for him.

She glanced around the dimly lit, crowded room, then turned to the windows and stared out. Chad followed her gaze. Directly below them, the Southwest Freeway was a glittering ribbon of lights from passing cars. Farther out, lights illuminated buildings from the Galleria area to the suburbs. "Nice view, isn't it?" he said.

"Yes, beautiful." She smiled at him, then added, "This is the first time I've been here."

I'll make sure it's not the last, he thought, but knew if he said the words, she'd retreat faster than a cornered rabbit. Instead, he chose the one subject he knew she'd be interested in. "I had an encounter with Lynn O'Donnell this afternoon."

Jenna looked up sharply, all business now. "What happened?"

"She came into the tape room while I was there." He summarized the episode and Jenna listened carefully. "She couldn't be Rose, could she?" he asked. "Rose made an appointment for ten."

Jenna chewed on her lip. "Maybe she couldn't wait. I don't like this. We'll station someone at your office, starting tomorrow."

"Damn! I was afraid you'd say that."

"He'll be in plain clothes. You can say he's doing some kind of internship in television. No one will know who he is."

"*I'll* know."

"You're not making sense," she said, annoyance creeping into her voice. "I thought we'd ironed this out. You have a crazy person stalking you. You asked for police help, and now you turn around and tell me you don't want us to do our job."

He sighed and frowned into his drink. "I don't like having someone run my life."

"*Rose* is doing a pretty good job of running your life. Why don't you cooperate so we can get her out of the way?"

"Give it another day or two."

She shook her head. "What if she shows up tomorrow?"

"I'll—"

"You'll what? Be a hero? The chief would have my head *and* my badge if I let you get away with that."

He sighed. "Okay. Send your man in tomorrow."

"Let's hope Rose surfaces soon," Jenna said. "I was so sure she'd turn up tonight. Something—I don't know what—must've spooked her."

"Maybe she's given up," Chad said hopefully.

"Maybe. Imagining a love affair is one thing. Living it is another. Maybe Rose couldn't deal with the reality." Jenna sighed. "These cases are confusing. I'll talk to our psychologist tomorrow. Maybe she'll come up with something, and we can go from there."

"Any other ideas?" Chad asked.

She shook her head. "Your architect's off the list, by the way. She checked out okay."

Chad smiled. "Told you so."

Jenna smiled back. Then she turned and stared out the window. From the piano across the room came the romantic strains of "Unchained Melody." Chad watched Jenna's face, silhouetted against the night sky. He wanted to reach out to her, put his hand against her cheek, and draw her gaze back to his. Instead, he folded his hands in his lap and asked, "What do you think about when you're on a stakeout?" Maybe he could learn something personal about her.

Her expression was pensive. "Sometimes when it's dark and quiet, I think about the people sleeping in the houses around me. I try to imagine what their daytime lives are like. If they're happy or lonely. What they want out of life. And sometimes," she said, turning back and smiling at him, "I think about how long it is till the stakeout's over and I can go home."

He liked her smile, the sparkle in those beautiful eyes. "You enjoy your work, don't you?" he asked.

"Yes, it's a challenge—solving problems, figuring a way to the end of the maze. Sometimes it's incredibly boring, like last night, sitting in that car waiting and nothing happening. But the payoff makes it all worthwhile. Most of the time," she added, and the light faded from her eyes.

"And the other times?"

She shrugged. "Other times, there's no way out of the maze." Before he could question that, she said, "How do you know the chief?"

He let her get away with the change of subject. "He's an old family friend and a poker buddy of my father's."

"Macauley plays poker?"

"Sure. It's not illegal."

She shook her head and chuckled.

"Anyway," Chad continued, "he and Dad played football together at UT."

"Your dad played football...? Martin Foster!"

"You've heard of him."

"Of course, I have. He's a University of Texas legend. I just never connected the name with you."

Pleased at her response, he said, "You'll have to meet him someday."

"Oh, no, I—"

"Sarge," he said softly, "don't back off. I'm not going to bite you. I just want to be friends."

"We're not friends," she objected. "We're professional acquaintances. A cop and a case."

"Even professional acquaintances can be friends."

"I...don't know."

"Scared, Sarge?"

As he expected, she bristled at his words. "Of course not."

"Good. Friends?" He extended his hand.

After a moment's hesitation, she grasped it. "I . . . uh, all right." As their hands touched, he knew he hadn't told her the whole truth. Yes, he wanted friendship, but now, as she pulled away, he realized he wanted more.

"Tell me how you decided to become a cop." He'd concentrate on the police officer and hope she'd lead him to the woman behind the uniform.

"Runs in the family."

"Your mother's a cop?"

She caught the teasing glint in his eye and laughed. The sound was mellow, sexy. He realized it was one of the few times he'd heard her laugh. "My dad," she said.

"Is he with the HPD?"

"He's chief of police in Plano."

He knew the city, a suburb of Dallas. "Is that where you grew up?"

"No," she replied. "When Dad took the position with Plano, we had to move."

Something in her tone told him the move hadn't been to her liking. "How old were you?"

"Sixteen."

"The change must have been hard for you."

She shrugged. "I got used to it."

He doubted that. "Where did you live before you moved?"

"Garland."

He'd worked at the Foster station in Dallas for a while, and he knew the city and the surrounding towns. Blue-collar Garland was a far cry from upper middle-class Plano. He wondered if the adjustment to Plano had been a difficult one for a sensitive sixteen-year-old, and he'd bet Jenna had been as sensitive as an adolescent could be. "What did you do after high school?" he asked.

"Went to college at Southwest Texas State in San Marcos, then moved here." She smiled at him suddenly—a smile that warmed him, made him want to see more of the relaxed Jenna Wakefield, not the businesslike cop. "You'd make a good detective. You've wormed my life story out of me."

"I don't think so," he murmured. "I think there's more to Jenna Wakefield than the stats you just gave me. A lot more."

Her dark brown eyes met his, wide and surprised. He held her gaze and saw uncertainty and a brief flash of longing that mirrored his own. "Jenna," he whispered and captured her hand. This time she didn't pull away but let her fingers rest in his. They sat silently, their gazes locked, Chad's thumb gently tracing circles on her palm. He wanted her closer, her arms around him, her mouth on his. He wanted to taste her, touch her. . . . *Too soon.*

He knew when to let go. Reluctantly, he drew his hand back and said lightly, "We have something in common. I followed in my father's footsteps, too. In fact, all of his kids did. I already told you Ariel's in Corpus Christi. My brother Daniel manages the El Paso station."

"Really?"

"When Dad decided to retire, he pitted us against each other, told us the one whose ratings increased the most that year would get Houston."

"And you came out on top."

"No, Ariel did, but by the time the contest was over and she'd won, she decided she didn't want to leave Corpus. Meeting her future husband there may have had something to do with it."

She smiled, obviously at ease again. "I don't have to ask if you enjoy your work."

"The enthusiasm shows, doesn't it? I like the challenge of a new position—taking over a station and molding it my way. Even though all the stations in the Foster chain are basically similar, each one has its own personality, created by a combination of community needs and the station manager's leadership."

Jenna rested her chin on her hands. "What are your plans for Channel 6?"

"Houston's a dynamic city, a true melting pot with different ethnic groups, different cultures. I want the station to reflect that. Not just by having the politically correct mix of news reporters, but through our programs, like 'The Public Soapbox.' And, of course—" he grinned "—I want to kill the competition."

Jenna grinned back, then her expression turned serious. "And when you've accomplished your goals, will you move on?"

"No. Houston's home, and Channel 6 is our lead station. After I have it where I want it, I'll do more with the overall management of the chain."

"Are you sure you won't . . . lose interest?"

He shrugged. "I guess we won't know that until it happens."

She nodded and took a sip of mineral water.

They continued talking until he saw her stifle a yawn. "I'd better get you home," he said. When he turned to signal the waiter, he was surprised to see that the room was almost deserted. A glance at his watch told him it was nearly one o'clock. They'd been here well over an hour. He liked talking to her, sharing his goals and aspirations. In his busy life, he didn't have much time for conversation or confidences.

On the way to Jenna's, only the purr of the motor broke the silence. When he pulled up in front of her house, he turned and saw that she'd fallen asleep. He started to call her name, then paused. The light from the streetlamp cast her face in soft shadows. Thick dark lashes lay against the smooth ivory of her cheeks. Her breasts gently rose and fell as she breathed. Chad gazed at her, drinking in his fill. His body tightened with a desire the strength of which surprised him.

She'd given him no sign that she was interested in him as anything more than a case, one that had been thrust into her unwelcoming arms. Their relationship, if he could call it that, was destined to be brief. She'd find Rose; he'd thank her and be on his way. She'd be glad to write "Solved" next to his case number, and he'd be relieved to get on his with life. Right? Then why did he have this inexplicable yearning to touch her, to draw her against him, to kiss those gently parted lips?

As he wrestled with his thoughts and needs, she stirred and her eyes fluttered open. "Oh," she murmured, "we're home."

He came around and opened the door for her, took her arm and was pleased that she didn't pull away. At the door he let her go.

She fumbled for her key, inserted it in the lock, then said, "Lock your doors on the way home."

"Yes, Sergeant."

"I'm serious," she said, her expression solemn. "You have to watch out. If you have a message from Rose when you get home, call me."

"Yes."

"I'll let you know tomorrow what we'll do next." She pushed the door open.

"All right. Good night."

She stepped inside, and he started down the sidewalk. "Chad."

"Yes?"

"Be careful."

"I will."

She stood in the doorway and watched until he got into the car, locked the door, and turned on the engine.

He drove home slowly, his thoughts confused. Why, of all women, had Jenna Wakefield sparked his interest? Since his divorce, he'd limited his relationships to women who liked a little fun, a little romance, with no strings attached. Jenna wasn't like those women. She was too serious, too controlled, too distant. Maybe that was the reason. Her aloofness made her a challenge, and he'd never been able to resist one. But more than that drew him to her—the sound of her voice, the scent of her perfume, the vulnerability behind the tough-cop exterior. He enjoyed being in her company. This wasn't the time, but he knew that with very little provocation he could come to care for her. Very much.

He turned down his street, parked his car in the garage, and after double-locking his door, went upstairs to bed.

JENNA'S ALARM CLOCK woke her far too early the next morning. Her first thought was of Chad. Was he all right? He hadn't called, so he had to be. Or maybe he hadn't phoned because he couldn't, because Rose—

She reached for her phone and called him. "H'lo," a raspy voice answered.

He was home in bed. Safe. More relieved than she wanted to admit, she said brusquely, "Jenna Wakefield. Just called to be sure Rose didn't show up."

"Everything's fine."

"Good. Go back to sleep." Before he had a chance to respond, she hung up.

On her way to the shower, the thought crossed her mind that in the past twenty-four hours she'd become considerably more interested in the Foster case. Well, of course. The letter writer was about to reveal herself, bringing the case to a climax. That always got her adrenaline flowing.

She turned the shower on cold. With the late hours she'd been keeping—not just last night but the night before, too—she needed a good icy blast to wake her up. She scrubbed herself briskly and stepped out.

As she toweled dry, she predicted that she'd likely have Rose in custody within the next day or so. Then she could close the Foster case, and get on with her real work. No more camping out in front of Chad's town house, no further obligation to watch him on the ten o'clock news. No more listening to his voice or feeling the touch of his hand. She thought of the music playing last night, the dim room, the way he'd said her name as if— No! She mustn't think that way. Chad Foster wasn't right for her, no matter what she was beginning to feel. He would hurt her, she was certain. Hadn't Mona Switzer said he had a short attention span? Mr. Love 'Em and Leave 'Em. "No," she told herself again, marching into her bedroom to dress.

The first pair of panty hose she pulled out of her drawer had a run; so did the second. She mumbled an expletive, grabbed a third pair and yanked them on. She took a uniform out of her closet and surveyed it with distaste, wondering why it suddenly seemed so drab. Why couldn't police officers wear bright colors once in a while, she wondered crossly. God, she was crabby this morning. Lack of sleep was certainly telling on her. She'd better have a cup of strong black coffee, maybe two, before she went to work.

Fortified with caffeine, she drove to headquarters. She scheduled an appointment with Dr. Sonia Overstreet, the psychologist, to discuss Rose, then dialed Larry Knowland, the student who was to confirm Peter Chu's alibi.

This time she got lucky. "Yeah," a voice mumbled.

Was the kid still asleep? At practically...eight o'clock? She'd wake him up fast. "Larry Knowland?"

"Yeah."

"Sergeant Wakefield, Houston Police."

He came to attention, voice clearing immediately. "Yes."

"I'm checking on the whereabouts of Peter Chu on the afternoon of May third. Do you recall seeing him that day?"

"Yes, ma'am. At the Coke machine in the dorm. Around five o'clock." His answer was quick. *Too* quick.

"Have you spoken with Peter in the past two days?"

There was a long pause. "Um, yes, ma'am."

"And he told you I'd be calling?" When Larry didn't reply, she said, "*Did* you see him on May third?"

"I...don't remember."

"Thanks, Larry. Go back to sleep." She hung up and shoved the phone away with a sigh of frustration.

As she muttered irritably, the door opened and Gracie poked her head in. "Talking to yourself?"

"Was I?"

"Sure sounded like it, unless you have someone stashed in your desk drawer." When Jenna grimaced, she said, "You look like you could use a break, maybe talk to a real person. Can I come in?"

"Sure."

Gracie sat down and reached into her pocket for an envelope. "I brought some pictures."

Jenna took the packet of snapshots. The first showed Gracie, her arm around a handsome, dark-eyed man with tousled black hair and a sexy grin. "Ah, this must be

Jorge." Gracie nodded, and Jenna asked, "When are you two going to get together?"

Gracie sighed dramatically. "When he realizes I'm not an extension of his little sister. When he decides he can't live without me. I'm trying to help him along, but he's so dense."

Jenna smiled for the first time that morning and flipped through the rest of the pictures. "Where were these taken?"

"At a family picnic. See, there's his mother. She likes me."

"That's good."

"His father likes me, too," Gracie went on. "And his sisters and his brothers *and* his grandmother. Jorge likes me, too."

"That's good, too."

Gracie shook her head vehemently. "No, it's not. I want him to *love* me. I think he does, down deep, but he just doesn't know it yet. I wish I could think of a way to make him pay attention."

"Send him a love note. Send him roses."

Gracie snorted. "You're thinking about your case."

"Yeah. Maybe it'll wrap up this week."

Jenna fiddled with a pencil while Gracie studied her intently. "Funny, you don't look very happy."

"Of course, I'm happy." She drew a rose on her notepad, studied it, then added a couple of thorns.

"Ouch," Gracie said. "Those thorns look nasty. The celebrity getting to you?"

Jenna ripped the page off her pad and wadded it up. "Lack of sleep's getting to me. Night before last I was staked out in front of his house for eight hours and nothing happened. Last night I waited at the TV station until after eleven, then he didn't get me home until nearly two...."

"Two. Mmm-hmm. Sounds fascinating."

Jenna looked up into her friend's knowing eyes and scowled at her. "He needed some company, so we had a drink and talked. I was off duty."

"Of course, you were. No need to make excuses."

Jenna lifted her chin. "I'm not."

"Good. What'd you talk about?"

"Our families, all kinds of things. He's... he's interesting."

"What happened to arrogant, self-absorbed and, let's see, what else? Rude?"

"I never said he was rude."

"You never said he was interesting, either."

Jenna tossed the wad of paper at Gracie and scored a direct hit. "I didn't know him before."

"So is this the start of a relationship?"

"No way." Jenna shoved her chair back from the desk and got up, wishing she had room to pace. "Not in a million years. I know his type. He's the kind of guy that shows up at the country club with a new woman on his arm every month. Women are interchangeable. Drop one, replace her with another."

"You don't really know that, do you?" Gracie said.

"I can tell. He flirts with every woman he sees—store clerks, hostesses in restaurants. I've spent enough time with him to know. And we ran into one of his castoffs, a woman he'd 'lost interest in.' That's a direct quote. And *she* told me his attention span was short." She glanced at the windowsill. "I need to water these violets."

"I think I've been dismissed." Gracie got up, too. "Want to meet me at the gym one morning this week, maybe work off some of that nervous energy?"

"Sure. Day after tomorrow, 6:00 a.m." She followed Gracie out, went to the water fountain and filled a pitcher for her plants. When she returned, she found Corey Phillips seated at her desk.

"Where were you last night?" he said. "I tried to find you all evening."

"On a stakeout." Forgetting the violets, she set the pitcher down and sat across from him. "You have news?"

"Yeah. Yesterday our friend Peter took a ride on his lunch hour. He drove out South Main about thirty miles, almost to Richmond, pulled off at a roadside park, and got out of the car."

A roadside park. This might be... Oh, God, she didn't want to think what it might be. "What'd he do there?"

"I couldn't see everything from where I was because the park is lower than the highway and I didn't want to get too close. What I saw was this. He got out and looked around, seemed real edgy, too. I don't know if he thought he was being followed or if he was waiting for someone. Anyway, after a while he walked farther into the park. I lost him for a few minutes, then he came back."

"Did he take anything with him?"

"A plastic bag, the kind you get in grocery stores. He brought it back with him, too."

"How long was he back in the park?"

"Not more than five minutes," Corey said. "Then he got in the car, waited another few minutes, and drove back to school. What do you think?"

"I think," Jenna said, "we're going to get a few of our buddies together, take a ride out to that park, and search it from one end to the other." *And we're going to pray to God we don't find Nicolas Morales's body.*

CHAPTER SIX

JENNA STOOD in the middle of the rocky path into the roadside park, waiting for the rest of the patrol cars to arrive so she could direct the search. The sun glared down. Despite the leafy oak trees that shaded the picnic area, she could already feel sweat seeping down her back and chest.

Two men in scraggly jeans and faded T-shirts sat at one of the cement picnic tables, sipping beer from cans. Country music blasted from a boom box on the table. They eyed the small knot of police officers with curiosity.

Jenna walked over to them. "We're conducting a search here. You'd better find another spot."

"Whatcha lookin' for?" The younger of the two smiled at her, displaying a chipped tooth.

"That's police business." She gave him a cool stare and saw his cockiness disappear. He stood and motioned to his companion, and they headed for their pickup, gunned the motor and roared out, raising up a cloud of dust and gravel.

Jenna was relieved they'd gone. If the search revealed what she feared, the sight wouldn't be pretty. She shivered and watched as three more blue police cars pulled up.

When they were assembled in the drive, she divided the searchers into teams and assigned each an area to investigate. "Okay, everyone." She gave them a rundown on Peter Chu, then continued. "We're looking for Nick

Morales's—'' Saying the word hurt, but she forced it out. "Body. Go over every inch of ground. Check that creek down there," she added, gesturing toward her left, "and look around for anything—shoes, buttons, even a pencil—any evidence that he's been here. Let's go."

She and Corey combed the far end of the park, working slowly and systematically. Nothing. No sign of a burial, nothing under any of the bushes. Only disposable cups, remains of a Kentucky Fried Chicken dinner and a nest with three eggs in one of the low bushes. A mockingbird—probably the owner of the nest—chattered angrily as Jenna pushed the leaves aside.

She smelled nothing more ominous than sun-baked earth and leaves, heard no shouts of discovery from her colleagues, and after two hours called off the search.

"If there's nothing around, what the hell was the Chu kid doing way out here?" Corey said, kicking at a rock.

Jenna wondered the same thing. "You'll just have to keep an eye on him, follow him all the way in here if he comes again." Could Peter have come back at night, she speculated, moved whatever he'd left, if indeed he'd left something? But they'd seen no evidence.

Frustrated, feeling she was always a minute too late, Jenna climbed into the car again and drove back to town. Corey rode with her. When they reached headquarters, he gave her a friendly hug. "Maybe this weekend you ought to get your mind off this case. We could get together and have a few drinks or see a movie—whatever you like."

Corey was a good friend. They'd gone out a couple of times and she liked his company. But right now... "Thanks. I'm so overrun with work, I'll be lucky to come up for air. You know they put me on a stalking case."

"Yeah, I heard." He got out of the car, came around and met her beside her door. "If you get some time, give me a call." He headed across the parking lot toward his own car. "I'm going over to the Rice campus again."

She waved and went inside to her office. At her desk she caught up on paperwork, trying to lose herself in the mindless routine. By midafternoon she gave up. She'd had a couple of guys checking out the Morales's neighborhood, searching for the gray van Arthur Green had mentioned. Maybe she'd drive out and look around herself.

She glanced up as Nate Harris appeared in her doorway. She motioned to him to enter. From the look on his face, she knew this would take a while.

"Macauley wants to know how the Foster case is coming," Nate said without ceremony, easing himself into a chair.

"I'm working on it," Jenna said with a grimace. "Foster signaled the letter writer. She made an appointment to meet him last night, but she didn't show."

Nate raked his fingers through his sparse hair. "Macauley wants results."

"He wants a miracle," Jenna corrected him. "Don't you think I want results, too? You think I enjoy having this hanging over me?"

"Macauley says—"

"I don't care what Macauley says." She took a long breath and tried to calm herself. "Look, Nate, I know he's putting pressure on you, but tell him we're doing the best we can. I'm not a mind reader or a shrink. I don't know why the woman didn't turn up last night."

Nate cracked his knuckles, a sure sign of agitation. "What about today?"

"I checked with Foster this morning. Nothing happened during the night and I don't have any messages from him, so I imagine nothing's gone on today, either."

"Who've you got over at the TV station?" Nate asked.

"I've started a couple of people on shifts. No messages from them, either."

"Nothing!" His knuckles cracked again. "How about the lab? Fingerprints on the letter check out?"

"No, but we really didn't expect them to, did we? Rose may be a loony, but I doubt she has a criminal record. I'm sorry, Nate. I guess Macauley gave you a rough time."

Nate sighed and nodded, swiping at the sweat that beaded his brow. "He did. You know, the man's a master of the carrot-and-stick technique. He sort of hinted he'd keep both of us in mind for prime assignments if—"

"*If* the Foster case is wrapped up. And if not?"

"He didn't say."

"Of course not," Jenna retorted. "That's the stick. We know Macauley's like an elephant. He never forgets—especially lousy work on a case involving his friends. Right?"

"Right. I told him you're doing your best, and I know you are. You're a damn good cop."

"Thanks. I promise you, Nate, I'm doing everything I can for Foster. I'm supposed to talk to Dr. Overstreet in the morning. Maybe she'll give me some insight into Rose's mind. I—"

The phone rang.

She was tempted to ignore it, but Corey could be calling with news of Peter Chu. "Sergeant Wakefield."

"Jenna, this is Chad."

"Yes." Nate started to get up, but she shook her head and pointed at the phone, mouthing Chad's name. "Lieutenant Harris is in my office. Do you mind if I put this on Speaker?"

"No, go ahead." His voice boomed into the room. "I have another letter."

"Read it."

"It's hard to make out. The writing is sloppy." He cleared his throat.

"Darling Chad,
I'm sorry, sorry, sorry I didn't come last night. I couldn't. Spirits stood between us. I tried to come to you, but they held me back. But I will come in a day, in a week, whenever they let me go. I will contact you by letter, my darling, so you can expect me. Now that I've seen the rose, I know that you understand what is meant to be. Even though roses have thorns, even though there might be pain or blood first, we will be together.

Rose, your phantom lover."

Pain or blood! "I don't like the sound of this one," Jenna muttered.

"Neither do I," Chad agreed. "What do we do?"

"Can you drop that letter off to us this afternoon?" Nate asked. "I want the lab to take a look at it, and Sergeant Wakefield will take a copy to our psychologist in the morning."

"All right."

Nate continued. "Let's meet in my office tomorrow afternoon, say two-thirty, and discuss the next step."

"I'll be there."

After they hung up, Nate said, "I'll let Macauley know the latest development. You wait for Foster."

"Okay."

Chad arrived an hour later, looking like an ad from *Gentlemen's Quarterly* in a navy suit, crisp white shirt and red Paisley tie.

Jenna scrutinized the letter he handed her. She hadn't liked the sound of it; she liked the look even less. The penmanship was indeed sloppy, almost illegible. Lines wavered up and down with drunken abandon. She looked up and met Chad's eyes.

"Not good," he said.

"No, it isn't. Hopefully, we'll come up with a plan tomorrow. Meanwhile, go home, stay calm, and—"

"Whoa, Sarge. I agreed to having someone watching my office, but I'm not going to barricade myself in my house and let some demented fan take control of my life." His eyes flashed with anger and frustration.

"Just for tonight," Jenna suggested in a tone meant to be soothing.

"I feel like a caged animal."

He looked like one, too. Jenna felt a stirring of sympathy. "I know this must be hard for you."

"Yeah." His sigh was deep and ragged. "Look, I'm sorry. I don't mean to be uncooperative, but I resent this... this phantom presence in my life."

"We'll meet tomorrow, figure out a way to make Rose come forward, and it'll be over soon." She wasn't sure that was true, but she sensed it was what Chad needed to hear.

"Yeah, thanks." He got up and started to leave, then paused with his hand on the doorknob. "What if I went out this evening, with police protection?"

"Um, sure. That'd be okay, but I'd have to arrange for someone—"

"I was thinking of you."

Oh, Lord, she'd walked right into that one. "I, uh—"

"C'mon, Sarge. The Houston Symphony's playing at Hermann Park tonight. 'The B's of Summer—Bach, Brahms, and Beethoven.' You like music. Come with me."

"You shouldn't go to the park. It's too crowded. Rose—"

"Said she'd write before she comes. Any reason to believe she's following me?"

"No, but—"

"See? Besides, I'll have a bodyguard."

She grasped at the first excuse she could think of. "I'm in uniform."

He glanced down at his business attire. "So am I. Go home and change, and I'll pick you up at eight."

She hesitated. She loved the symphony. In fact, she'd thought about going to the park concert herself. But to go with Chad? She was already far too attracted to him to risk another evening in his company. But the chief wanted his pal to get the royal treatment. Okay, she'd give it to him. "All right. I'll see you at eight."

CHAD SPREAD A BLANKET on the hill behind the amphitheater, and they sat. On the stage below, musicians tuned up. Around them, families cleared away the remains of picnic dinners, lovers cuddled close together, two children tickled each other and giggled. Jenna drew her legs up and leaned back for a moment to look at the sky. A full moon rose, a couple of stars glittered through the twilight. Even this late in the day, the air was heavy with heat and humidity. The faint odor of grass mingled with the smells of popcorn and humanity.

"Glad you came?" Chad asked.

She turned to smile at him. "Yes."

"So am I." His voice was deep, soft.

The conductor strode to the podium, the crowd applauded, then a hush fell, broken only by a few latecomers. The maestro raised his baton, and the music began.

Jenna leaned forward to listen; Chad stretched out beside her, propped on one elbow, running a blade of grass between his fingers. He seemed totally relaxed. Watching him, she would never guess the stress he was under. He had to be wondering who was stalking him, if she would come nearer, and what she might do.

Jenna loved the clean elegance of Bach's music, but as the sky darkened, she found her eyes straying from the orchestra and lingering on Chad. He had a face that might be found on a Greek statue—finely chiseled features, a strong jaw, the hint of a cleft in his chin. The arrogant man she'd met in Nate Harris's office was gone, replaced by someone who could be a friend...a lover. And, oh, she was tempted to let that happen. As the passionate strains of a Brahms concerto drifted into the night, she thought it would be so easy to say yes to the desire starting to build inside her.

She watched his strong profile, realizing that he was absorbed in the music. A tiny smiled played on his lips. Her pulse quickened and she leaned closer to him, barely conscious of the movement. Suddenly he turned. Their eyes met, and his glittered with the same desire she felt. All she had to do was lean closer, take his hand. But she was afraid. She turned back toward the stage, concentrated on the Brahms, and let her emotions settle.

At intermission, they wandered down the hill to the concession stand and bought popcorn, which they shared companionably while waiting for the concert to continue.

The second half of the program featured Beethoven's Ninth Symphony. As the music rose and swirled around them, Jenna forgot Chad, forgot the rustling of movement around her, forgot everything but the beauty and power of the masterpiece. In the final movement, when the Houston Chorale sang Schiller's "Ode to Joy," their voices soaring into the night, the glory of it brought tears to her eyes.

The final notes died away, the audience thundered its appreciation, but Jenna sat transfixed, unwilling to break the spell. She turned to Chad, and their eyes met for a moment of silent understanding. He brought his hand to her cheek, caught a tear on his fingertip, and Jenna's breath stopped. She felt as if a roller coaster had catapulted her into space. Neither of them spoke, neither moved until the departing crowd intruded on their space. Chad rose, offered his hand to help her to her feet. He folded the blanket, then took her arm, and still silent, they walked to the car.

When they reached her house, the street was dark. Automatically Jenna glanced around, wondering if Rose could have followed them. She hadn't thought of Rose in the park but now, in the shadowy street, her police officer's vigilance returned.

As she took out her key and opened her front door, she felt compelled to warn Chad. "Lock your car doors on the way home. When you get there—"

"Jenna, stop," he interrupted gently. "Stop being a cop, at least for tonight."

"I am a cop. And you could be in danger."

He shook his head. "Yes, but tonight I want to forget about Rose, think of other things." His eyes caught hers and held them.

"Wh-what?" she whispered.

"This." His hands settled on her shoulders and drew her forward. Closer. Her lips parted of their own accord, her eyelids fluttered closed, she held her breath.

And then he kissed her—gently, tenderly, as if she were made of crystal. And in truth, she felt she might shatter as he drew her closer.

"Jenna," he whispered against her mouth.

She heard herself moan; a sound of yearning, of desire. Oh, God, she mustn't let this happen. She pulled away.

"Jenna," he said again.

She stared at him in longing, in confusion. "Chad, I...I can't."

"You can."

He reached for her hand, but she yanked it back. "No, I can't. Really. I... Good night, Chad." Carefully, firmly, she shut the door and listened as his footsteps died away.

Legs weak, breath shallow, she leaned against the wall. She'd done the right thing, stepping away from him. Getting involved would be a mistake. For him, it would be a short-term fling. For her, much more. And what would she get in return? Hurt. For that moment in his arms, though, with his hands caressing her skin, his lips covering hers so sweetly, she'd wanted. She'd ached.

No! Forcing herself, she pushed away from the wall and went into the bedroom. She didn't allow herself to think or to feel as she stripped off the clothing still suffused with Chad's scent, scrubbed the skin still imprinted with his kisses. In bed, she squeezed her eyes tightly shut to blot out the memory of his face. Mercifully, within a few minutes she fell asleep.

THE NEXT MORNING, Jenna sat at her breakfast table, sipping coffee and reading the morning paper. Good news from city council: A raise for police was in the offing. Bad news from the crime reporter: Violent crime was up. And, of course, the Department got the blame.

She turned to the life-style section, read the lead article on Houston's best coffeehouses, then scanned the society column. Her eyes were drawn to the news of Houston's Beautiful People.

Halfway through the column she spotted an item about Chad. "Sighted at Mario's, huddled over a power lunch—Channel 6's Chad Foster, Chamber of Commerce Prexy Ralph McDermott, and Bio Corp's CEO, Marshall Stokes."

"Oh, nice," she muttered. "Now everyone in Houston—Rose included—knows he lunches at Mario's."

Irritated with Chad for making her job more difficult, she switched to the comics but didn't find them amusing. After a minute, she turned back to the column with Chad's name in it.

Reading it again, she clenched her jaw until the muscles screamed. She'd been right last night, she thought. Right to push him away. He was toying with her, amusing himself with the cop, using her to take his mind off Rose. If she let him, he'd hurt her, as sure as the sun would rise tomorrow.

She wasn't his kind of woman. She remembered those kinds of girls from her high school days: girls who grew up to be rich society snobs with time on their hands, girls who'd snubbed her because she wasn't *their* kind, either. She was working-class, not Chad Foster's class, and she was lucky the society columnist had reminded her. No matter how she felt, no matter what she yearned for, she'd keep that fact firmly in her mind. And put Chad Foster out of it, starting now. She finished her coffee and headed for police headquarters.

When she arrived in her office, she found a message from the crime lab and hurried downstairs. Hank O'Malley, director of the lab, met her at the door, eyes snapping the way they did when he'd found something. "Come into my office." She followed him through the lab, wrinkling her nose at the smells that reminded her of her high school chemistry lab.

O'Malley's office reflected his life—sparsely furnished and devoid of personal items. He was a forty-five-year-old bachelor whose life revolved around his work.

Jenna declined a seat. Instead she stood, tapping the floor with one foot. She knew Hank would take his time telling her. When it came to his work, he had a flair for the dramatic and enjoyed keeping people waiting, building up the tension. Today, though, she didn't have the time or the patience. "What is it?"

"The ice-cream truck."

"You found something? What?"

"Blood."

"Blood!" But she hadn't seen any bloodstains the other day. How could she have missed them? "Where?"

"Back of the truck, near the freezers."

Had Arthur Green dragged Nick into the truck? Stabbed him?

A picture of Anita the last time she'd seen her, sobbing on her living room couch, flashed through Jenna's mind. "How much blood?"

"Not much. A few drops here and there."

"Not enough, then," Jenna murmured.

Hank nodded. "Not enough for a murder, at least not in the truck."

"But a man with blood on his hands could go back to the vehicle, get in and drive home. What blood type is it?"

"O positive," Hank replied. "What's the kid's?"

Jenna had to force out the words. "O positive, too." She backed toward the door. "I'd better get the driver down here for blood matching."

"If his is the same, we'll request DNA testing," Hank said.

Jenna nodded. "Thanks, Hank."

Upstairs she stopped by Zack's office to bring the head of Juvenile up to date on the lab findings, then put in a call to Nate Harris and told him to take her appointment with the staff psychologist. Finally she headed for Arthur Green's apartment.

He wasn't there.

He wasn't at the dairy, either. Or out on his route.

"I need to speak to someone who knows where he is," Jenna told the receptionist at Sendak's.

The young girl's eyes widened. "Is he in trouble with the police?"

Jenna ignored the question. "Who does he report to?"

The girl's eyes slid to the pistol in the holster at Jenna's waist. "I'll get Mr. Shanks."

A few minutes later, she returned, followed by a corpulent middle-aged man who looked as if he sampled all of Sendak's calorie-loaded products. "I told him you're lookin' for Mr. Green," she announced with an air of importance.

"Come in my office and I'll check on him," Mr. Shanks said.

As she followed him out of the waiting room, Jenna read disappointment on the receptionist's face. She'd probably been hoping for a juicy tidbit with which to regale her friends. Too bad.

Mr. Shanks eased his bulk into the chair behind his desk and Jenna sat across from him, masking her impatience. "Arthur Green," Shanks muttered. "Ah, here we are. Green called in yesterday and asked for a couple of emergency days off. Death in the family."

"Let me know as soon as he gets back," she said, handing Shanks her card. She thanked him and left, the frustration she'd felt earlier now increased tenfold.

Death in the family? she wondered. *Or in the ice-cream truck?*

BY THE TIME JENNA returned to headquarters it was well past two. She only had time to wolf down a cardboard-tasting sandwich and a soda from the vending machine before she headed for Nate's office and the meeting with Chad Foster.

No matter how strong her determination to shut off her feelings for him, when Chad walked in, her resolve threatened to crumble. Their eyes met, and something electric zinged between them. If she'd been standing, it would have rocked her back on her heels.

"Well," Nate began, unaware of the silent communication between Chad and her, "thank you for coming down, Mr. Foster. We've been in touch with Dr. Overstreet, our consulting psychologist, and she agrees—"

A sharp knock on the door interrupted him. "Yes," Nate called.

The door opened, and Chief Macauley entered the room.

Automatically Jenna straightened though she already sat as upright as a soldier. *Major pressure,* she thought.

After Macauley had greeted Chad and taken a seat, Nate began again. "Sir, I just told Mr. Foster here that I've spoken with Dr. Overstreet to get her input on this matter. Now, according to her, we have two options. Number one, we keep on as we have, letting Rose call the shots. We continue to have someone inside the TV station. If Rose makes a move, we nab her. Second option is, we make the move, do something that'll grab her attention, something that'll flush her out."

"I vote for the second option," Chad said. "I believe in being proactive."

"I agree," Macauley said. "What's your plan, Lieutenant?"

Nate cleared his throat. "The way I understand it, this woman's fixated on Mr. Foster, thinks she's in love with him and vice versa. We need to make her angry, make her jealous of someone."

Macauley nodded. "Rose sees him with another woman, we plant a few items in the paper suggesting a relationship. Good idea."

Jenna disagreed. Who would play the other woman? Would Mona Switzer agree to being the decoy in a scheme like this? Would anyone?

"Are you seeing someone now?" the chief asked Chad.

Before Chad had a chance to reply, Jenna jumped in. "No disrespect, sir, but it would be dangerous to use a civilian as bait." *Not to mention unethical,* she added silently.

She heard the unmistakable sound of knuckles cracking. "Let me finish," Nate said, shooting Jenna a quelling look. "*Are* you seeing someone, Mr. Foster?"

"No."

"Good. Of course, we don't want to use a civilian. You'll do it, Wakefield."

"Me?" she croaked. "B-but—"

"Excellent," the chief said.

Nate smiled. He looked like the cat who'd swallowed the canary. Jenna wanted to throttle him.

He turned to her. "You and Mr. Foster can meet for lunch, go out together a few evenings, someplace where you'll be visible. You can drop by the TV station a couple of afternoons."

"Better yet," Macauley said, "she can move in with him."

Had he actually said that? Jenna's mouth opened, but nothing came out. Words of disbelief, of anger, stuck in her throat.

Three pairs of eyes fastened on her: the chief's with approval, Nate's with warning, and Chad's with a gleam of speculation.

She was cornered. Trapped, with no way out.

"I don't—"

Nate paid no attention. "Sergeant, move some things into Mr. Foster's place tonight. We'll let this fan think he has a new live-in relationship. What do you think of that, Mr. Foster?"

"Fine with me."

Jenna sat immobile. If she moved, if she so much as opened her mouth, she'd let out a shout of rage that would echo all the way to Dallas. Instead she kept still, biting hard on the inside of her lip, barely aware of the conversation going on around her. They could take the Foster case... take this *job* and shove it!

This job—the only career she'd ever wanted. All she'd hoped and planned for—to make her father proud, to achieve something for herself. Could she give up all that? She'd very likely have to if she turned down this assignment.

All right. She'd put up with Foster if she had to die trying. But she didn't have to like it. And, damn it, she intended to say so. "I'm not comfortable with this."

Nate looked surprised. The chief's eyes narrowed dangerously. "Are you turning down this assignment, Sergeant?"

"No, sir. I just want to go on record as saying I object."

She waited nervously, but Nate merely said, "I'll note that." Macauley didn't comment. Obviously he didn't intend to let her off the hook.

"...key?" Chad said.

She realized he'd spoken to her. "What?"

"I said, if you'll come out to the car with me, I have an extra house key in the glove compartment."

She stood without answering and followed him out. He said nothing, letting her simmer in silence.

He knew how angry she was, she thought, and it probably amused him. Oh, he was lucky they weren't somewhere private where she could give in to her desire to take a punch at him. She could hurt him. The thought pleased her and should have alleviated her anger. But it didn't.

When he handed her the key, she snatched it from him and hissed, "Two weeks, Foster. Then your new live-in's moving out."

"We'll talk about this later," he said. "You can put your things in the bedroom at the end of the hall. I'll be home around eight. I'll stop on the way and pick up something for dinner."

"Don't bother," she muttered, but he got into the car without answering.

Before she could give in to her urge to kick a dent in the side of his Porsche, he'd driven away. She watched him pull out of the parking lot, hurling silent curses after him.

When she returned to Nate's office, the chief had left. Nate welcomed her with a pleased smile. "Wakefield—"

She bared her teeth at him. "Don't you 'Wakefield' me! How dare you, *how dare you* sit with that smug grin on your face while you and Macauley play havoc with my life? 'Move in with Foster,'" she repeated, clenching her fists. "Why didn't you put a stop to it? Don't you know I have other cases to work on? Damn it, I'm just starting to get somewhere with the Morales kid. I have two serious suspects, and now I'm supposed to drop everything and play hearts and flowers with Chad Foster. Is that the way Macauley wants this department run? No wonder he's getting bad press—"

"Cut it out, Wakefield. Calm down," Nate ordered. "I've noted your objection, but you don't have to quit the Morales case or anything else."

Did he think her time was all she was angry about?

Apparently so, for he said, "Spend your days doing what you always do. Just be visible. Go out with Foster, meet him for lunch—"

"And live at his house? That's...that's asinine."

Nate shook his head and smiled at her placidly. "No, it's sensible. It'll give this Rose something to worry about. She may be watching his house."

"Damn it, Nate!"

"I don't know what you're so riled about. You've gone undercover before. Didn't you once pose as a nanny to a kid after his family got a kidnapping threat?"

Jenna suppressed the urge to laugh hysterically. Living with Chad Foster could hardly be compared to spending her time with a four-year-old child. Chad Foster was dangerous—attractive, appealing...and sexy. How would she reconcile her responsibilities as a police officer with her feelings as a woman? Maybe it was a good thing Nate didn't understand. She tried once more. "Can't someone else do this?"

"Impossible."

Disgusted, Jenna stomped to the door. Arguing was useless. "I'm going back to my office," she said. "I'm putting out an APB on Arthur Green, the ice-cream man, and checking in with Corey Phillips. Then I'm going home."

When Nate glanced at his watch, she snarled at him. "Don't mention the time to me. I'm not leaving work early. I'm on duty now twenty-four hours a day. I'll be putting in for overtime."

She gave herself the pleasure of slamming the door in his face.

CHAPTER SEVEN

WHEN CHAD CAME HOME, he found Jenna in the kitchen, pulling jars out of a plastic grocery bag and shoving them into his refrigerator. She was still furious, he thought, watching her, and she'd be angrier still if she knew he was standing behind her, enjoying the way her uniform molded her curves. Tendrils of shimmering brown hair had escaped from her braid. God, how he longed to undo that glorious mane and bury his face in it. How he longed to bury himself in her. One taste last night had awakened a fierce hunger, a need that astonished him with its intensity.

He moved closer, listening to her mutter as she rearranged his groceries to make room for hers. She'd even brought her own mustard. He touched her shoulder.

Instantly, she whirled. Her hand whipped downward to grip her gun. She stared him in the face, her eyes sizzling with naked rage.

Stunned, he stepped back and raised both hands. "Take it easy, Sarge," he cajoled. "I'm not going to jump you."

"Make sure you don't." In her eyes he saw more than anger; he saw fear.

"I brought dinner," he said, "and a peace offering. Come into the dining room."

She followed him, stopped in the doorway and stared at the table. Two places were set; take-out containers at both. Beside one was a bouquet of pastel-colored carnations in a crystal vase. "For you, Sarge. I didn't think you'd like roses...."

She laughed and buried her nose in the flowers, then turned to him. "Thank you." Her cheeks flushed. "I'm sorry I overreacted just now. You startled me."

She'd been more than startled, he thought, but didn't comment. Instead he pulled out her chair. "Shall we?"

She took her seat and opened the container. "Mmm." She sniffed appreciatively at the spicy aroma of Tex-Mex that pervaded the room. "Tacos *al carbón*."

For a few minutes they both concentrated on their food, then Chad said, "I know you're angry about this assignment. Buster didn't give you much choice."

"Cops don't get choices. We get orders," she muttered, looking down at her plate.

"I could let you off the hook."

Her head shot up. Surprise and hope shone in her eyes, then resignation dulled them. She returned to her meal. "No, thanks. It's already done."

"But—"

"Forget it," she said, her voice flat. "I'd look bad to the chief, and so would Nate." She took another bite.

"Look," he continued, wanting to reassure her, "we can do everything possible in public to make Rose jealous, but in private, we won't—"

"I wasn't worried about that," she insisted, lifting her chin.

"Then what's the problem?"

"Time." Frustration bubbled in her voice. "I'm working on a case that takes a lot of it."

"Another stalker?"

She shook her head. "I haven't worked on stalking cases for two years. I'm in Juvenile."

He frowned. "Then why did Buster put you on this one?"

"I did a good job with a couple of stalkers. He remembered and yanked me out of my division."

"I see." Her attitude, the anger that seemed to permeate the very air between them, made more sense now. "Tell me about your case."

"It's a kid, a ten-year-old boy—"

As Chad listened, he heard more than Jenna's words. He heard her commitment to her work, her compassion for a family touched by tragedy. He also saw a new side of Sergeant Jenna Wakefield.

"So," she finished, "I wasn't as flattered as you might think to have this case dump—uh, handed to me."

"Stick with 'dumped.' I'll make a deal with you," he said, putting out his hand. "I'll try not to take too much of your time."

She hesitated a moment, then took his hand. "Okay."

"You know," he said thoughtfully. "I remember that case. We covered it on the news a couple of times. I remember thinking at the time that losing a child, not knowing what happened, must be the ultimate tragedy. Would doing another story help?"

"It might. It certainly couldn't hurt."

"Okay. Talk to the parents and we'll send someone out as soon as we can."

"Thank you. That means a lot." The look she gave him made him feel like a hero.

She returned to her dinner, tasted the guacamole, then said, "This is delicious, but you don't have to provide dinner while I'm here. We'll each do our own cooking."

He thought that ridiculous but decided not to argue. "Are you a good cook?"

"Lousy."

He took another bite of taco. "Me, too."

"I usually pick up something from Souper Salads."

"Helps keep you in shape, I suppose," he said.

"I work out for that."

He thought her shape was fine. She reminded him of Wonder Woman, whom he'd once been madly in love with—tall and strong, with fascinating curves. When he was about eleven, before he'd discovered real girls, he'd constructed lavish fantasies about the comic-book heroine. Of course, *he'd* been the one to rescue her. Now here she was in the flesh, at his dining room table, only prettier, feistier and a lot more vulnerable than a two-dimensional cartoon character ever could have been. He smiled to himself and said, "I have workout equipment if you want to use it."

"Thanks. Tomorrow I'm meeting a friend at the gym, but after that I may take you up on it."

They ate in silence for a while, then Chad said, "Friday night there's a party at the River Oaks Country Club. We need to go."

She frowned. "Can't you go without me?"

"Do you have something to take care of on your other case?"

She shook her head.

"If you're supposed to be my new love interest and we want people to believe it, you need to go with me." When she grimaced, he said, "You wound me, Sarge. Is the idea *that* unappealing?"

"I don't enjoy cocktail party chitchat." She sighed. "But it's part of my job. I'll go." She pushed back her chair and stood, picking up her carton.

He caught her wrist before she could leave. "Jenna," he said quietly, "it's part of my job, too. Making contacts, keeping up with what's going on in the city is important to the station. You and I aren't so different. I'm not fond of the society circuit, either."

She stared down at him, an expression he couldn't fathom in her dark eyes. "Seems like you'd fit right in."

"Fitting in and liking it are two different things. Why do you say that about me?"

"You're... smooth."

He chuckled. "From anyone else, I'd take that as a compliment. From you, I suspect it isn't."

She shrugged and pulled her hand away. "Take it however you like. I'm going to clean up and go upstairs."

"This early? It's barely nine."

"I like to go to bed early," she said, as if that proved something.

"Fine." He waited until she'd gone upstairs, carrying the carnations with her, to take his own things to the kitchen. Then he returned to the living room where he settled down, notepad in hand, to wait for the news.

He kept the volume low so he wouldn't disturb her. She probably needed all the sleep she could get. He thought of the concern in her eyes as she spoke about the missing child, her dedication to solving the case.

He could hear her moving around upstairs and pictured her in a skimpy gown. He remembered those long, slim legs, that enticingly rounded bottom. *Oh, hell,* he thought. He'd better keep his mind on other things. The newscast, for one. He watched intently and when it was over, headed for his room.

As he reached the top of the stairs, she came out of the bathroom, wearing a clingy silk robe of vivid emerald. Her face was scrubbed clean, her hair unbound and flowing past her shoulders.

He stood still and swallowed, though his throat had gone suddenly dry.

"Good night," she said, and went into her room, shutting the door after her.

He strode through his bedroom and into the adjoining bath, turned the shower on ice cold and stood under it for a long time.

"YOU'RE LATE," Gracie noted, as Jenna climbed on the stationary bicycle next to hers.

"Mmm." Jenna programmed an uphill ride and began to pedal.

"And grouchy, too."

Jenna shot her friend a disgusted look. She was always grouchy in the morning, and Graciela knew it. "Thanks, Miss Perky. What are you so cheery about?"

"Jorge kissed me last night. Not a brotherly kiss but an honest-to-goodness *kiss* kiss."

"Well, congratulations. When's the wedding?"

Graciela giggled. "We have to get through the courtship first. I'm looking forward to it."

"How'd you finally convince him to go beyond 'brother'?" Jenna asked.

"I bought a new bikini."

"And that's all it took?"

"Well—" Gracie grinned "—I used a little coercion, too. I got him to put suntan lotion on my back and while he was doing it, I told him I was crazy about him. It worked."

"Good for you." Jenna smiled at her friend. "A little police brutality never hurts." She concentrated on pedaling, then said, "I have a new love interest, too."

Surprised, Gracie stopped. "Who?"

"Chad Foster. I moved in with him last night."

Gracie's mouth dropped open. "You don't seem very happy," she ventured.

"Happy? I'm livid. It's all part of the plan to catch the woman who's been writing to him. Talk about coercion. He and Nate and the chief cornered me, and I couldn't say no. I should have. I wanted to, but damn it—" her legs worked furiously "—I couldn't get it out."

"So you're not—"

"No!" She pedaled faster.

"I thought you said you were interested in him."

Jenna glared at her friend. "I said he was interesting, not that I was interested. Two different things."

"Uh-hmm."

"Don't get any ideas, Gracie. I may be living there, but the part about being lovers is just pretend." And she intended to keep it that way. Kiss or no kiss, she thought, remembering the way his lips had tasted the other night. "Tonight we're going to the River Oaks Country Club." Her voice dripped disdain.

"Sounds nice."

"Not to me. I know those kinds of people. When I moved to Plano in high school, we were assigned to ability levels, then each level was broken into groups that had all their classes together. Maybe if I'd been in a different one... But all of a sudden, there I was with a bunch of girls who bought their clothes at Neiman Marcus. I bought mine at J.C. Penney. They talked about Ralph Lauren and Calvin Klein as if they were members of the family. I once asked a girl in my English class who Mary Quant was, and she laughed at me. That story made the rounds."

Jenna's face burned with remembered humiliation. She slowed her bike and got off. "Five miles. That's enough." Without waiting for Gracie, she stalked to the upright row bar. After a few minutes, Gracie followed and took the machine beside her. She made no effort to continue their conversation, and Jenna was grateful. She'd already said too much. For the next half hour she concentrated on exercising, pushing herself harder than usual, until her muscles ached and she was bathed in sweat.

Afterward, she and Gracie sat side by side in the sauna. The faint smell of cedar mingled with the odor of perspiration. The heat relaxed Jenna. She leaned back on the bench and shut her eyes.

"Feeling better?" Gracie asked.

"Mmm. I'm supposed to meet Chad at Mario's for lunch."

"Now that doesn't sound too bad."

"No, they have good salads," Jenna agreed.

"I, ah, was thinking more about the company."

"*I* wasn't. He's a case, Graciela. A case is a case."

Gracie wisely didn't argue with that.

WHEN JENNA WAS DRESSED again, she headed for her office. As she drove, she berated herself for her reaction when Chad had surprised her last night. She'd been ready to pull her gun on him and had caught herself just in time. She wasn't sure why Chad seemed to elicit strong emotions—emotions she didn't want or understand.

In her office, she checked first on Arthur Green. No news. He hadn't turned up.

Then she called the school district for information on Franklin Reeves, the substitute teacher who'd been at Nicolas's school. He was in his early forties, had taught history at the high school level full-time in Houston for fifteen years, then had requested a change to substitute status. No one could say why.

On the chance he wasn't teaching today, Jenna called him at home, but got no answer. Maybe she'd go out and drive by his house. She had plenty of time before she needed to change into the silk dress she'd brought along and join Chad for lunch.

One of the dispatchers rapped at Jenna's door, then opened it and stuck her head inside. "Corey Phillips just radioed in. He wants to talk to you."

Jenna hurried out and took the mike. "Wakefield."

"Peter's on the move again. He's just left the campus, heading west on South Main."

"I'm on my way," Jenna said. "Keep him in sight."

She took only a minute to call Chad. "Something's come up on my juvenile case. I can't meet you today."

"I'll see you tonight, then."

Jenna hung up, dashed out to her car and headed for the Southwest Freeway. Maybe today she'd luck out, catch Peter in the act of... of what? She flipped on the radio to a classical station and let Handel's *Water Music* calm her. Just past the roadside park she spotted Corey's unmarked car, pulled up behind him, and got out. "What's going on?"

"Nothing. When he got here, he sat down at one of the tables and watched the road. He waited about five minutes, then he got back in his car, and I followed him to a strip mall in Richmond. He made a couple of calls at a pay phone, went inside, bought a soda and a bag of chips, and came back here. Since then he's been waiting." He handed Jenna a pair of binoculars.

She focused on Peter. He scanned the highway, checked his watch, got up and paced. "He's agitated, that's for sure."

"He's been back here ten minutes," Corey said. "Whoever he's waiting for is late."

"I wonder who he's meeting and why he picked such an out-of-the-way spot."

"Maybe he's got a drug deal going," Corey suggested.

"I wouldn't have pegged him for a junkie, but you could be right," Jenna said. "Uh-oh. Here comes someone."

A tan Honda pulled into the park, and Peter hurried toward it and opened the door on the driver's side.

Jenna didn't know who she expected to get out—a sleazy-looking drug dealer or a sinister gangland character. Certainly not the person who emerged from the car: a slender blonde in shorts and a skimpy T-shirt, who looked about as menacing as a Barbie doll.

She stared in astonishment as Peter and the girl embraced, then added a passionate kiss. Jenna's mouth went dry as she watched the lovers. Against all logic, her mind flashed back to Chad and the way he'd kissed her the other night.

Berating herself for her foolishness, she handed the binoculars to Corey. He stared, then whistled softly. "Man, when are they gonna come up for air?"

Jenna cleared her throat. "It seems innocent enough—"

"Yeah, *real* innocent."

"But I think we should go over and ask a few questions."

"Better hurry, then," Corey said, continuing to watch, "because they're heading for her car. Yeah, they're both getting in. Wanna stop them?"

"No. Let's see where they go."

The Honda, with the girl at the wheel, shot out of the park, gravel spitting in its wake, and turned west. "Too bad we're out of our jurisdiction, or we could get 'em for speeding," Corey remarked.

"Just follow them," Jenna ordered.

In a couple of minutes, the Honda reached the city limits of the small town of Richmond and slowed. A few minutes more, and it stopped across from the Fort Bend County Courthouse. Peter and the blonde got out and hurried inside.

Corey parked beneath the shade of a giant oak tree, and he and Jenna looked at one another in mute amazement. "Well," he drawled, "I guess, whatever they're doing, it's legal."

"Yeah, but what?"

They waited, and fifteen minutes later, the couple emerged. Faces wreathed in smiles, they strolled down the sidewalk to the Honda and drove back to the roadside park. Peter got out, fetched an overnight bag from his car and stowed it in the trunk of the Honda.

"I gave him strict instructions not to leave the city," Jenna muttered from her vantage point in Corey's car. "Let's get over there."

The Honda pulled onto the highway as they started for the park. Corey glanced at Jenna but she shook her head. "Forget the girl. I want to talk to Peter."

He was walking back to his car, and paid no attention when they pulled in behind him.

Jenna got out and slammed her door. "Peter."

He jumped. When he turned and saw her, his face went pale. "Wh-what are you doing here?"

"That's my line, Peter. What are *you* doing here?" Jenna came abreast of him on one side, Corey on the other. "Let's sit on that bench over there and have a little chat."

Peter sat and stared up at the two police officers. His mouth opened, but no sound came out. Finally he croaked, "My lawyer—"

"If you want your lawyer with you, fine," Jenna said. "He can meet us down at headquarters. Or we can talk here, now. It's up to you."

Peter hesitated, glancing from Jenna to the highway
and back again. Then he covered his face with both trem
bling hands. He uttered a sob. "Please, don't give me any
trouble. I haven't done anything wrong. I swear it." He
dropped his hands and raised tear-filled eyes to Jenna.

"You'd better start talking, then," she said coolly
"You've got a lot to explain—trips into the country, a
packed suitcase."

"Okay, I'll tell you everything. Only...only you won't
tell my uncle...or...or anybody? I...I don't even want
my attorney to know this."

"No promises," Corey said. Peter bit his lip and stared
at the ground. "Come on, kid, you're wasting time,"
Corey prodded. "What's going on?"

Peter took a shaky breath, swiped at his wet cheek, then
began. "I came out here to meet Marcy."

"The blonde?"

"Yeah. We always meet here. It's the only safe place."

"Safe? From what?" Jenna asked.

"Her parents. They...they don't approve of Marcy
getting involved with an Asian. My family...they feel the
same way. But we won't let that stop us." His voice
strengthened. "We love each other. We're getting married."

Jenna and Corey looked at one another. "The courthouse," Corey muttered.

"Yeah," Peter said. "We got a license."

"And the suitcase?"

"We...we aren't going to leave town, I promise. We're
getting married tomorrow. Then we're going to spend a
couple of nights at a hotel before we tell our folks, that's
all. You have to believe me," he said, his voice breaking
again. "I'll do anything you want—come down and take
a lie-detector test, whatever. Only don't screw up my

plans. Marcy's parents hate me enough as it is. What would they think if I got arrested? What would *Marcy* think? Besides," he added, his voice stronger, "I already told you, I don't know anything about the kid you're looking for. I saw his picture in the paper and I recognized the address in my uncle's neighborhood, that's all."

"And the afternoon of May third," Jenna continued. "Where were you, really, after you finished your final?"

"With Marcy," he said in a voice so low she could hardly hear.

Jenna believed him. She glanced at Corey, then back to Peter. "You want to take a lie-detector test?"

He nodded, hope springing into his eyes.

"Okay, get in your car and we'll drive down to headquarters. One of us will be in front of you, the other behind, so don't try any funny stuff. You can call the physics department when you get there and say you need the afternoon off."

"Yes, ma'am." Peter got up and started for his car.

A few minutes later, as she followed Peter toward town, Jenna hoped for his sake and for Marcy's that he'd pass the lie-detector test.

Then where would that leave her on the Morales case? One out, two to go. She'd better talk to Nick's parents so Channel 6 could do that news story.

CHAD STOOD WITH Derek Adams beneath the portico in front of Mario's, waiting for the valet to bring his car. Noon sunlight reflected from the pavement and sent rivulets of sweat down the inside of his shirt.

Jenna would have been bored stiff during the lunch, Chad reflected. He and Derek, a representative from the network, had discussed business and little else. He wondered whether Jenna had made any progress on her case.

"Hot," Derek commented. "How do you Texans survive?"

"With lots of air-conditioning."

"Thank God, network headquarters are in New York."

Chad grinned. "And that you'll be back there tonight, huh?" He glanced at his watch. "I should have you at the airport in less than an hour."

"I enjoyed the visit," Derek said. "Channel 6 is up to its usual high standards, and I'm impressed with your future plans. And by the way, this restaurant is as good as anything Manhattan has to offer. Hey, what's that on your car?" he added, as the Porsche arrived. "Their version of the after-dinner mint?"

"Hmm?"

"They've gone one better. A rose on the windshield."

A rose!

If Derek said any more, Chad didn't hear. His eyes were riveted on his car. Tucked under the windshield wiper on the driver's side was a long-stemmed red rose. Its scarlet petals rested against the windshield like a smear of blood on the glass.

Perspiration streamed down, soaking Chad's shirt. For a moment he stared, unbelieving, at his car. She'd been here, watching him, stalking him. This time she'd even left her mark. Was she still here, watching his reaction?

His eyes swept the parking lot. Nothing out of the ordinary. Just the usual well-dressed shoppers going in and out of nearby stores. No one lurking about or staring at him.

Anger surged through him. Rose was closing in, taking control of his life, manipulating him like a puppet on a string. He couldn't even have a routine lunch without her specter skulking in the background, always out of reach. He strode to the uniformed young man who stood waiting by the driver's-side door. "Where did you park this car?"

"Around the side of the building, sir, where we always do. Is . . . is something wrong?"

"Did you see anyone hanging around the lot?"

"No, sir. Nobody was back there." The attendant shook his head earnestly and peered into the car. "Is anything missing?"

"No." Chad realized that Derek was beside him, staring at him curiously. Ignoring Derek, he lifted the windshield wiper and held up the rose. "Where'd this come from?"

The valet thought for a moment, frowning, then his eyes brightened. "A new florist opened on the next block last week. Maybe they put it there."

The florist would have attached a business card. "Any other cars have roses on their windshields?"

"I didn't notice. I'd be glad to go back and check."

"I'll do it." Chad thrust a tip into the young man's hand, then scanned the parking lot again before he got into the car. "Wait," he called as the attendant walked away. "What space was it parked in?"

"On the end, sir, next to a white Mercedes."

Chad got in the car and noticed the grin on Derek's face. "Looks like you have a secret admirer, Chad. Any idea who she is?"

Chad blinked. Derek's amusement was such a stark contrast to his own feelings, he could hardly comprehend it. He forced himself to chuckle. "Your guess is as good as mine."

He drove slowly back to the parking area, looking in both directions as he went. Where was Jenna when he needed her? Damn her, she was supposed to be here with him.

He pulled up behind the Mercedes and got out. He glanced inside the white car though he didn't really expect Rose to be there, then walked back down the line of automobiles, hoping at least one or two had flowers on their windshields. None did.

Next he checked the back alley. He walked a little way along the buildings past trash bins and piles of boxes. Someone could spring out from behind one, knife in hand. He felt a crawling sensation on the back of his neck, as if someone were watching him, and swung around. No one there.

He turned back, and from the corner of his eye, caught a movement behind one of the bins. He edged toward it, wishing he had a weapon. An empty bottle lay on the pavement. He picked it up; it would have to do. Jenna, he thought, damning her again, would have had her gun.

He moved closer. Saw the movement clearly this time. Held his breath. Sweat dripping into his eyes, the stench of garbage in his nostrils, he reached the trash bin, inched around it . . . and came face-to-face with a kitchen worker from Mario's emptying garbage.

The man's face went white. The trash-can lid fell to the ground with a clang and rolled away. *"Qué pasa?"* the man croaked.

"Um, *perdóneme,*" Chad mumbled, and backed off. He strode back to his car, got in and slammed the door. Damn Rose for getting in his head and making him behave like an idiot.

"Find your secret admirer?" Derek asked.

Chad shrugged; casually, he hoped. "No, but whoever she is, she has good taste in flowers." He'd laid the rose on the dash. Now he tossed it on the back seat. The scent nauseated him.

He reached for his car phone as he pulled out of the parking lot. "Excuse me a minute." He punched in Jenna's number and asked for her.

"I'm sorry. Sergeant Wakefield is out," the police operator informed him.

"Nate Harris, then."

The lieutenant wasn't in, either.

"Do you know when, ah, Ms. Wakefield will be back?" He didn't want to use her title. No use giving Derek a tale to carry back to the network.

"No, sir. Would you like to leave a message?"

"Tell her Chad Foster called," he said. If she didn't get back to him, he'd have to contain his temper until he saw her this evening. He knew he was being unfair. He understood she had other cases, but seeing the rose on his windshield had unnerved him, and damn it, he intended to let the sergeant know how he felt about her leaving him to deal with Rose alone.

JENNA PARKED IN FRONT of Chad's town house and got out. She leaned into the back seat and pulled the silk dress she'd intended to wear to Mario's off the hook, then locked the car and started up the sidewalk. Halfway to the door, she stopped. She'd forgotten her shoes. She swore as she backtracked and retrieved the shoe box, then trudged back up the walk.

As far as the Morales case was concerned, the day had been a washout. Arthur Green was still out of town, Franklin Reeves didn't answer his phone, and she'd crossed Peter off her list of suspects. Actually, she was relieved he'd passed the lie-detector test. She'd wished him luck with Marcy when he'd left the station. He'd need it.

Hoping Chad wasn't home yet, she fumbled for the key he'd given her, shoved the front door open and went inside. She needed some time alone, but the sound of a news show coming from the living-room television told her he'd already arrived. She tried to slip past the room and go directly upstairs.

No such luck. He came into the entry hall, blocking her path. "I'm going up," she said, glancing pointedly at the stairway.

"I have something to show you first," he said, his expression stern. With a resigned sigh, she followed him into the living room.

She smelled the perfume before she saw the single red rose on the coffee table.

She dropped her things in a chair. "Where'd this come from?" If a florist had delivered it, she thought hopefully, they might be able to track down the purchaser.

"It was on my car, stuck under the windshield wiper when I came out of Mario's."

"You should have called me."

"I did. You were out. So was Lieutenant Harris."

"They could have radioed me."

"Would you have come?"

Probably not. She'd been in the park questioning Peter Chu about the time Chad would have finished lunch. She shook her head. "They could have sent someone else."

"I'm dealing with you."

"When I'm not available," she snapped, "another officer can take my place."

"I—"

"Save it, Foster. Did you search the parking lot?"

"Yes. I didn't see a thing."

"Was Lynn O'Donnell in the restaurant?"

He considered a moment. "I don't know."

"Didn't you go back and look?" she asked, her voice rising.

They stood eye-to-eye now, almost nose-to-nose, glaring at each other.

"No, that didn't occur to me. I'm not a police officer. *You* were supposed to be there."

She turned away. "I had an emergency call on the Morales case. I thought you understood how important that was." If she *had* been at Mario's, maybe she could have caught Rose, she reflected. Or maybe not. "I can't be everywhere," she murmured.

"Apparently Rose can." He sat down on the couch and sighed heavily. "Sorry about the outburst. If Rose keeps this up, I'll end up as crazy as she is. What do we do now?"

She wished she knew. "Rose will show up again," she said. "Meanwhile, we keep to our agenda."

"Which means dinner and dancing at the country club," he said, rising and checking his watch. "We'd better get ready."

"Darn!" she muttered. "I forgot." Just what she needed to top off a rotten day.

"So I'm reminding you."

She scowled at him, then stalked to the window and stared out, wishing she could make a run for it and go home.

"Lighten up, will you?" Chad ordered. "An evening of dinner and dancing should be a damn sight more enjoyable than what you usually do at work."

She whirled around and glowered at him. "How would *you* know what I enjoy?"

"Why don't you tell me?"

"Not the same things you do, that's for sure. I like classical music, you like rock. I go to bed early, you were up till all hours last night."

He shrugged. "Superficial differences."

"I'll tell you another. Our friends are different. My friends are on the police force, yours are at the country club."

"Only a few of the people at the club are friends. The rest are business contacts."

"Sure," Jenna said. "Contacts. That's what this evening's all about. Power, connections, a way to make your station number one."

He leaned forward, his air of amusement gone. "No, that isn't what this evening is all about. I thought I made that clear last night. Of course, I want Channel 6 on top, and yes, it takes connections. But I want more than that. I have... a mission. To accomplish something for the viewers, for the city, not just to rack up Nielsen points." He picked up the rose and twirled it in his hand. "That's why I have to get Rose out of my hair, so I can get on with my work. So, come on, Sergeant Wakefield," he added more quietly. "Your assignment for the evening is the River Oaks Country Club."

She knew she had no choice, but she mumbled, "I don't have anything to wear."

"Wear that." He pointed to the dress she'd tossed on the chair.

"That was for Mario's."

"You didn't go to Mario's," he reminded with infuriating logic. "You can wear it tonight."

She stared at the turquoise silk print. Like all her clothes, it came straight off the rack at Foley's. She'd probably look as out of place at the country club as a dandelion in a formal garden. She'd *feel* out of place, too. She fought back a sudden desire to cry.

"Get dressed, Sarge," Chad said firmly.

"Oh, all right." Jenna snatched her dress and shoes from the chair and stomped out of the room.

His voice floated up the stairs behind her. "And wear your hair down." Not trusting herself to answer, she ran the rest of the way up before he could follow and see the tears already trickling down her cheeks.

CHAPTER EIGHT

"TRY TO LOOK LIKE you're enjoying yourself," Chad muttered in Jenna's ear.

Jenna pasted on a smile, but she doubted it would fool Chad. She glanced around the country club—the crystal chandeliers, the brocade draperies, the elegantly set tables. The surroundings intimidated her, felt heavy and depressing. They were a palpable reminder that she didn't belong here, and so were the people. She felt gauche, clumsy, as if any minute she'd trip over her feet.

She reminded herself she was a police officer. She'd stared down assailants with guns, juvenile gang members, even rescued a baby once from a crazed woman holding a knife to his throat. Why should she feel ill at ease? Why had she never gotten over her teenage discomfort or her hurt over Ken's rejection? Her feelings tonight had nothing to do with the people here and everything to do with her. Realistically, she knew that many of the members here were pleasant, congenial people; but collectively they overwhelmed her.

When she and Chad had entered the ballroom earlier, she'd had an intense desire to turn and run, but she'd fought it down. Instead, she'd clutched Chad's arm until she realized what she was doing and loosened her grip.

She'd smiled and nodded and done her best to participate in some of the small talk that Chad engaged in so easily, but mostly she'd been silent, feeling like a kid who'd accidentally wandered into the wrong class at school. Out of her element. She was on duty, she reminded herself, and spent her time scanning the crowd. Chad, of course, was at home here. He exchanged light-hearted banter with the men and effortlessly charmed the ladies.

The orchestra returned from a break and began a ballad. Chad leaned toward her. "One dance, and then we'll leave."

Relieved, Jenna accompanied him to the dance floor. He drew her against him and she stiffened, but he whispered, "Love interest, remember?" and she let him pull her close.

The music was slow and sensual, and Chad was as smooth on the dance floor as he was everywhere else. Jenna had never thought of herself as a particularly good dancer, but Chad led her so expertly, she seemed to float across the floor.

She drew in the musky scent of his cologne, felt his warm breath on her cheek, and suddenly she didn't care whether Rose was in the crowd or not. She forgot that none of this was real.

She shut her eyes and let herself imagine that the man whose arms held her close, whose cheek rested against hers wasn't pretending, either. Maybe Chad had forgotten, too, for his hand caressed the small of her back. She felt his heartbeat accelerate. His body hardened against hers.

When the song ended, she opened her eyes and tried to step back, but he held her tight. "One more," he murmured against her cheek.

The music began again, slower now, richer, a melody that whispered of moonlit nights, tropical beaches, heated bodies pressed together. As they glided across the floor,

Chad's lips skimmed across her temple, and she shiv
ered.

When the last notes died away, he drew back and stared
into her eyes with a long, smoldering look. "Ready?"

For what? she wondered, but merely nodded.

He kept his arm around her as they crossed the room
and she let her dream continue.

"Chad!" A man's voice stopped them before they
reached the door.

Chad turned. "Trevor! Jenna, this is Trevor Mc
Gowen and his lovely wife, Kay. Jenna Wakefield."

The McGowens were the kind of people who regularly
appeared on the pages of the *Houston Post's* life-style
section. A handsome couple—well-dressed, confident,
rich; everything she wasn't.

They acknowledged Jenna with friendly greetings, then
Kay put her hand on Chad's arm. A diamond-encrusted
tennis bracelet sparkled at her wrist. "We haven't seen
you in ages."

Chad flashed an enigmatic smile and drew Jenna closer.
"I've been busy."

"So I see." Trevor scrutinized Jenna with interest, then
turned back to Chad and frowned. "I notice you've made
time to appear on TV."

"I never let an issue I'm concerned about pass without
comment."

"Don't you know what's going to happen to property
values in the Montrose area if that halfway house goes
in?"

"I do. I own property there myself. There's bound to be
some fallout, but the facility has to go somewhere and
Montrose is the logical place."

"Logical?" Trevor said with a snort. "If you want logical, let them put it in the Third Ward. People out there are used to felons in the neighborhood."

"That's why we don't want to send these parolees back there," Chad countered. "How can they change if they're thrown back into their old environment?"

Trevor shrugged. "I don't know about that. All I do know is I don't want them in my environment."

"I talked to Ellen Lattimer," Kay remarked. "You know, they live near the Museum of Fine Arts, and she's afraid they'll have to move. Of course, they've considered it for a long time anyway."

"The neighborhood's changing," Trevor added. "You wouldn't believe the element that's moving in."

Kay nodded. "The Lattimers want to be closer to the better private schools. A bachelor like you," she went on, tossing her expertly coiffed honey-blond hair, "can't appreciate the problems involved in educating children. Of course, public school's out." She wrinkled her nose. "The Houston schools are simply overrun with kids you don't want sitting in the same classroom with yours, let alone associating with them."

"Yes. One even has to choose a private school carefully. A lot of blue-collar types are applying for scholarships," Trevor added, scowling.

"Trevor, I'm sure we're boring Chad with all this school talk. His mind's on other things." Kay flashed Jenna a teasing smile. Jenna noticed her teeth were perfect. "You two must come by and we'll barbecue by the pool. Jenna, are you from Houston?"

"Dallas, but I live here now."

"I'm surprised we haven't run into each other before," she said. "Have you been in Houston long?"

"A while."

"Well, we'll let you go." She stood on tiptoe to kiss Chad's cheek. "Don't be strangers, you two."

Jenna stood silently as the couple walked off. Trevor said something to his wife, and the tinkle of Kay's laughter floated back toward them.

"Jenna?" Chad interrupted her thoughts. "You look like you're a million miles away."

"No, I'm right here." Back in the real world. The illusion she'd indulged in on the dance floor evaporated like mist in the harsh glare of the sun.

Chad took her arm, and she tensed. "What's wrong?"

"Nothing," she snapped. "I've had enough, that's all."

He may have wondered at the change in her mood, but he only said agreeably, "So have I. Let's go."

They waited in front of the club for one of the eager young parking attendants to bring the car. From inside came the sounds of music and laughter. No one else was leaving early. Chad put his arm around Jenna. His fingers brushed seductively across the bare skin of her upper arm. "Stop," she ordered, ignoring the goose bumps his touch produced.

"Why?"

"The evening's over. I'm off duty now."

"Sarge." He let out an exasperated sigh and shook his head.

The car arrived. On the way home, Jenna was silent. She stared woodenly out the window, her hands locked tightly in her lap. When they reached the town house, she got out quickly and surveyed the street. She checked Chad's mailbox and as soon as they came in the front door, opened the entry-hall closet and peered inside.

Chad watched her with a bemused expression. "What are you doing?"

"What does it look like? Searching the premises." She marched through the living room and headed for the kitchen.

"I thought you were off duty." He sounded amused as he followed her through the dining room.

She didn't appreciate the joke. Rounding on him, she slapped her hands on her hips. "I'm assigned to your case, and I take my responsibilities seriously. I'm checking this apartment for signs of a break-in. What my job does *not* include is necking in front of the country club." She brushed past him and started up the stairs.

Chad followed her as far as the foyer. "We weren't necking. On the dance floor maybe, but not out in front of the club."

She marched up the stairs. "Check your answering machine," she ordered, without bothering to look back. She took a quick tour of the upstairs rooms, then came halfway down the steps. "Any messages?"

"No."

"Good. I'm going to bed now."

"Jenna, wait!" She met his eyes, which were no longer teasing but dark and serious. "Come down here and talk to me for a few minutes. Please."

Warily, she came into the room and took the chair across from his. "What about?"

"This evening. You hated the country club, didn't you?"

His quiet words sparked her anger. "Not that it's any of your business, but you're wrong. I don't hate the club, I hate the members. They're so full of themselves, so superior." She knew her voice was shaking, but she didn't care. "They talk about 'blue-collar types' as if they're . . . as if *we're* filthy scum. They think because they have money they can step on anyone."

"Is that what happened to you?" he asked gently, his gaze intent.

She turned away from those knowing eyes. "Who cares what happened to me?"

"I do."

Surprised at his words, she glanced at him to see if he was teasing her, but his expression showed sincerity and concern. Too much concern. "I don't want you to care."

"Why?"

Because I don't want anything personal between us. Because then I may begin to care...too much. "I don't know."

He came to her, sat on the ottoman at her feet, and took her hands. "Tell me."

His soft words and gentle touch were her undoing. "I don't fit in with the jet set," she blurted. "I didn't from the beginning."

"When you moved to Plano."

"Yes. Those girls lived in a world I could only dream about. They spent their summers at ritzy Camp Waldemar, their winter vacations skiing in Colorado or Vermont. Everyone talked about Christmas trips. One was going to London, another to Williamsburg. Someone was going to the family cabin at Sun Valley. One of them asked me where I was spending Christmas one year and I said, 'My grandparents'.' What they didn't know was that my grandparents lived thirty minutes away, in South Dallas."

Chad's thumbs stroked her hands. "High school must have been tough."

"It wasn't a total disaster," she said. "I made friends with a couple of girls in other classes, and we got together after school. But I had to spend six hours a day with a snobby clique, and it was rough. I didn't even look right," she added bitterly. "I was taller than everyone else, and gangly. I looked like a stork."

"The ugly duckling who turned into a swan." When she looked at him without comprehension, he said, "You're beautiful. Don't you know that?"

"No, I—"

"Trust me. I know a beautiful woman when I see one." He smiled at her and she couldn't help but smile back. "Jenna, everyone at the country club isn't like the kids from your high school class or the McGowens."

"Aren't they?" she asked. "I had another exposure when I was in college. My sophomore year I started dating a boy from a rich west Texas oil family. We were crazy about each other. At least, I was crazy about him. We talked about getting married, even looked at rings. Then he invited me to spend Thanksgiving with his family."

She shut her eyes and remembered. The big house, the elegant rooms, the table set with expensive china and crystal and so much silverware she didn't know which fork to pick up first. "I felt like I was on the hot seat at dinner. 'Where are you from? What does your father do? Do you know this person or that person in Dallas?'"

Chad sat listening silently, his hands still clasping hers.

"I was coming down to breakfast the next morning when I heard his mother talking about me—'That Wakefield girl, or whatever her name is, seems pleasant, but she's rather...colorless, don't you think? Well, after all, with her background...' After the holiday, Ken and I never saw each other again."

"Jenna." Chad's voice was gentle. "Nothing I say will erase those experiences from your mind. But give me a chance to show you that all people with money aren't the same. My parents are leaving on a cruise in a couple of weeks. They're having a bon voyage party a week from Sunday. I want you to come with me."

No matter what Chad thought of his family and their friends, she was certain she'd dislike them. She didn't want to endure another evening like tonight. "I don't think so."

"You'll enjoy yourself," he urged. "You'll even know someone there."

"Who?"

"Chief Macauley."

Oh, Lord! If she didn't attend, Macauley would have her head. "I'll think about it...if I'm still working on your case." If she wasn't, Macauley's presence wouldn't matter.

His lips curved into a pleased smile. "Even if you're not. You won't be sorry." She didn't answer, but he let it pass. Instead he said, "We'd better plan to spend tomorrow someplace where we'll be noticed."

She sighed. "That's what I'm here for."

"Right. But we'll make the day fun, too." He got up and drew her to her feet. They were very close. For a breathless moment, he stared into her eyes and she thought he was going to kiss her. But he simply brushed his hand very gently across her cheek and said, "Sleep well."

SHE SLEPT LIKE A BABY. She'd expected to lie awake reliving the day and the evening, but when she opened her eyes to find morning sunlight streaming through the window, she realized she'd slept better than she had in days. More peacefully than she had since Nicolas Morales had been missing. Telling Chad about her past heartaches— something she had never shared with anyone, even her parents—had been cathartic. But now, in the clear light of a new day, she felt embarrassed for having blurted out her teenage anguish. What would he think of her?

Oh, what did she care? Once the case was solved, she wouldn't see him anymore.

She threw on a blouse and a calf-length khaki skirt, tied her hair back in a ponytail and wandered downstairs to find Chad at the breakfast room table, reading the newspaper. "Good morning," he said, glancing up.

Self-consciously, she crossed to the coffeepot and poured herself a cup. She felt strange to be sharing the morning with a man she hardly knew. But she might as well get used to it. "Have you had breakfast?" she asked, noticing only a coffee cup at his place.

"No, I thought we'd have a picnic."

"For breakfast?"

"Mmm-hmm. We'll go to the park and have some quiet time before we have to go public, okay?"

"And then?"

"Then we go to The Galleria. It's a good place to be seen. Besides, my brother's birthday is coming up, and I want to get him something."

"All right." She wondered what Chad would buy for his brother. Something expensive and useless? She drained her coffee cup. "I'll go up and get ready."

Chad's gaze raked over her. "You look ready to me."

She shook her head, hesitated a moment, then added, "I need to get my gun."

"Your gun?"

"Yes. For a cop, carrying a pistol is as natural as you taking your house keys. I don't go out without it. I took it last night, too." She saw the shock in his eyes and continued: "We're dealing with a loony here. She followed you to a restaurant yesterday. She could do the same thing today. And if she sees you with another woman, she might get violent. My job's to draw her out in the open *and* to protect you. For that, I need a weapon.''

Chad grimaced and shoved his coffee cup aside. ''Do you have any idea how I feel, having a woman protecting me?''

''Don't think of me as a woman, then. Think of me as a police officer.''

''I'm not sure that's possible,'' he muttered, but he folded the newspaper and got up with a sigh of resignation. ''Go get your gun.''

She ran upstairs, decided her pistol would fit in the deep pocket of her skirt, and came back to find Chad at the front door, a wicker picnic basket in one hand and a camera in the other.

They drove to Hermann Park and chose a secluded spot beneath the trees. While Chad spread a blanket on the ground, Jenna circled the area. She saw nothing suspicious or threatening; just summer sunshine and a faint breeze stirring the trees. A scene for lovers ... or pretend lovers.

Enjoying the tranquillity of the park, she wandered through the trees, knelt to watch a duck with a trio of ducklings waddle by on their way to the pond. The mother duck quacked with each step as if giving directions to her offspring. Jenna grinned with delight.

''Perfect shot.'' She heard Chad's voice and the click of a shutter and looked up. When she rose, he snapped again. She laughed and threw up a hand. ''Enough.''

Chad shook his head. ''I'm an addict.'' He continued taking pictures—some of her, others of the scenery—as they returned to the blanket.

Jenna sat down and tucked her legs under her. ''This is nice.'' Spying a clump of pink primroses in the shadow of the tall trees, she plucked one, and ran her fingers over the velvet petals. Chad broke off another flower, leaned toward her and tucked it behind her ear.

The touch of his fingers on her sensitive skin, the compelling look in his blue eyes, both intrigued and frightened her. Determined to resist his appeal, she said, "Why don't we have breakfast?" Aware her voice was too high, too bright, she reached past him, opened the basket, and began unpacking it. She turned her attention to the food as if it were of major importance—a thermos of coffee, another of orange juice, bagels, cream cheese, butter and jam. "Looks delicious," she babbled. "I never eat breakfast, but this morning I'm starved."

Nervously, she reached for a bagel, spread cream cheese on it, and began to eat. Chad picked up his camera again and focused. "Oh, don't," she begged, but he laughed and took a shot of her with a mouthful.

He continued snapping pictures. "Your face is so expressive, it's a photographer's dream. You could be a model."

"Stop saying things like that."

"Why? They're true." He set the camera down, stretched out on his side, and nibbled a bagel. After a while he asked, "What do you do on your days off?"

"Relax. Catch a movie, go bike riding."

"We'll do that another Saturday."

Jenna didn't answer. If they were lucky, there wouldn't be another Saturday. She buttered the other half of her bagel, added jam, and looked up to find Chad's eyes on her. She took a bite; he watched. She licked a trace of jam from her lips; his eyes darkened.

As she watched him, too, Jenna felt the air sizzle with an electric current that flowed and sparked between them. She watched his hands, drank in the sight of his hair, ruffled by the breeze. She followed the movement of his mouth, the flash of teeth as he bit into his bagel. Even the act of chewing seemed suddenly erotic.

He set the half-eaten bagel down, moved toward her—

"Excuse me." A woman's voice. High-pitched, shrill. Startled, they turned.

She was short, squat, with lanky hair and vapid brown eyes. A canvas bag hung over one shoulder.

"I think I'm lost." She took a step forward, fixed her eyes on Chad. "I'm looking for... Could you, um, could you tell me where the rose garden is?"

Jenna sprang to her feet, her hand inching toward the gun she'd stashed in her pocket. Beside her, she heard Chad's sharp intake of breath as he, too, stood.

Automatically, Jenna assessed their position. No one around. Open space beyond the trees. A good twenty yards to their parking spot.

"Get to the car," she ordered under her breath. Chad didn't move. Jenna stepped in front of him.

The woman reached for her bag. Jenna's fingers closed around the handle of her gun. She tensed, ready to pull it out, ready to fire if need be.

The woman's hand disappeared into the bag. Jenna concentrated, held her breath.

"My friend drew me a map. See?" From the bag she pulled a scrap of paper and held it out.

Just as she'd said, it was a map of the park.

Jenna heard Chad expel a long breath, felt it flutter against the back of her neck. She took the paper and glanced at it. "You're turned around," she said, flipping the map sideways and gesturing to their left. "You need to go that way."

"Thank you so much." The woman smiled at them, turned and walked away.

Jenna watched until she disappeared behind the trees, then swung around. "I told you to go back to the car."

"And leave you here alone?"

"Yes. I'm trained to deal with these kinds of people. You're not." Angry beyond reason, she shoved at his chest. "Don't give me the macho routine, Foster. If that woman had been Rose, and she'd had a gun, you'd have been dead meat."

"What about you?"

"*I'm* the cop and the one giving orders. You asked the police to intervene, you'd damn well better cooperate."

His face flushed, and she suddenly remembered his comment earlier. *Do you know how I feel, having a woman protecting me?* He was more embarrassed than angry, she realized, perhaps more humiliated than embarrassed. She stepped back. "Sorry."

"Yeah. Me, too." He bent down and began gathering the picnic supplies.

Jenna knelt beside him and picked up the jar of jam. "That could have been a close call. I guess we both overreacted."

As Chad silently stuffed picnic supplies in the basket, he wondered if Jenna had any idea what his reaction had been. Fear! When he'd heard the words "rose garden," he'd been scared out of his wits.

And he hated it. He hadn't had much experience with fear. Now that he did, the terror belittled him, made him ashamed. He felt like the seven-year-old Chad who'd awakened whimpering in his bed whenever his recurring nightmare stalked him. Now the stalking was real, and he didn't know how to deal with it.

Jenna hadn't appeared frightened. She'd stared that woman down with the cool assurance displayed by cops on the TV shows on Channel 6. Was it training, or was her bravery inborn?

Funny, she could face a possible assailant with aplomb but she'd been terrified of going to the country club. He, on the other hand, who never shrank from a confrontation at work, never avoided an issue no matter how controversial, had felt like a wimp when that woman had approached them.

At least Jenna thought he was being macho. She had no idea he'd been frozen in his tracks. And he didn't intend to tell Wonder Woman the truth. He hated admitting it to himself.

He tossed the blanket and picnic basket in the back seat of his car and drove through the sparse Saturday traffic to The Galleria.

People thronged the three-story mall, some of them laden with packages, some window-shopping, gaping at expensive clothes and jewels displayed in the elegant shops. The noise of a hundred conversations sounded against the backdrop of a waltz. The music blared from the lower-level ice rink where skaters skimmed, or tried to, in time to the beat. The commotion was a shock after the serenity of the park.

He wondered if they were safer here, mingling with the crowd, than they'd been in the deserted park. Jenna seemed unconcerned. Though she kept her hand in her pocket, ready to draw her pistol, outwardly she was just a shopper like the others. She slowed as they passed Tiffany and stopped to admire the gems sparkling in the windows.

Behind them footsteps shuffled, coming closer. Then Chad heard the cackle of a woman's laughter. To his ears the sound was sinister, almost maniacal. He tensed, waited.

In the window before him, he saw the reflections of two women, their faces misshapen, surreal. One of the women stepped closer. Distorted by the glass, her nose was elongated, her mouth crooked. She might have stepped out of his old nightmare. He felt her breath at the back of his neck. His skin prickled, his hands clenched.

The woman peered around his shoulder, slowly raised a hand and fluffed her hair, turning sideways to preen as if the window were a mirror. Then she stepped back, said something to her companion, and the two of them walked away, their raucous laughter echoing behind them.

Chad let out his breath and glanced at Jenna. She showed no trace of apprehension. Did cops have a sixth sense about danger? The shopper behind them hadn't raised Jenna's antenna even a millimeter. Instead, she eyed the display of jewelry before her.

Chad was relieved to have something else to focus on. "You should wear a ring like that," he told her, pointing to a cocktail ring shaped like two flower petals with emerald chips mounted in their centers.

Jenna shook her head, but he noticed her wistful expression as she turned away.

As they meandered along, she asked, "What are you getting for your brother?"

"Sunglasses, to start with."

"That's an unusual gift. Doesn't he already have a pair?"

"He told me the other day he'd lost them." Chad led the way to Optica.

"Maybe they'll turn up."

"Not likely. He dropped them out of a balloon."

She turned and stared at him. "Are you serious?"

"Yep. Daniel's into ballooning. Has his own craft."

"That sounds like fun."

"You can ask him about it. He'll be at my parents' party next week. Remember, I asked you to come."

"I didn't give you an answer."

He halted in midstride and caught her hand. "Give me one now."

She repeated what she'd said last night. "I'll think about it." Someone jostled them from behind and Jenna tugged at his arm. "You're holding up traffic."

"Even cops don't give tickets here," he said. His voice softened as he brought his hand to her cheek. "I want you to come with me. Please."

Her eyes were wide and startled. "Why?" she whispered.

"I want to spend time with you."

She stared into his eyes for a moment longer, then nodded. "All right."

"Good." He tucked her arm in his. "Let's buy that gift."

After purchasing an expensive pair of sunglasses, Chad led the way to Brentano's bookstore, where he selected a book of poetry and an adventure story. "Daniel's a paradox," he told Jenna. "He's quiet, intense, sort of a dreamer, but he has an adventurous streak. I think he'd secretly like to join the Foreign Legion or become a Texas Ranger."

"I'm looking forward to meeting him," Jenna said, and Chad smiled in satisfaction.

"I have a meeting at the station in half an hour," he said, glancing at his watch, "but I have two tickets to the Astros-Giants game this evening."

"Lots of people, lots of noise, and we'll be seen."

"Right. Do you want me to drop you off at my place, or will you come to the station and wait?"

"I'll wait for you. What's your meeting about?" she asked as they turned into the parking garage.

"'The Public Soapbox.' We're moving on it. The first show should air in about two weeks."

"Isn't that fast?" she asked.

"Yes, but I have a top-notch staff and 'Soapbox' is an important show." He unlocked the Porsche. Inside the car, he continued. "I want to focus on topics that are meaningful, that affect Houstonians. We'll start with the Montrose facility, of course, and then I want a program on education. School taxes go up every year but test scores are still abysmal. Too many kids are dropping out. I've lined up the president of Bio-Tech Industries as a guest. They've established a mentoring program in which their employees sign up to sponsor children who are at risk. They develop personal relationships, act as role models, tutor—whatever they feel is needed. I think their program is one of the best to come along, but it can only reach a small number of students. I have a couple of other guests in mind, too. I want the public to hear some innovative ideas.

"Then I want a program on crime. Even though the rate is down, people perceive the city as dangerous enough to make them change the way they live. They're afraid to go out after dark."

"It's a complex problem," Jenna said. "What's your solution?"

"Personally, I don't think you can put an end to crime without better education and more jobs," Chad said. "But *my* solution isn't what matters. I don't want to slant the program one way or the other, even on issues I feel strongly about. For this series to work, it has to be open and objective, a forum where everyone has a voice." He pulled onto the freeway. "Tell me, what issues do you think we should address?"

"Juvenile crime," she said without hesitation. "It's becoming more and more violent. Twenty years ago, kids were arrested for playing hooky or stealing hubcaps. Today it's armed robbery, even murder. We need to change the system to deal with juvenile offenders more effectively."

"You're right," Chad said. "How would you like to appear on the show when we discuss it?"

"Are you serious?" When he assured her he was, she said, "Yes, I'll do it."

"No stage fright?"

She looked surprised. "Of course not."

Chad chuckled. "Sarge, like my brother, you're a paradox, too. Nervous about meeting some inconsequential folks last night, but you're willing to take on a whole television audience."

She frowned, then joined in his laughter. "I guess I am."

Ten minutes later, they arrived at Channel 6. Jenna declined Chad's invitation to sit in on the meeting. Instead, she made herself comfortable in the waiting room and read the latest issue of *TV Guide*.

She'd been there for half an hour when the sound of approaching footsteps drew her attention. She looked up to see Lynn O'Donnell heading for Chad's door. "Hello," Jenna said.

Lynn started and stared at Jenna in surprise. "You must be waiting for Chad. I saw his car in the lot. I wanted to talk to him."

"He's in a meeting."

Lynn took a seat across from Jenna. "I guess you're ahead of me. Have you been here long?"

"Thirty minutes." If this woman was Rose and their goal was to make her jealous, she'd better let her think she and Chad had a relationship. Jenna gestured toward the door. "He's with Bryan and Tina, going over 'The Public Soapbox.'" When Lynn looked blank, Jenna added, "It's a new show in the works. Chad told me about it on the way over."

She watched with interest the various emotions that played across Lynn's face. Surprise first, then dismay.

"You came with him?" Lynn gasped.

"Mmm-hmm. We were on the way back from shopping."

Lynn clamped her lips together, then rose abruptly. "I'll talk to him Monday." She strode away, her heels clicking sharply on the floor as she turned into the hall.

Moments later, Chad's door opened. He said a few words to Bryan and Tina as they came out, then smiled at Jenna and put out his hand. "Ready?"

As they walked outside, he said, "We're really moving. By the way, you get the day off tomorrow. I called my dad and I'm going to spend time with him, filling him in on the 'Soapbox' plans."

"It's nice of you to keep him informed."

"Even though he was looking forward to retirement, Dad misses this place. Besides," Chad said seriously, "I owe him a lot."

As they crossed the parking lot, Lynn O'Donnell came out of the building. Chad waved at her, and she nodded as she got into her car.

"I let her know we're seeing one another," Jenna told him.

"How'd she react?"

"She seemed displeased, but she didn't actually say anything."

Chad sighed. "God, this is frustrating."

"This is what I live with every day. By the way, thanks for doing another story on Nick Morales. Maybe, just maybe, it'll jog someone's memory."

"Glad to do it," he said.

On the way to the baseball game, Chad stopped at a camera shop, and Jenna waited in the car. Through the shop's front window she watched him hand over the roll of film he'd taken this morning and chat with the clerk. Afterward, they stopped at Becks Prime for a hamburger, then headed for the Astrodome.

Fans surrounded them as they ambled across the parking lot. Inside the stadium the smell of popcorn mingled with the odors of hot dogs, roasted peanuts, and beer.

They had box seats directly behind first base. As they made themselves comfortable, Chad waved to people in nearby boxes. *Good.* That was what they were here for—to be seen. "Do you come to the games often?" she asked.

He shook his head. "Don't have the time. I'm usually working late."

"A workaholic," she teased.

"Guilty." He narrowed his eyes. "You are, too."

"Guilty, too, but I love baseball."

"So do I," he said. "I played on my high school team."

"Really?"

"Yes. I can instruct you on the fine points of the game." She raised a brow and he continued. "For example, you have to eat peanuts and drink beer."

Jenna chuckled. "Okay."

"I'll get us some. Be right back."

"I'll go with you."

He grimaced and muttered, "Let's hope Rose isn't a baseball fan," but he didn't protest. They returned from the concession stand in time for "The Star-Spangled Banner."

After the lineup was announced and the Astros took the field, Jenna remarked, "Petrovich should add some muscle to the team."

"Hey, you really do follow baseball."

"My dad used to take me to Rangers games in Dallas— Oh, no!" she groaned as the Giants' leadoff batter slammed a long ball into center field.

"Oh my!" squealed a feminine voice behind them. "What happened?"

"See that guy running?" her companion explained. "He's going to make it all the way to second base."

"Is that good?"

"Not for the Astros."

Jenna met Chad's eyes, and they both laughed. "She can't be that ignorant about the game," Jenna whispered.

"She's trying to make him feel important."

Jenna snorted. "Do men still go for that 'stupid little me' routine?"

"Not this man."

"Good," she said. "Because—" *Because what?* He wasn't a date or even a potential one. She didn't have to adopt some tactic to impress him—not that she'd do that with a man, anyway. She turned back toward the field.

At the end of the fourth inning the score was tied at three and the woman behind them was still asking questions, and Chad and Jenna were both hoarse from shouting. They argued over the fine points of the game, fed each other popcorn. Jenna forgot they were acting and enjoyed herself. The score stayed close, but in the bottom of the eighth a two-run homer by Petrovich put the Astros ahead. They jumped up to cheer, Chad hugged her, and they beamed at each other. "You should do that more often," Chad murmured, his arm still around her.

"What?"

"Relax. Smile." His eyes darkened, his thumb traced her lips. "You have a beautiful smile."

The noise around them receded. All Jenna could hear was his voice; all she could see was his face, moving closer. "Chad," she murmured.

"Chad," a masculine voice called.

Startled, they both turned. A smiling couple stood in the aisle. *Saved in the nick of time,* Jenna thought as Chad introduced them. They chatted for a few minutes, then the two left. Chad and Jenna turned back to watch the remainder of the game, the spell between them broken.

On the way home Chad tuned the radio to a rock station. Usually rock music got on her nerves, but tonight Jenna paid no attention. She wondered what would happen when they reached Chad's house. Her mind strayed to the evening of the symphony—to the feel of Chad's arms around her, the taste of his lips. And then to this evening at the ball game. Would he want to finish that kiss he'd begun? Would she let him?

The men she dated, most of them cops, were direct. Their messages were clear. Either they were buddies, or they wanted to go straight to bed. She knew how to deal with these men—pal around with the buddies, turn off the lechers. But Chad's messages were mixed. He confused her. One minute, he was a friend; the next, a would-be lover. She didn't know how to react. Worse yet, she didn't know how she wanted to react.

He pulled into the driveway. "I'll get out here," she said. "I want to check your mailbox."

She got out of the car and glanced around the street. It was quiet, drenched in moonlight. She opened the mailbox and thumbed through the mail. An envelope from Rose was at the bottom of the stack. She lifted it carefully and held it up as Chad came to her side. "Another one." He reached for it, but she shook her head. "I'll look at it first."

Inside, he switched on the lights and Jenna sat down on the living room couch and read the letter. "Chad," she asked, "has Lynn O'Donnell ever been here?"

"To my house?" He shook his head. "Never."

"Then she didn't write the letters. Because Rose *has* been in your house." She held the letter out to him. "Read it."

CHAPTER NINE

HE READ ALOUD.

"Darling Chad,
Did you get the rose? I picked the prettiest one. I wanted to bring it inside to you, but the spirits held me back again. They're still too strong, but I'll overcome them soon. I want us to be together. I know you love me, but I can make you love me even more.

Yesterday I planned how we would spend our first day together. I want to watch everything you do. You'll be my own private TV star. Only it won't be television anymore, my love. It will be real.

I'll lie under the comforter on the king-size bed and watch you work out on your exercise machine. Then I'll watch you shower. I'm so glad you have a clear glass shower door. I'll dry you off with one of those fluffy brown towels. Mmm! Just thinking about touching you sends me into spasms.

We'll go downstairs and I'll fix you breakfast. Do you like waffles? I'm sure you do because we're so in tune, we like the same things. We'll eat at that little table in your kitchen. Then we'll spend the whole day together. We'll cuddle under the navy afghan on the couch. We'll listen to our favorite songs on the CD player. We'll read each other love poems. And at night, we'll act them out. I want to touch your body all over, kiss you until you beg for me. I'll love you better than anyone ever has and we'll be together always. It will happen soon. Please be patient, my darling.

Rose, your phantom lover

"Good God!" Chad choked. "This is unbelievable. She knows everything about me, down to the color of my towels."

Jenna nodded. "What I want to know is how."

"I've never invited Lynn O'Donnell here. I told you, I don't get involved with people I work with."

"Have you described your home to her?"

"I may have mentioned something innocuous like my CD player, but not the kind of glass I have in my shower, for God's sake. Damn, I need a drink." He strode to the bar in the corner of the room and poured himself a liberal dose of scotch. "Want something?"

She shook her head.

He returned to the couch, took a gulp of liquor, and rubbed the back of his neck. "I thought we had Rose pegged."

"So did I," Jenna said. She reached into her purse for a notebook and pen. "Okay, we cross Lynn off the list of suspects. Who's been here?"

"Not many people," Chad replied. "As you know, I haven't lived in Houston long and I've been too busy."

"How about Mona Switzer?"

To Jenna's surprise, Chad flushed. "We went to her house."

"You didn't date her long. What about the next one?"

His glass clattered on the coffee table. "I haven't brought any women here."

"Friends in for the evening?"

"The McGowens, a few other couples."

"Someone who could be angry enough about the property values in Montrose to threaten you?"

He got up and poured another drink, gulped it down. "The McGowens are upset about the halfway house, sure, but they aren't the kind of people to stoop to this. I'd stake my life on it."

Jenna grimaced at his choice of words. "Let's hope you don't have to." She doodled on her notepad for a minute, then said, "Okay, tomorrow I want you to go over that list of names you gave me. Circle anyone who's been here, even if they just came to the door. I'll take it from there."

"What are you going to do?"

She hadn't the faintest idea. "See what we can find out about these people—their habits, their hang-ups. Maybe with a little luck, we'll figure out who Rose is."

He shut his eyes and shook his head. "I certainly hope so."

Jenna rose. She was tired, dispirited. She'd banked on Lynn being the crazy letter-writer. Now they were back to square one.

She glanced at Chad. His eyes were still closed, his face pale and drawn. "Are you okay?"

"Migraine," he muttered. "Just hit me. Shouldn't have had that last drink. Alcohol and stress are a lethal combination."

"I'll get you some aspirin," she offered.

"No, I have a prescription."

"Where?"

"In the bathroom upstairs."

"Let's go up, then," Jenna said. "You should get to bed."

He got out of the chair and stood gazing blankly at the stairs.

"Dizzy?" she asked.

"No," he murmured, but he stumbled after a few steps.

Jenna caught his arm. "Come on." She led him to the stairs, felt the weight of his body as they slowly climbed to the top. Chad stopped, groaned, and rubbed his right temple. "We're almost there," she coaxed.

In his room she reached for the light switch, but Chad's arm flailed out to stop her. "No light," he mumbled. He staggered to the bed, sank down, and stared at the wall.

Jenna went into the bathroom and found his prescription, filled a glass and brought it to him. He hadn't moved. She handed him the pill and he swallowed it. Then she knelt in front of him, unlaced his sneakers, and gently slipped them off. She left his socks on; the idea of holding his naked feet in her hands seemed curiously intimate.

"Take off your shirt," she told him.

His fingers fumbled for the hem. He pulled the shirt halfway up, then stopped with a moan. "Can't," he muttered, and started to lie down.

"I'll do it." She leaned over him, took the edge of the T-shirt in her hands, and slowly lifted it. She didn't want to touch him but couldn't avoid it. Smooth, warm skin. Sinew and muscle. Her finger skimmed over his ribs, and he drew in a breath. Her hands seemed to move in excruciatingly slow motion. She wanted to hurry; she wanted to linger, to savor every inch of the upward journey. Her knuckles grazed soft hair, the tip of a nipple. His collarbones were broad and strong, his body firm and sleek. Careful not to jar his head, she spread the shirt wide and slipped it off.

His eyes were still shut, his mouth set in lines of pain. "Thanks," he said. "I'll get the rest." He unbuckled his belt, pulled it off and let it fall, then reached for the snap at his waist.

Jenna stood frozen, wanting to leave, yet powerless to tear her eyes away. The rasp of the zipper sounded loud to her ears. Her eyes followed it down, centimeter by centimeter. Chad rose unsteadily, shrugged off his jeans, kicked them out of the way. His briefs, a flash of white against his tanned skin, came into view. She saw his thighs—muscular, powerful—and, God help her, she wanted to touch them, feel the muscles flex beneath her hands.

"Lie on your stomach," she said, her voice husky. "I'll massage your neck."

He said nothing but simply lay down, his head turned toward her, eyes closed, golden lashes feathering over his cheeks.

She bent over him and put her hands on his shoulders. She began to work at the knotted muscles, kneading firmly. Chad groaned. "Hush, it'll feel better soon," she murmured. "My mom used to have headaches. Working on those pressure points helped."

Faint light from the stairway filtered into the room, enough for her to see his body clearly. As she massaged at his muscles, she drank her fill of him. She thought of Rose's letter—*I want to touch your body all over*—and realized she and Rose weren't so very different. She wanted to touch him, too. To run her hands over smooth skin, down his back to the curve of his buttocks, along the length of his legs. And to follow the same pathway with her lips. She wanted to urge him over onto his back, rub her bare breasts against his chest, caress his stomach, his hips.... Take him in her hands, take him inside her.

His breathing deepened; hers became shallow, reduced to tiny pants. His skin cooled; hers heated. Her fingertips tingled from the touch of his flesh. Oh, Lord, she was losing her mind.

At last she felt his muscles go lax, heard a moan of relief. "Better?" she whispered.

"Mmm, thanks." His speech was slurred.

She let her hand brush over his back just once, then tiptoed out, hoping he hadn't been alert enough to notice her reaction to him.

She went to bed and dreamed she was Rose, doing all the things Rose had written about, feeling all the emotions Rose had described and she herself had experienced. She woke in the darkness, disoriented and edgy, afraid the lines between her and the crazy fan were blurring, that she might *become* Rose.

She went downstairs and made herself some tea, drank slowly until her emotions settled. She wasn't like Rose. She'd been carried away by the situation this evening—the darkness, the bedroom, the sight of Chad's body. It wouldn't happen again.

IN THE MORNING SHE WOKE early and listened to the sounds coming from down the hall. Apparently Chad had recovered from his headache and the meeting with his father was still on. She heard the shower run, drawers open and close, and Chad's footsteps on the stairs.

Thankful for a rare morning on which to linger in bed, Jenna turned over, hugged the pillow to her chest, and went back to sleep. She woke again at ten with a whole Sunday stretching before her. She could go home and do her laundry, walk in the park, shop for bargains at one of Houston's flea markets. Usually she savored a day like this. This morning she felt at loose ends.

She wandered through the house, trying to think of something to do. Her journey brought her to the door of Chad's room, and she went inside. He'd told her she could use his exercise equipment. She got on the NordicTrack, took a few steps and stopped. The room smelled of him. The bed bore the imprint of his body. The jeans he'd worn yesterday still lay where he'd tossed them, a sharp reminder of what she'd thought and felt when he'd taken them off.

Get out. Now! Jenna ordered herself and darted into the hall. She called Gracie. "Want to get together this afternoon?"

"Can't," her friend answered with a lilt in her voice. "Jorge and I have plans."

"This is getting serious."

"Mmm. I'm in love," Gracie sang out. "And how's your love interest?"

"I don't have one."

"Your case, then. How is life among the upper crust?"

Jenna considered that. "Some of it's good, some of it's bad."

"Tell me the good parts."

Jenna recited their Saturday schedule.

"Oh?" Gracie didn't sound impressed. "That sounds too common. I thought those arrogant, *interesting*, spoiled rich-guy types did fancier things—went cruising on the family yacht, sat around sipping champagne and discussing the latest on Charles and Di."

"'Fraid not."

"Did he at least buy something outlandishly expensive for his brother?"

"Sunglasses, two books."

"Oh, nuts!" Gracie said. "From the way you described him the other day I thought he'd do better than that. I picture him stepping out of *Gentlemen's Quarterly,* right down to his designer underwear."

An image of Chad's briefs clinging to his body flashed through Jenna's mind. "He doesn't wear it," she said without thinking. She could have bitten her tongue.

Gracie dissolved into giggles. "*Designer* underwear? Or any underwear? And how do you know?"

"I don't." Jenna sighed. "Forget it, have fun with Jorge, and I'll see you tomorrow."

She dressed and left Chad's house, drove to the Museum of Natural Science and spent the remainder of the morning browsing through the exhibits. She could have called Corey or one of the other guys she palled around with, but she didn't want to. Instead, she went to a tear-jerker movie and sniffled over her popcorn. She was lonely.

Afterward she treated herself to Chinese food, then drove back to Chad's. Light shone in the living room window, and the warm glow raised her spirits. No, not the light, she admitted. More likely the thought of the man who'd turned it on.

"Hi," he said when she came inside. "Have you eaten?" She nodded, and he asked, "Want some ice cream?" She filled a bowl with creamy vanilla and joined him at the kitchen table. "Thanks for last night," he said.

"I'm glad it helped."

He put down his spoon. "How was your day, dear?" he asked, his eyes gleaming with mischief.

Jenna laughed. "Fine. I went to the science museum and saw a movie."

"At the Imax theater at the museum?"

"No. *Summer Dreams.*"

"The reviews say it's a two-hankie movie. Is it?"

"Three," she said.

"Why do women like those things?" Chad asked sounding genuinely puzzled.

"For the emotional release, I guess." She finished the last spoonful of ice cream and took both their bowls to the sink.

Chad nodded. "Like men get from sports."

Jenna put the bowls in the dishwasher. "What men get from sports is vicarious machismo."

Chad grinned at her. "Low blow, Sarge. You think that's why I took you to the ball game last night? You think I feel masculine watching a bunch of guys whack a ball with a piece of wood?"

"You said that. I didn't." She shut the dishwasher and stretched. "I'm going to bed."

"See you tomorrow."

"Good night," she said. On the way upstairs, it occurred to her that this evening and last night, too, they'd actually had fun together. Fun with Chad Foster? A week ago she wouldn't have believed it.

Their camaraderie continued on Monday. Jenna stopped in at the TV station on her way to work to make sure Chad's staff was aware of his new "love interest." In the evening, they met at the Saltgrass Steakhouse for grilled-chicken salads.

When they got home, the telephone was ringing. Chad answered, talked for a few minutes, then hung up and grinned. "That was my sister, Ariel. She and her husband are coming in a few days early for the National Hurricane Conference."

"Are they interested in hurricanes?" Jenna asked.

"Jeff's a meteorologist," Chad explained. "Last year he did some spots for our TV station in Corpus Christi. The newspapers called him the Hurricane Hunk. Then, when Hurricane Ethan hit, he went on without a break for twenty-four hours, and they changed that to the Hurricane Hero.''

"Hey, I read about him."

"Ariel said they'll come over Saturday, so you'll get to meet him, but whatever you do, don't call him Hunk. He hated that nickname and all the publicity. He's back working for a private meteorology company now, but he's promised Ariel if, God forbid, another hurricane hits, he'll go back on the air."

Before Jenna could comment, the phone rang again.

Chad reached for it. "Hello."

His face paled. He gestured to Jenna. "Pick it up," he mouthed.

She ran into the kitchen and grabbed the extension.

"I can't hear you," Chad was saying.

"You heard me." The voice was a raspy whisper. "Who is she?"

"Who?" he asked.

"That woman. Get rid of her. You're mine."

"Rose? *Rose!*"

The line went dead.

Jenna punched in 57 for the phone company's tracing service, then slammed down the receiver. "Damn! Rose wasn't on long enough for a standard trace. At least it'll be recorded at the phone company *if* she's calling within the same phone system." She returned to the living room where Chad stood, staring at the receiver in his hand. She took it from him, replaced it, and motioned to him to sit down.

"I thought we had her," he muttered.

Jenna needed to reassure both of them. "Don't worry. Our plan's working. She's upset because she's seen me. We just have to figure out where. At least we're narrowing the field. We have to come up with someone who's seen me *and* been in your house.''

They retraced their steps over the last few days and could only think of Kay McGowen. ''She's not a logical choice,'' Chad said.

''I agree with you, but logic doesn't always apply. We'll put Kay on our list for now, and keep looking for clues.''

''And how do we do that?''

''Slowly.'' When his expression darkened, she explained, ''That's the way investigative work is. Unless Rose turns up on your doorstep, we've got to piece the clues together, one by one.''

Rose didn't turn up. And she left no more clues.

She sent letters, though. Plenty of them. In the next two days seven arrived, each more incoherent and bizarre than the one before. Each mentioned Jenna, beseeching Chad to break off his relationship with her. Jenna and Nate were stumped. The rookie policewoman assigned to do the legwork on the case went over the few names Chad had circled on his list. Not one of them fit the profile of an obsessed fan. They crossed off Kay McGowen and all the others.

''All we can do is wait,'' Nate said.

''Right,'' Jenna muttered. She had to admit she didn't mind. She was becoming more and more captivated by Chad. She looked forward to the evenings they spent together visiting his favorite haunts, making themselves visible as a couple. She looked forward to the sight of him, his scent, the sound of his voice, the rumble of his frequent laughter. She even relished their spirited debates about everything from politics to sports.

Though she enjoyed their good-natured arguments, she pointed them out to Chad as evidence of their differences. He laughed at her. "Life would be damn dull if everyone thought the same. I like arguing with you."

MEANWHILE, JENNA continued to work on the Morales case. No clues turned up there, either. Until Friday afternoon, when Sendak's Dairy called. Arthur Green had returned.

Jenna rushed to his apartment. He answered the door, again attired in his ratty robe, again looking weary and unkempt. His eyes widened with surprise when he saw her.

Jenna stepped inside and shut the door. "We've been looking for you, Mr. Green."

"Wh-why?" He backed up a step. "I was out of town."

"Yes, I know. Where were you?"

"Hey, I have a right to leave Houston," he said, crossing his arms over his chest. "I'm not a suspect in this case, am I?"

"Where were you?" Jenna repeated.

"Personal business." She raised a brow, and he continued. "My brother-in-law died. I went to Ohio for the funeral."

"For a week?"

"I stayed to help my sister. What do you want with me, anyway? I told you everything I know. I gave you permission to search the truck."

"Right. We searched the truck, and you know what we found?"

He waited impassively.

"Blood. We found blood."

A choking sound escaped from Arthur Green's lips.

"What we want to know," Jenna continued, "is whose."

His hands trembled, but he stood his ground. "It' probably mine. I...cut myself reaching into the freeze one day. I...I guess I bled on the floor."

"Where'd you cut yourself?"

"My...hand."

"Let me see."

He glanced down, turned his hand over as if he'd neve seen it before and stuck it in the pocket of his robe. "Th cut's healed."

"Healed," Jenna muttered with disgust. "Okay, mayb you did cut yourself, maybe the cut's healed by now. Yo could save yourself and the police a lot of trouble, M Green, if you'd let us take a sample of your blood, see i it matches the stains in the truck."

His eyes darted nervously around the room. "Yo won't say anything about that to Sendak's?"

"Not about the blood. They already know I was look ing for you."

His face turned gray. "I— All right. I don't want an more trouble. What do I have to do?"

She gave him instructions, then turned toward the door "For your sake, I hope it's a match."

He stuck his chin out. "It will be."

"We'll see," Jenna said. "Meantime, don't leave tow again for *any* reason."

SATURDAY, JENNA WAS edgy. She wanted to go home an hide, let Chad visit with his sister without her.

"That doesn't make sense," he said.

"Can't we tell your sister nothing's going on betwee us?"

Chad looked up from his newspaper. "You know bet ter than that. We decided no one should know."

"Who's she going to tell?"

"Nobody, but if she knows the truth, she'll behave differently toward us, and people will figure out that something fishy's going on."

He was right, but she didn't like the idea of putting on an act in front of his sister. And the thought of meeting his entire family, especially the formidable Martin Foster, at the next day's party, was as appealing as infiltrating a juvenile gang.

At two in the afternoon, a car door slammed out front. A minute later, the doorbell chimed. Chad shook his head. "That's Ariel."

He opened the door and lifted a tiny blonde off her feet for a hug, then turned to shake the hand of the dark-haired man beside her. Jenna watched as they came through the entry hall. They were a striking couple. Ariel looked like a fairy-tale princess with a cloud of golden hair around her elfin face. Slender, almost fragile, and no more than five feet tall, she was the kind of woman who always made Jenna feel like an awkward giant.

Jenna could see why Ariel's husband had earned the title "Hurricane Hunk"—midnight black hair, smoky gray eyes fringed with thick lashes, and a body that would catch the eye of any woman.

Ariel sailed into the room, caught sight of Jenna, and stopped short. "Hello."

Chad came to Jenna, put his arm around her shoulder and drew her close. "This is Jenna Wakefield. My sister and brother-in-law, Ariel and Jeff McBride."

Ariel cocked her head. Her eyes assessed them. Then she grinned. "Well, *hello.*"

"Um, hi," was all Jenna could manage.

"Sit down," Chad invited. Before Jenna could scoot away from him, he tightened his grasp on her shoulder and steered her toward the living room couch. He sat so close they might as well have been Siamese twins. Jenna shot him a warning glance, but he blithely ignored her.

Ariel flopped onto the armchair across from them and curled her feet under her. "So, how long have you two known each other?"

Jeff choked back a laugh, and Chad said, "Ariel's nothing if not direct."

He could say that again, Jenna thought. She felt the way she did when she testified in court.

"Jenna and I met a few weeks ago when she came to the station to interview the staff," Chad said. "She's writing a book on television careers."

"Love at first sight," Ariel cooed. Jenna squirmed under her approving gaze.

"I told you, she has a platitude for everything," Chad said out of the corner of his mouth. He patted Jenna's hand.

"Have you written other books?" Ariel asked Jenna.

"No, I, uh, mostly do . . . investigative reporting." She felt Chad's silent laughter.

"What's new at Channel 6?" Ariel inquired, turning to her brother.

Chad launched into a description of "The Public Soapbox," and soon brother and sister were deep in conversation while Jeff sat back and listened with a benign smile on his face. Ariel asked questions and made suggestions, and even though Jenna's knowledge of television was scanty, she could tell the ideas were good ones. Ariel's fragility was clearly an illusion. This woman knew her business. Jenna realized her impression of Chad's sister from the picture she'd seen in his office had been totally inaccurate. His sister wasn't a social butterfly like Kay McGowen; she was a businesswoman, as committed to her career as Chad was to his. Ariel had won the ratings contest between the siblings, Jenna remembered, and she could see why. Chad's sister was five feet of pure energy.

When they'd exhausted the topic of their respective TV stations, Jeff said, "We got the last set of pictures of the new house. Looks like it's coming along well."

"I should be in by fall," Chad said.

"Sure it's hurricane-proof?" his brother-in-law asked.

"My husband, the meteorologist," Ariel teased, laughing. "By the way, you've done a nice job with the town house, even though it's temporary. I liked the pictures of your bedroom."

That got Jenna's attention. "You've seen photos of the bedroom?"

"Chad takes pictures of everything, alive, dead, and in-between," Ariel said. "I've seen every room in this place, even the closets."

Jenna felt like kicking herself. Why hadn't she thought about Rose seeing *photographs* of the town house? Photography was Chad's hobby. Hadn't he spent last Saturday snapping innumerable shots of her at the park?

"Want a snack and something to drink?" Chad asked after a while. There were yeses all around, and he excused himself to go into the kitchen.

"I'll help," Jenna offered and followed him from the room. In the kitchen, he opened the refrigerator and reached in, but she caught hold of his arm. "How many other people have seen pictures of this place?" she asked urgently.

Chad shrugged. "I took a few snapshots to the office along with the roll of the new house. Why?"

"Don't you see? Rose doesn't have to have been here. She could know everything about this place from seeing the pictures."

He turned to stare at her. "My God, you're right."

"This puts Lynn O'Donnell back in the picture," Jenna warned.

"Yeah, but now we know where she could have gotten her information. You're a genius, Sarge." Before she could stop him, he caught her in an exuberant hug.

"Let me go."

The devil himself couldn't have grinned more charmingly. "Why? I like to hug you."

"Stop it anyway," she ordered. "And you don't have to sit so close."

"Yes, I do, Sarge. Love—"

"Interest. Yes, I remember. But you're overdoing it."

He brushed his finger across her cheek. "You can never overdo love."

She narrowed her eyes, wishing she could think of something to say that would wipe that smirk off his face, something that wouldn't cause too much commotion. Unable to come up with a suitable reprisal, she snatched up a tray of tortilla chips and guacamole dip and returned to the living room. Ariel declined the snack but accepted a glass of iced tea from her brother.

"How's the hurricane conference going?" Chad inquired.

"Very well. There's new technology this year that'll make tracking storms easier," Jeff said and went on to explain the advances.

"He forgot to mention that he helped develop that technology," Ariel interjected, giving Jeff an adoring smile. "My husband believes in hiding his light under a bushel. He also forgot to say that he's getting an award tonight for his work during Hurricane Ethan last year."

"Congratulations," Chad said, getting up to shake his brother-in-law's hand. When he sat down again, he put his arm around Jenna and began a lazy caress of her upper arm. She gritted her teeth and endured it. *Endured?* She wanted to purr like a kitten.

Ariel's knowing gaze was riveted on her brother's hand. "We have some other news, too," she said, turning to grin conspiratorially at Jeff. She took a breath. "We're going to have a baby."

"Maybe two," Jeff added. "The doctor thinks he hears two heartbeats."

Chad got up again and enveloped his sister in a bear hug. "Congratulations, squirt." His voice was husky. "Twins, huh?" he said to Jeff. "Good work, McBride."

Jeff's gaze slid to his wife, and he grinned like a Cheshire cat. "It was a pleasure."

Watching the three of them, Jenna felt her heart contract. She'd like a baby someday and a husband who adored her the way Jeff did Ariel.

They visited for another half hour, discussing their parents' cruise, the party tomorrow, and Ariel's plan to have a bon voyage "telegram," complete with balloons and a racy song, delivered by Eastern Onion.

"They should get a kick out of that," Chad said. He laid his hand on Jenna's knee. His touch raised goose bumps, and she flushed crimson when she realized he noticed. Just wait until Jeff and Ariel left! She'd fix Chad good for torturing her like this when she couldn't fight back.

Finally Jeff said, "We'd better go, honey, so you can rest before the banquet this evening."

Ariel agreed. "Being doubly pregnant makes you doubly tired . . . and doubly morning sick."

"I need to take off, too," Chad said. "I have to go by the station for a while." He turned to Jenna and ran a finger down her cheek. "I'll be back in an hour or so."

"Don't rush," she said sweetly. *Damn him.* He'd made it patently clear they were living together.

Ariel beamed at them. "Love makes the world go 'round."

Chad pulled Jenna close as they walked Ariel and Jeff to the door. "See you tomorrow."

They waited in the doorway, watching the McBrides' car disappear down the street. When it turned the corner, Jenna sighed with relief and tried to pull away. "Let me go."

"Uh-uh."

"Come on, Foster. Your family's gone. You can stop pretending now."

Something flashed in his eyes. Still holding her, he backed up a step and shut the door. Then he turned her firmly in his arms and drew her against him.

With unerring aim, his mouth captured hers. His lips moved over hers with gentle pressure; teasing, seducing, effortlessly surmounting every barrier she'd built against him, against this.

She wanted to push him away, *needed* to, but she couldn't. His arms encircled her so warmly, his hands moved over her so surely. And his kisses spawned a roaring in her head, a thunder in her blood. He kissed her until she couldn't think, couldn't breathe. Then he pulled back and stared into her eyes. His voice husky, his breath as shallow as hers, he held her gaze. "I wasn't pretending, Sarge. That was real." He opened the door again, pulled his keys from his pocket and went outside.

As she stood in the doorway, frozen with shock, her knees buckling, he glanced at her over his shoulder. "I'll see you later, Jenna," he said softly. "Think about it." And he disappeared into the garage.

CHAPTER TEN

THINK ABOUT IT! She could do nothing else. As afternoon drifted into evening, she relived everything that had happened since she'd met Chad, everything that had led up to that searing kiss. When had her feelings about him started to change? When had she begun to want him with an urgency that tempted her to rush headlong into his bed?

The night of the symphony, when he'd first kissed her, held her so sweetly? Or the evening at the ball game when they'd laughed together like carefree kids? He'd sympathized with her feelings about the Morales child, even done another news feature to try to help. She'd shared the anguish of her teenage years with him, and he'd listened and understood. He'd told her of his hopes and dreams for his TV station—his mission, he'd said. And she'd seen he wasn't a rich dilettante playing at being a television executive, but a man who cared, who wanted to make the community a better place. She'd seen how he worked . . . and how he played. And, God help her, she was falling in love with him.

But did he return her feelings? He liked her, perhaps he even cared for her in a way, but she couldn't forget Mona Switzer's bitter, "He has a short attention span." Maybe that was sour grapes on Mona's part, but Jenna suspected the statement was true. She could make love with Chad tonight, but what about next week or next month when Rose was history? Jenna Wakefield would be history, too. She'd be "the cop he'd slept with," nothing more.

This afternoon when he'd kissed her, she should have stopped him. *Could* have. She'd had courses in self-defense. She could have had Chad Foster on his knees in an instant. But she had no defenses against his kisses.

Well, she'd build some. She made a mental list of all the reasons a relationship with Chad was wrong. Then she decided her first strategy was to put the man out of her mind. She went upstairs and found the book she'd started the other evening. She'd concentrate on the hero—a dark, dangerous drifter from the wrong side of the tracks, as unlike Chad as a man could be. She'd sit in the living room and read.

Halfway down the stairs, she heard Chad's key in the lock. She froze.

The door opened. He stepped inside, saw her, and started up the stairs. "Jenna." His voice was deep as night, soft as a caress. He moved toward her. Up one step, two, three.

She gripped the banister as if it were a lifeline. "I, um, was just going to—" *To what?* "Fix some coffee."

He reached the step below her and stopped, his mouth level with hers. "All afternoon I thought about you. About this." He took her face between his hands and urged her toward him.

"No, I..."

"Please." He waited an instant, giving her time to resist, but she did nothing. Then his arms were around her, his lips moving on hers.

So much for defending herself. The book slipped from her grasp. The hand that should have pushed him away slid around his neck, the other tangled in his hair.

"That's right," he murmured against her mouth. "Kiss me back."

She did. And lost herself in him. In the wine-dark taste of his mouth, the warmth of his lips, the rough surface of his tongue.

"Come upstairs," he breathed. "Make love with me."

With all her strength, she forced herself to resist. "No. No, I can't."

He let her go. "We have to talk," he said and took her hand.

He led her to the couch and sat beside her, keeping her hand in his. He raised the palm to his lips and when she tried to pull away, he held on firmly as if he couldn't bear to let her go. With his eyes on hers, he kissed the tender tips of her fingers. "Why?" he asked. "Better yet, why not?"

"Because," she began, and all those logical reasons she'd cataloged earlier vanished from her mind. She struggled to remember. "Because I can't begin a relationship—"

"We already have a relationship."

"A professional one."

"Jenna," he chided, "do you really believe our relationship is only professional?"

"No." They'd begun as antagonists, but somewhere along the way, they'd slipped into the role of friends, even confidantes. "But it *should* be."

"It hasn't been for some time." He laced his fingers through hers. "I care about you, Jenna."

She wanted to ask him what that meant. Instead, she said, "You can't. We're . . . we're too different."

"Are we? Because I like rock music and you like classical? Because I eat breakfast and you don't? That's trivial."

"You're forgetting the biggest one," she said. "We come from different worlds. Mine is beer and barbecue, yours is champagne and caviar."

"You sound like Ariel," he said. "Spouting clichés."

"Sayings become clichés because they're true." She didn't tell him the other reason—that she knew he didn't go in for long-term relationships; that she was afraid he'd leave her and break her heart.

"You're building a wall that doesn't have to exist," he argued.

She shook her head firmly. "I'm not. The wall's been there from the beginning."

"Then let's tear it down."

"I can't."

"Jenna, look at me." He put his free hand under her chin so that he could look into her eyes. His gaze was so warm, so inviting. His eyes sent messages she was afraid to believe. "Tell me what you feel."

"I...don't know."

His lips curved into a half smile. "At least you're not sure, so you've left me some hope. I'll wait, but I'll do everything possible to level that wall you've built between us, everything I can to change your mind."

A tender threat. She didn't know how to respond. "I should go up," she muttered.

"A good-night kiss," he said softly and drew her against him.

He kissed her with gentle patience, his tongue teasing hers lightly, his hands stroking her back. As seconds ticked by, he continued to hold her mouth captive with his. He kissed her as if he wouldn't let her go, as if they had forever.

If only she could believe that.

JENNA STARED AT THE imposing River Oaks mansion and swallowed. She'd almost rather be visiting a crack house. Behind her, the street was filled with BMWs, Mercedeses, and a Lexus or two. Azalea bushes flanked the walkway and bordered the wide, manicured lawn. The house itself, a two-story white brick with a graceful columned veranda, intimidated her.

Chad squeezed her shoulder reassuringly. "Relax. You'll have a good time."

She didn't believe him for a minute, but she took a deep breath as they approached the door. Chad rang the bell and Jenna was surprised when Martin Foster himself opened it.

"Chad! Your mother's been wondering when you'd show up."

Chad drew Jenna inside. "Dad, I want you to meet Jenna Wakefield."

Shrewd eyes sized her up as Chad's father took her hand.

"Jenna remembers your name from University of Texas lore," Chad said.

"Are you a UT fan, Jenna?"

"Yes, sir."

Martin smiled, his grin a replica of Chad's. "Longhorn fans are always welcome here. Come in the living room and tell me what you know about my football career."

"Well, I've heard the story about the ninety-seven-yard run against A. & M."

"That one's still making the rounds, huh?" Martin looked pleased.

They talked football. Here, Jenna could hold her own. She'd spent countless afternoons in Dallas's Texas Stadium, cheering the Cowboys. Since she'd lived in Houston, she'd attended Oiler games.

"You'll have to meet one of my old teammates, Jenna." Martin scanned the crowded living room. "There he is." He beckoned to Ed Macauley, who stood by the bar. The chief ambled over, clapped Chad on the shoulder and gave Jenna a polite, I-don't-believe-we've-met smile.

"Buster," Martin said, "meet Jenna Wakefield, a Longhorn fan. Buster, here, opened those holes in the line for me when we played together. I got the glory and he did the work."

"It's a pleasure to meet you, Mr.—"

"Oh, none of this 'mister' stuff," Martin advised her. "Just call him Buster."

Jenna glanced sidelong at Chad. His eyes gleamed with mischief. Unable to contain a grin, she stuck out her hand. "Nice to meet you . . . Buster."

"Ms. Wakefield."

"Call me Jenna."

"Buster, why don't you keep these two company while I get them something to drink," Martin said. He took their orders and left.

Chief Macauley waited until Martin was out of earshot, then asked softly, "Anything new?"

Jenna told him about the recent barrage of letters and her theory about the photographs.

"Good thinking, Sergeant. Pursue it. You still have someone stationed at Chad's office, right?" When she assured him she did, he added, "I want someone with Chad at all times—you, or the plainclothes officer. Make sure you keep a close watch."

"Yes, Chief Macauley."

He grinned at her suddenly. "You can call me Buster . . . here."

"Uncle Buster!" Ariel appeared beside them and gave the chief a smacking kiss on the cheek.

He hugged her, then held her away from him and scrutinized her thoroughly. "I heard a rumor a while ago."

"It's true. I'm pregnant, maybe with twins."

The chief rolled his eyes. "Double trouble. Two little hellions like their mother. You gave Virginia and Martin fits. I remember when you fell out of the tree house—"

"And split my chin. See? I still have the scar." She tipped up her face and Buster chuckled.

"Jenna," Ariel asked, taking Jenna's arm, "have you had anything to eat?" Jenna shook her head. "Come on, you two, grab some plates." She stood on tiptoe and gave the chief another peck on the cheek. "'Scuze us, Uncle Buster. I have to get these two fed."

Jenna wasn't hungry, but Ariel tugged her along through the elegant living room with its Oriental rugs, graceful antique furnishings, and windows looking out on a patio and pool. As they approached the dining room, a spicy odor met Jenna's nostrils.

Chad handed her a plate and gestured to the table. "What would you like? Barbecue?" He nodded to an ice-filled tub. "Beer?"

Their eyes met, his alight with triumphant laughter. Jenna smiled at him. The Fosters were a surprise.

The surprises continued throughout the afternoon. She met Virginia Foster, Chad's mother. Small, blond, lively, she was Ariel, twenty years hence.

Daniel, the third Foster sibling, was just as Chad had described him—dark, intense, with dreamy brown eyes. He told Jenna about his love of ballooning. "I like the quiet, but I enjoy the challenge, too. A couple of guys I know are talking about a cross-country flight. I may join them."

Jenna sensed the spirit of adventure Chad had mentioned and felt an immediate liking for Daniel. She loved adventure, too. You could hardly be a police officer if you didn't.

"Maybe you can encourage my workaholic brother to take up a hobby," Daniel continued.

Jenna guessed his sister must have filled him in on Chad's new "relationship." She shifted uncomfortably. She didn't enjoy deceiving Chad's family. "He, uh, likes photography," she said.

"Too tame."

"Oh, yeah?" Chad said. "What about the time I fell out of a deer blind taking pictures and busted my ankle?"

Daniel laughed, dark eyes gleaming. "I'd forgotten that." He grinned at Jenna. "Climbing into a deer blind's about as high up as Chad gets. I thought about inviting him to join my crew in the next balloon race, but he likes to keep his feet on the ground."

As they continued talking, several other guests joined them. The Fosters' guests were another surprise to Jenna. Oh, a few seemed typical society types, but the majority were unpretentious and friendly. Laughter and good-natured conversation filled the house as waiters kept the glasses filled and the table groaning under the supply of barbecue, baked beans, and coleslaw.

"Enjoying yourself?" Chad whispered.

"Yes, I am."

He grinned and flicked her dangly earring into motion. "I won't say, 'I told you so.'"

"Please, don't," Jenna replied, laughing.

MIDWAY THROUGH the afternoon, the doorbell rang. Ariel hurried to answer it, and in walked an outrageous trio—a ship's captain, a well-endowed girl in a bikini, and a large chicken. The chicken blew a horn and announced, "All aboard for the Greek Isles," as Ariel pushed her mother and father forward. The chicken danced, the girl in the bikini pranced, and the captain sang a bon voyage song set to a tune from *H.M.S. Pinafore*. There was much noisy laughter and applause, and the performance ended with the chicken presenting a bottle of champagne to the senior Fosters.

"More champagne," Ariel called, and waiters passed out glasses to the guests. "A toast to Virginia and Martin." She raised her glass. "May they continue to sail through untroubled waters."

Jenna nudged Chad. "Champagne."

"But no caviar," he whispered, hugging her and planting a lingering kiss on her cheek.

Jenna felt her face flame. "The chief's watching."

"He'll think we're playing our roles well." Chad raised his glass to her. His eyes held hers and, though he said nothing, she read his silent message: *I want you*. Her blood fizzed like the champagne in her flute.

"Hey, you two. Break it up." Ariel's voice intruded. "Jeff and I are leaving. We have a long drive back to Corpus."

As they walked to the door with the McBrides, Ariel turned to Jenna. "Why don't you all come down for the Fourth? The station always has a picnic."

"Um, we'll see," Jenna said. She'd enjoy seeing more of Ariel and her husband, but July Fourth was a long way off. She'd probably be spending it at the annual police barbecue—alone.

When she and Chad left a short time later, she said, "I like your family. Their friends, too."

"I knew you would. Jenna, I told you, the time I spend at the country club is for business. I serve on committees, and network because I have to. The connections I make are important. But that's not how I spend my leisure time. Today was for friends and family. This afternoon you saw my real world."

Jenna considered his words. "I think I understand."

"Good." He reached for her hand, and this time she didn't shrink from his touch.

As they drove along, Jenna was absorbed in her own thoughts. Had she been wrong to judge Chad so harshly? She'd always prided herself on being fair. She thought of Peter Chu and Marcy and the prejudice they'd run up against. Had she in her own way been just as bigoted as Peter's and Marcy's families? Didn't she judge people by the size of their bankrolls? Chad's family had money; therefore, she'd assumed they were cold, haughty, self-absorbed. The Fosters were anything but. She'd been too quick to condemn. It was something to think about.

"You're awfully quiet," Chad observed.

She smiled at him, seeing him with new eyes, and he lifted her hand to his lips. "Whatever happens with Rose," he said, "I want you to stay with me next weekend. We won't worry about being seen—we've done enough of that. We'll spend the time enjoying ourselves, exploring the ways we're alike. All right?"

Why not? Why not be reckless, give herself a chance to get to know him better? She took a breath. "Yes, all right."

He continued touching her as the rest of the evening passed—laying his hand on her shoulder, brushing his knuckles against her cheek, twirling a curl that escaped from her braid. When they went upstairs, before they parted to go to their separate bedrooms, he pulled her close and kissed her—one of those deep, drugging kisses that was over much too soon, that left her lonely and aching long into the night.

MONDAY MORNING JENNA drove Chad to work. They'd decided, because of the rash of letters in the past few days, that they'd better heed Buster's advice. Someone would be with Chad at all times, even on the way to and from the TV station, in case Rose followed him.

He chafed under the restrictions. He missed having his car. He missed the freedom to come and go as he pleased. He missed his privacy.

As he sat in a production meeting, he tried to hide a yawn. He'd been up half of last night and the night before, tossing and turning, thinking of Jenna lying in bed only a few steps down the hall. He wanted her, desired her with an intensity that shocked him. He spent the nights imagining her in his bed, moving beneath him, crying out his name. When he fell asleep at last, he dreamed about her and awoke heated and unfulfilled.

In just a few weeks he'd become enchanted with Jenna. He'd begun by thinking of her as a challenge, then he'd wanted to prove to her that he wasn't the arrogant bastard she imagined. Somewhere along the way, all that had changed. She'd moved into his house and he'd wanted her in his bed. But now he wanted more. He'd come to see the many facets of Jenna Wakefield—her passionate commitment to police work, her courage and strength, and her vulnerability and sweetness. He had to admit that, as much as he hated having Rose breathing down his neck, he owed the woman a debt of gratitude; she'd brought Jenna into his life.

After the meeting, he spent the rest of the day in his office, ordering a sandwich from the deli around the corner for lunch and eating at his desk. No matter what, he probably wouldn't have gone out. He had too much to do on "The Public Soapbox." The first show was due to air in just under two weeks. A fifteen-second commercial announcing the debut was appearing eight times daily. Next week they'd switch to a thirty-second spot.

He checked to see that interviews were set with both the *Houston Chronicle* and the *Post* for Hugh McIver, who was to moderate "Soapbox," and reviewed guests for the initial program with Tina, who informed him the switchboard was already getting requests for tickets.

"We may have to move to a bigger studio to accommodate the audience," Tina said.

"Great! Do it."

The day went well. Lynn O'Donnell kept her distance. He did, however, receive another note from Rose, pleading with him to give up "that woman."

"Can't you see she's a prostitute?" Rose wrote. "No woman with morals wears her hair in a braid." Chad chuckled over that one and put the note away to show to Jenna.

At five, Catherine buzzed him. "Mitchell Nabors is here to see you."

Of all the people he didn't care to encounter, his ten o'clock news anchor topped the list. He'd had several more discussions with Nabors about his on-camera arrogance, and so far, Nabors had made no effort to change his behavior. Chad was surprised he wasn't staying as far away as possible. No such luck. "Send him in."

The door opened and Nabors marched in. He wasn't a big man, but he had presence—the deep voice, the chiseled features, the assurance that audiences expected in an anchor. Trouble was, along with his sterling qualities, the nan had an over-inflated ego, which also came across on he screen.

Chad stared at him coolly. "Sit down. What do you need?"

Nabors ignored the proffered seat. He planted his hands on the desk and leaned over, his face a dull red. "I heard McIver's hosting 'The Public Soapbox.'"

"That's right."

"That two-bit hick! He has a voice like an adolescent frog and the personality to match. McIver belongs on a 3:00 a.m. show in the boonies."

Chad held his temper in check. "Thanks for your observation. Anything else?"

Mitchell leaned farther across the desk, his face contorted with rage. "That job should have been mine, and you damn well know it."

"Sorry. People *earn* jobs around here."

"And I haven't earned it? Anchoring the top news show. Pulling up your lousy ratings."

"You haven't done a damn thing for the ratings, Nabors. If anything, we've lost viewers because of your know-it-all attitude. I've talked to you about this before. If you want prime assignments, change your style." He gestured toward the door.

But Nabors wasn't ready to leave. Fists clenched, he came around the desk and loomed over Chad. "I can walk out on this job—"

"And I can replace you."

Nabors's face turned crimson. "Watch out, Foster," he said, his voice loud and angry. "You be careful what you do to me, or—"

"Or what?"

"Just watch out." He swung around and stomped to the door.

Jenna stood outside Chad's office, her hand raised to knock when she heard the loud voices. She didn't wait to hear what might happen. She grabbed the doorknob.

Before she could open the door, someone yanked it out of her hand. Mitchell Nabors shoved past her, almost knocking her down. His face was mottled; the veins in his neck stood out. Seemingly unaware of her presence, he stalked across the waiting room and disappeared.

Jenna peered into Chad's office. He stood behind his desk, a bemused expression on his face. She ran to his side. "What happened?"

"The star—soon-to-be ex-star—threw a tantrum."

She grabbed his arm. "Are you all right?"

"Of course. Don't I look all right?"

Her eyes swept over every inch of him. Not a scratch on him, not a hair out of place. She took a breath and sat down, realizing her legs were shaking. "What was that all about?"

"Nabors is a prima donna. He was angry that he wasn't tapped to host 'Soapbox,' and he let me know it. This isn't the first time we've clashed."

"Not the first time," she repeated. "Why didn't you tell me?"

"Why?"

Wasn't the reason obvious to him? "He isn't Rose, but he could be angry enough to put someone up to writing those letters."

Chad shook his head. "I don't think so. He's the type to blunder in and blow up on his own, like he did just now."

"Has he seen the pictures of your town house?"

"No. Believe me, Nabors and I don't spend any more time together than we have to. He hasn't been in the office in a couple of weeks."

"I hope you're right about him. I wouldn't want you to tangle with that guy." Now that her legs were steady, she stood. "Ready to go?"

He stuffed some folders into his briefcase. Arm in arm, they walked out to the parking lot. They stopped for a pasta dinner, then went home and attacked their respective paperwork. When the late-evening news came on, Jenna stayed to watch. "This isn't like you," Chad said. "Staying up past ten."

"I want to watch Mitchell Nabors."

The anchor was his usual haughty self. "I see what you mean," Jenna remarked. "He acts like he's doing the audience a favor just sitting in the chair."

"I'm going to have to fire him," Chad said, making a note.

"You know that reporter, Brett Sloan? He'd make a good anchor."

"You're right," Chad agreed with a bemused smile. "You have a good feel for what works on TV. Want to come work at the station?"

Jenna leaned back and stretched. "Not a chance. Who'd catch the bad guys if I left the HPD?"

Chad stared at her thoughtfully. "Have you caught many...bad guys?"

"A few. Mostly gang members. I once nailed the leader of a gang called the Hawks, a real charmer who called himself the Great Falcon. Nabbed two of his lieutenants, too, while they were on their way to a showdown with a rival gang."

Chad shuddered. "I don't like thinking about how hazardous your job is."

"Well, it's not *West Side Story*. These kids don't go dancing down the streets. Don't even carry baseball bats like they used to. Nowadays they go in for knives if they're a second-rate gang, guns if they're first-class.''

"And you like this kind of work!"

"I like making the city a safer place," Jenna said. "Besides, my job's not all danger. I work on crime prevention, too. Talking to schools, consulting with programs to get kids off the streets, preventing child abuse."

"I admire you," he said solemnly.

"Thanks. That's the way my father saw police work. Not bopping guys over the heads but upholding the law, making the community work."

"I'd like to meet your dad someday."

She wondered if he meant that. Those were easy words to say, but she doubted Chad and her father would ever get together. She stood, stretching again. "I think I'll go up."

He smiled and reached for her, pulled her into his arms for what had become their ritual good-night kiss. Afterward, while he held her, he tugged gently at her braid. "Did you know only loose women wear their hair like this?"

She leaned back and frowned at him. "Where'd you pick up that piece of information, Mr. Foster?"

"From Rose. She mentioned it in her latest letter."

She pulled away abruptly. "What letter?"

"The one that came this afternoon."

"You got a letter and didn't tell me? Damn it, Foster!" She gave him a shove. "Let me see."

"I forgot about it in all the uproar over Nabors." He opened his briefcase and took out a sheet of the familiar stationery.

Jenna read quickly. "She's getting angrier at me. Maybe that'll draw her out."

"Maybe." He pulled her back into his arms.

"Chad—"

"Shh." He toyed with the end of her braid. "One night I'm going to undo your hair, spread it on my pillow—"

"Chad."

"Hmm?" He ran his tongue along her throat.

"You don't play fair."

He blew gently on the place he'd licked. "As Ariel would say, all's fair in love—"

But was this love—to him? She forgot her question as his lips covered her ear. A moan sounded deep in her throat.

"Am I wearing you down?" Chad's breath tickled, his voice rumbled in her ear.

She pulled away from him. "No."

"Liar. Your pulse is racing."

She pecked him on the cheek. "Good night." Then, before she could change her mind, she ran up the stairs.

In her room, she sat on the bed in the darkness. He *was* wearing her down. She was losing sleep over him, knowing all she had to do was walk a few steps down the hall to his room, to his bed. Why couldn't she be like many of the women she knew—take a chance, take what he offered and enjoy it while it lasted? Then when they parted, she'd at least have the memories. If she kept refusing him, she wouldn't even have those. "Do it," she whispered and stood. She started toward the door, then turned back and flung herself on the bed. She couldn't. She wasn't ready to take those steps down the hall. Maybe she never would be.

THE NEXT MORNING, the crime lab called with the results of blood matching on Arthur Green. As he had predicted, the bloodstains in the ice-cream truck matched his own.

Two of her suspects were off the list. One to go. Jenna drove to Franklin Reeves's house again, determined to wait until he got home. Or maybe he'd be there, now that school was out.

She parked in front of his house, a neat brown brick, the tan trim freshly painted but the yard surprisingly overgrown. Didn't the man believe in mowing? The grass, which had been short the first time she'd come by, was now high and choked with weeds. Soon the lawn would look like a jungle.

Jenna rang the doorbell. No answer. She rang again and knocked. No response.

Maybe Reeves was in the backyard. She walked around, peered through the slats in the wooden fence but saw no one. She turned back to the house, stood on tiptoe and tried to see in a window but couldn't. Frustrated, she returned to the front. Damn it, where could Reeves be? Trying to decide on her next step, she started toward her car.

"Looking for Mr. Reeves?"

Jenna swung around. A woman in a cotton robe and slippers stood on the driveway next door, the morning newspaper in her hand. "Yes, I am."

"I've seen you before from my dining room window. Couple of times. Last Wednesday, right?"

A nosy neighbor. The best possible informant. Jenna smiled at her. "Yes, I've been looking for him. Maybe you could help me out, Mrs.—?"

"Kramer." The woman eyed her suspiciously. "You're not a bill collector, are you?"

Jenna laughed. "No, I just need to talk to him."

"Well, you're not going to find him here." With the self-importance of a born gossip, the woman tossed out that tidbit of information and put her hand on her hip, waiting to be asked for more.

Her cop's radar on alert, Jenna obliged her. "Do you know where he is?"

"I know he's left town."

"Did he leave an address where he could be reached?"

"I don't know," Mrs. Kramer said. "He's a private sort of person. Doesn't let on much about his plans. Gotten even quieter since the trouble."

"Trouble?"

"Why, yes. Poor man lost his wife and son in an accident about five years ago. Since then, he's pretty much kept to himself. The neighbors used to try to draw him out, you know, but he just shut us all out. Gave up his full-time teaching job, started substituting. Once in a while I go over and see how he's getting on, but everyone else leaves him alone. Too bad."

Jenna nodded. "The grass has gotten mighty tall," she observed. "Mr. Reeves must've left before school was out."

"Quite a while before. Early May, first week."

Jenna's blood began to pump. *The right time!*

Mrs. Kramer continued, "I talked to him the day before he went away. Said he was going on vacation."

"But he didn't mention where?" Jenna pressed.

"No. Just said he'd be gone for the summer. But I wondered why he was leaving before school was over, especially since he took his nephew with him."

"His...nephew?"

"Yes. Sweet-looking little fellow. Dark, curly hair. Maybe about ten or eleven, near as I could tell. 'Course, I couldn't see him very well. He was asleep on the couch when I came over."

Jenna felt her heart rate shoot up. "Mrs. Kramer, if I showed you a picture, could you tell if it was the same boy?"

The woman frowned. "A picture? Why would you have a picture of Franklin's nephew?"

Jenna pulled out her identification. "Sergeant Wakefield, Houston police. I'm looking for a missing boy. Dark hair, age ten. I have the picture right here in my car. Would you mind taking a look?"

The woman's eyes lit up with excitement. "I'd be happy to help you out if I can."

Every muscle screaming with tension, Jenna went to the car, returned with Nick's picture, and handed it to Mrs. Kramer.

The woman studied it for a moment, then looked up. "That's him. Lord have mercy, that's the boy I saw in Franklin's living room!"

CHAPTER ELEVEN

JENNA TRIED TO CONTAIN her excitement. "Are you sure this is the same boy, Mrs. Kramer?"

"As sure as I'm standing here."

"Would you mind if I came inside and we talked?"

"Not at all." Mrs. Kramer led the way across the yard and into a living room that might have come straight out of the 1930s. Jenna sat down in an overstuffed flowered chair with lace antimacassars on each arm. Mrs. Kramer settled on the matching sofa. "Now, what can I tell you?" the woman asked.

"When did you first see them together?" Jenna asked.

"Let me see, now." Mrs. Kramer lifted a liver-spotted hand and patted her hair. "It was a...yes, a Tuesday, late in the afternoon, when I first saw Franklin with the little boy. I was standing in the dining room, just happened to be looking out the window when they drove up."

"The child I'm looking for has been missing since May third."

"Why, I do believe that was about the time I saw him." Mrs. Kramer considered for a moment. "Yes, I remember because I left Wednesday afternoon to stay with my sister for two weeks after her gallbladder operation."

So Mrs. Kramer had missed the media blitz about Nick's disappearance. "Tell me what you saw when he brought the boy home."

"Well," the woman said, "they got out of the car and went into the house. Later, around dinnertime, I went over there. I'd made spaghetti—it's one of my specialties—and I had extra, so I took a serving dish over. You know how crazy children are about spaghetti. Franklin was never very hospitable, but I went inside."

Jenna thanked God for a professional busybody like Mrs. Kramer, who could probably finagle her way in anywhere.

"The little boy was asleep on the couch. Franklin said he was tired from his trip, but you know—" She frowned and tapped a finger on the arm of the sofa. "Now that I think of it, I didn't see Franklin bring in a suitcase or even a duffel bag for the boy. And I wondered why he'd come on a visit before school let out, but Franklin's not the sort of person to confide, so I didn't ask."

"Did Mr. Reeves tell you the boy was his nephew?"

"Yes, from Corsicana. And that wasn't hard to believe. Such a strong family resemblance. In fact, that little fellow was a dead ringer for Franklin's boy, the one who got killed a few years back."

Inwardly, Jenna cringed. Had Franklin Reeves kidnapped Nicolas to take the place of his dead son?

Mrs. Kramer chattered on. "I said to Franklin, 'Well, your nephew will be nice company for you, won't he? Maybe he can get together with my little grandsons.' Anyhow, Franklin thanked me but said he and the boy were leaving in the morning and they'd be gone all summer. And he said he had packing to do. Well, I got the message, so I left them the spaghetti and went on home."

"And that's all you saw?"

"Well, no. I happened to be out getting the paper the next morning when they left. It was early, and the little boy was still asleep. Franklin carried him out and put him in the van.''

''Franklin has a van?''

''Yes, a gray Toyota.''

The gray van Arthur Green had mentioned!

Jenna tried to phrase her next question discreetly. ''You said he carried the boy out. Did he . . . wake up when they got to the van?''

''Well, Franklin laid him on the back seat and I saw him thrash around a little like he was having a bad dream, but Franklin kind of patted his head and quieted him, you know.''

He'd been alive then, when they'd left the house. Thank God!

After a few more questions, Jenna decided Mrs. Kramer couldn't tell her anything more. She declined the offer of a cup of coffee. She was impatient to get back to headquarters and step up the search. ''Thank you for your help, Mrs. Kramer. You may have given us a very important lead in this case.''

The woman basked in Jenna's praise. She'd have a story to tell about this day. ''Well, you just let me know if I can help you any other way.''

''Just let me know if Franklin turns up, with or without the boy.'' She handed Mrs. Kramer her card.

''Yes, I'll do that.'' Mrs. Kramer walked Jenna to the door. ''Good luck finding that poor child. I'll be praying for you.''

''Thanks.''

On her way back downtown, Jenna told herself not to get too excited. They knew *who* to look for but not *where*. And they had no assurance that Nicolas was still alive.

As soon as she arrived at headquarters, she set the wheels in motion. She got the license number of Reeves's van and put out a bulletin, checked with the Houston school-district office for more background on the substitute teacher, sent Corey Phillips to the administration building to pick up a photograph of Reeves. Then she called Lila Sterling at home.

The principal of Nick's school had little information to add. "He was such a quiet, unassuming man." Lila sighed. "Ironic, isn't it? That's what we always say about people who go off the deep end and do something terrible."

Satisfied that she'd done everything she could, for now, Jenna drove to the Morales's house to see Anita.

Thinner now, her skin sallow, eyes devoid of even the faintest trace of hope, Anita opened the door. From the living room behind her, the TV blared. "Come in, Sergeant."

The two youngest Morales daughters lay on the floor, absorbed in early-afternoon cartoons. Veronica, the sister just a year older than Nick, sprawled in an armchair, reading. She looked up, turning anxious eyes on Jenna as she came into the room.

All the way over, Jenna had pondered what she should say, how she should handle this situation. Now that the time had come, she simply reached for Anita's hands. "We have news."

Anita's fingers tensed, then clutched Jenna's. "Is he . . . is he . . . ?"

"I wish I could give you an answer, but we don't know yet."

The little color that remained in Anita's cheeks drained away. "Then, what . . . ?"

"We think we know who took him."

Anita's nails dug into Jenna's hand. "Who?" Veronica's book dropped to the floor as she came to kneel beside her mother. Both daughter's and mother's eyes were wide with fear . . . and hope.

"A substitute teacher at his school."

Anita gasped. "A teacher!"

Who expected such news about someone to whom you entrusted your children? "A neighbor of his saw him in his home with a dark-haired boy the day Nick disappeared. She identified Nick from his photograph."

"And . . . and he was all right?"

"He seemed to be."

Anita made the sign of the cross over her breast. "Sweet Mary, be praised."

Now Jenna had to tell her the rest. "She also saw them leave the next day."

"Wh-where . . . ?"

"She doesn't know where they went. We're working on finding out."

Anita covered her face with her hands. A desperate, keening cry tore from her lips, from her heart. "A month, Sergeant. He's had my son for a month. Will we ever find him?" The two little girls turned to watch, wide-eyed and scared. Veronica put her arms around her mother as tears flowed down Anita's cheeks.

Jenna pushed back her own tears and answered in the only way she could, "We're doing our best." A futile response, but it was all she had.

After a few moments, Anita wiped her eyes. "I know you will do everything in your power to bring Nicolas back. But sometimes a human being's power is not great enough. I will call my husband now and we will go to the church, ask Father John to pray with us."

Jenna nodded. "I'll call you the minute I know something." She rose, and Anita walked her to the door. Jenna put her arms around Anita's thin shoulders. "We're closer now. We have to keep hoping."

She waited until she was in her car and around the corner before she let her own tears spill over.

BACK AT THE TOWN HOUSE Jenna went into the kitchen and sat at the table. She was grateful for the quiet. Chad had a meeting this afternoon, and she'd made arrangements for the officer on duty at Channel 6 to take him and bring him home. Thank goodness. She was too exhausted to drive across town, too tired for surveillance, too weary even to fix herself a cup of tea.

Why hadn't she pursued Franklin Reeves more diligently? She'd given him an overwhelming head start. If only she'd checked with his neighbors. Mrs. Kramer had been out of town, but someone else might have seen Nick. Oh, Lord, was Nick going to be another Avery Sullivan? She put her head down and shut her eyes.

"Jenna." Chad's voice at her shoulder startled her. She must have dozed, for as she sat up and rubbed her eyes, she saw that evening shadows had stolen across the kitchen.

"Honey, what's wrong?" He hunkered down beside her chair. "You're not sick, are you?"

"No, just tired, and I've . . . I've made a mistake. At work."

"Mistakes can be corrected." He pulled up a chair, straddled it, and reached for her hands.

"Not this one."

He tightened his grasp. "The little boy who disappeared?"

"Yes." He listened while she told him about Franklin Reeves, about her visit this morning with Mrs. Kramer.

Even about Avery Sullivan and her awful fear that Nicolas's case would end up the same way.

Chad warmed her icy hands with his. "I wish you'd told me about the Sullivan boy."

She shrugged her shoulders, but she wished she had, too. Sharing her problems with Chad made them seem easier to bear.

"Let me help you."

Jenna stared at him in surprise. "Thanks for offering, but we're doing everything we can. There's not much anyone can do."

"You're wrong. Now that we know Reeves may have left town, it may be useful to broadcast Nick's picture throughout the Foster television chain—that's fourteen stations all over Texas, Louisiana and Arkansas. Do you know how many people we can reach that way?"

Her heart speeded up. "A lot."

"I'll tell you what else. I'll call the network tomorrow, get them to do a spot about the boy on 'Police Files' next week. They get hundreds of calls after that show, and one of them might lead you to Nick."

A last shaft of sunlight shot golden highlights through Chad's hair, and touched Jenna's heart with a warm ray of hope. "How can I thank you?"

He grinned—that teasing roguish smile she'd come to love—and kissed her cheek. "I'll think of a way." He rose and pulled her to her feet. "Have you eaten?"

"No." And she realized she was starving.

"Let's go out, then. Hamburgers and fries?"

She'd begun to realize he really wasn't the champagne-and-caviar type. Thank goodness. "Sounds good to me."

At Burger King they ordered the works—juicy Whoppers, french fries, even thick chocolate milk-shakes—and ate every sinful, cholesterol-laden bite, joking with one another, forgetting for a while that Jenna didn't yet know what had happened to Nick, and that Rose might be lurking just beyond the bright lights of the fast-food restaurant.

When they returned home, Chad, as usual, watched the news, notepad in hand. Jenna wasn't sleepy. She curled up beside him on the couch.

"I talked to Brett Sloan today, told him the anchor position might open up," Chad said. "He was very interested."

"Hear anything from Lynn O'Donnell?"

"Nope. She's either lying low for a while, or she's realized she's no competition for my love interest." He smiled at her, a possessive smile that made her feel as if she were...wanted. Of course, Chad had made it clear he wanted her in bed, but what she felt from him tonight was a different kind of wanting. A desire for companionship, for sharing.

THE NEXT MORNING Franklin Reeves's gray van was found in the economy parking lot at Intercontinental Airport. Jenna spent the rest of the day questioning airline employees, showing them Nick's picture and Franklin's, to no avail. No one remembered seeing the pair, nor did any of the airline computers have records of a man and boy traveling together on May fourth.

"They could be anywhere," Jenna said to Zack as she sat in his office late that afternoon.

The head of the Juvenile Division grimaced. "The trail's cold. We may never find the kid." He shook his head. "It's a tough one, I know. I hate these cases, too."

That was no consolation. Only a stroke of luck would lead her to Nicolas, she thought as she threaded through afternoon traffic. In some ways, this case was worse than

Avery Sullivan's. At least, they *knew* what had happened to Avery.

Chad was already home when she reached the town house. Harv, the plainclothesman on duty, sat in the living room watching a rerun of "I Love Lucy." Jenna dismissed him and turned off the TV. Lucy's and Ethel's antics didn't amuse her today.

Chad came downstairs, a broad smile on his face. "Good news! Starting tomorrow, we'll have Nicolas's picture running on all our stations. And, pending the Morales family's approval, 'Police Files' will run a special segment Tuesday night."

"Oh, Chad. This is wonderful, the best news I've had all day."

"The only stipulation is, if you find the boy, we get to film his reunion with his family. I've talked to Buster and he okayed it, but I told him the final decision's yours."

She thought for a moment. "As long as the TV people keep me out of the scene."

"I've already told the producers you're working undercover on a different case."

"I'll call Anita."

The Morales family greeted her news with cries, this time of hope.

She hung up the phone. "They said go for it. Oh, Chad, thank you!" And she surprised them both by flinging herself into his arms. His rough afternoon stubble scraped her cheek, but she was too elated to care.

A rumble of laughter sounded in her ear. "See?" Chad said. "I'm not such a bad guy after all."

"I never thought you were a bad guy."

He leaned back and smiled at her. He brought his hand up and traced her mouth. "Funny. That was the impression you gave me at first."

"No, I thought—" She stared into his eyes, watched them darken and forgot what she'd intended to say.

"Thought what?" he whispered.

"I...don't remember." Her eyelids fluttered closed, her lips parted, and his mouth came down on hers.

Though he'd kissed her many times by now, this was different. Today he kissed her as if she were the center of his world, as if he would draw out her very essence. She felt as though every other kiss she'd had was a pale imitation. This was real; this was tenderness and yearning and passion all wrapped in one.

How many nights had they kissed? How many times had he whispered, "Make love with me," and she had refused? All the reasons she'd said no melted away now in the heat of this kiss. "Chad . . . Come upstairs."

He drew back and looked into her eyes. "Jenna, are you sure? You're not doing this out of gratitude because I—"

"No!" She urged his mouth back to hers. "No," she said against his lips. "I want you."

"I've been waiting for you to say that." His arm around her, he led her upstairs. "That first morning when I sat in your office in front of that old rusty desk, with the music playing and your perfume filling the room—I wanted you then. I've wanted you ever since."

They went into his room. It was cool and still, the blinds drawn against the summer sun.

Chad undressed her slowly, button by button, inch by inch, with kisses in between. He stopped to run his tongue along her collarbone, to trace a nipple, to lift an aching breast to his mouth.

"I want to take your hair down." He sat beside her on the bed, turned her so he could take the braid in his hands, and began to part it, strand by strand. "I've dreamed of doing this." He kissed her shoulder. "The first night you stayed here, I saw you with your hair down, and I ached for you." Her hair touched her shoulders now. He ran his hands through it. "Like silk."

Twining her hair around his hand, he pulled her back against him. His shirt buttons pressed into her back, but she hardly noticed. He kissed her hair, dipping his tongue into her ear, then massaged her breasts with slow—agonizingly slow—strokes.

He returned to her hair, freed the last strands, and buried his face in the loosened mane. "It smells like you—sweet. . . ."

He pulled her across his lap to cradle her in his arms. He touched her, stroked her, played her as if her body were an instrument made for his pleasure.

"Undress me," he said at last.

With sighs and murmurs, she did. He was beautiful. Lean and strong. She'd seen him the other night, but now her hands were free to touch wherever she wished, her lips free to taste the roughness of his cheeks, the salt-tinged skin of his shoulder, a pebbled nipple. "Oh, yes," he groaned as she took it in her mouth and sucked eagerly. "Kiss me there." Through the curtain of her hair, she saw his face—his eyes shut, his lips spread in passion.

She undid the fastener at his waist, helped him tug off his trousers, then his briefs. His body now revealed to her hungry gaze, she stayed her hands, let her eyes drink him in—all male hunger, primitive desire.

He pulled her into his arms again, but now his kisses were more urgent, his tongue plunging into her mouth in a preview of what was to come.

Pressing her down on the bed, he nudged her legs apart, and knelt over her. His mouth moved unerringly to the moist bud between her legs. He kissed her there with his lips, with his tongue, setting a rhythm, driving her higher until her movements became wild thrashings and her sighs, cries of longing.

He raised his head, moved between her thighs and slowly positioned himself. She felt the touch of him—the hardness, the heat—and gasped.

He entered her, then paused, holding himself back. "More?"

"Oh, God, yes." She wanted more. She wanted *all*.

But he teased her, moving deeper only centimeter by centimeter, until she couldn't bear any more. With a sob, she arched upward and took him fully inside her. Joining him in a fierce rhythm, she instantly climaxed, his name on her lips in a hoarse cry. Seconds later he followed her over the edge.

They lay face-to-face, sweat-soaked bodies tangled together, as the aftershocks of their passion receded. Chad lifted a hand to her cheek. "Jenna." In his eyes, she saw the same dazed wonder she felt. "Are you as stunned as I am?" he whispered.

"Yes, but—"

"Shh. No buts, not now. Just let me hold you."

She nodded, not sure what would have followed the but. Drained, sated, she closed her eyes.

Chad watched her as she drifted into sleep. Her breasts rose and fell gently, her lips parted slightly on a sigh. Her shining hair brushed his shoulder, tickling his chest.

He thought of the businesslike cop in her starched, creased uniform and smiled. Who, seeing her in her daytime milieu, would imagine the wanton woman he held in his arms? Even in his fantasies he hadn't come close.

What had she started to say just now? Whatever her fears, whatever her reservations, he'd make them disappear. He had to. This wasn't a superficial relationship. He wanted to make it last, and he would. Determination was his strong suit. Somehow he'd convince his Wonder Woman that their differences were meaningless. What they had together—their laughter, their arguments, and this incredible lovemaking—was what counted. He gathered her closer; then he, too, fell asleep.

When they awoke later, they wandered downstairs, nibbled on cheese and crackers between kisses. Chad knew he had a silly grin on his face, just looking at her across the table, but he didn't care.

"Let's go to Galveston Saturday," he suggested. "My family has a beach house. I want to make love to you there—"

The telephone rang.

Reality. With a sigh of resignation, Chad got up to answer.

"She's there with you, isn't she?" rasped the voice he'd come to know too well. "Get rid of her. Send her away. You're mine."

The line went dead.

Chad put the receiver down. "Rose," he said flatly.

Even in life's sweetest moments, she intruded, like a sinister shadow, a portent of evil. When would he be rid of her?

SATURDAY MORNING DAWNED clear and sunny, a perfect day for the beach. An ideal day, Chad thought, to get away from Rose and to give Jenna a break from her case. He'd begun to learn how to compartmentalize his life, to put difficult situations out of his mind and relax. The lesson had been hard for him, but he was gradually improving. Jenna needed to do that, too. She took her work to heart. He understood how important the Nicolas Morales case was to her, but she needed a respite. This weekend he'd give her one.

"I have to stop at my new house on the way," he said as they got in his car. "The painter wanted me to look at some samples. Besides, I want you to see the place."

They drove west on Memorial Drive, through neighborhoods with large, tree-shaded homes, and turned onto a cul de sac. He pulled up before a framed structure. "This is it."

The Saturday-morning quiet was broken by the noise of drilling and hammering, but in a few months, Chad knew nothing but breezes and birdsongs would intrude. Jenna got out of the car and stood, taking it in. She walked around to the back, where the yard sloped away to a wooded area surrounding a creek. "Oh, Chad, it's lovely."

"Come inside. I'll show you around." He introduced her to the contractor and let her wander while he discussed the paint. Then he caught up with her and took her arm.

The smell of wood shavings surrounded them. They shuffled through sawdust and skirted nails and bits of wood. "Here's the fireplace," he told her, picturing wintry nights, a fire crackling, and Jenna in his arms. He showed her the plans, pointed out the darkroom, took her upstairs to the master bedroom with its balcony overlooking the woods and creek. He imagined his bed there, with Jenna in it.

He wondered if she was imagining them here together, too. Her eyes were dreamy, so perhaps she was. She looked longingly at the peaceful scene outside. "It's hard to believe we're ten minutes from shopping malls and fast-food restaurants."

"When the house is finished, you'll come back with me," Chad said.

"Oh, Rose will be out of your hair by then."

"This has nothing to do with Rose." He took her arm, pulled her closer. "Jenna—"

"Mr. Foster." The contractor cleared his throat.

Chad let Jenna go. "Yes?"

"What finish do you want on the front-door hardware?"

"Do you have to know right now?"

"Yes, sir. We have to order in advance."

"Then get brass."

"I'll take care of it."

The man left, but Jenna had wandered off. Chad found her staring out what would be the front window. "Let's get going. I want to pick up some sodas and something for sandwiches later. We have bikes at the beach house. We can take a picnic dinner and ride down the beach." He'd talk about the future another time.

A few minutes later, Chad pulled into a shopping center with a supermarket and several other stores. They went into the grocery and made their selections. In a hurry now to get started, Chad headed for the car, with Jenna trailing behind.

Suddenly, she grabbed his arm and stopped him. "Look!" She pointed to a woman coming out of a store two doors away.

Chad recognized Sandra Townes from his accounting department, one of the women Jenna thought might be Rose. His eyes swerved to the sign over the store's entrance: Leaves and Petals. She'd been shopping at a florist's.

CHAPTER TWELVE

SANDRA STOPPED dead still. She stared at Chad and her face flushed, then went pale, as she looked away.

"Come on," Jenna whispered to Chad, taking a step forward. "But get ready to move if I tell you."

"Okay."

They walked toward Sandra. She seemed frozen in place.

Chad's eyes fastened on the capacious bag Sandra carried—big enough to conceal a weapon. He knew Jenna was eyeing it, too. What would they do if Sandra pulled out a gun?

He didn't want to die in a parking lot, especially not now on a brilliant summer day when he had so much to live for—a woman he cared about, a job he loved. He wanted to make a run for his car, get in, and speed away. But he found himself moving forward while Sandra Townes stood waiting.

They reached her side.

At a nod from Jenna, he spoke. He tried to make his voice normal, but he couldn't get enough air. The words came out breathless. "Sandra—hi. Nice to—see you."

Sandra's face reddened. Her eyes darted to the ground, focused on his shoes. Finally, as if it took a prodigious effort, she looked straight at him. "Hello, M-Mr. Foster, um, Miss Wakefield."

"Buying flowers?" Jenna asked.

Sandra's eyes stayed fixed on Chad's. Color came and went in her cheeks like a flashing neon sign. "Um, sort of."

"Flowers. Good idea. What do you recommend?" Chad asked too heartily. Would she say roses?

She twisted her hands. "Oh, um, they have lots of different kinds. Whatever you like, I guess."

"Roses?" The word felt like acid in his mouth.

"Um, maybe. I didn't notice any, but I...I guess you could ask." She took a step back.

"Let's go in and see," Jenna said.

"Sure." But he wasn't anxious to turn his back on Sandra, not with that odd look on her face and the enormous bag on her shoulder. He stalled, willing her to leave. "See you Monday, Sandra."

"Have a nice weekend," Jenna added.

"Um, you, too." Sandra turned, started to move away.

Chad took a breath. He watched Sandra scurry across the parking lot and get into a battered Chevy.

"Come inside," Jenna said, heading for the florist's. "I want to see what she bought."

Chad waited until Sandra pulled onto the street, then followed Jenna into the shop. She already had her ID out. "Sergeant Wakefield, HPD. That woman who just left—what did she buy?"

The clerk stared at Jenna curiously, but apparently impressed by the badge, she didn't question why Jenna wanted to know. "She ordered a kalanchoe."

"Did she have it delivered somewhere?"

"Yes, to Southwest Memorial Hospital. To—" she checked a receipt "—a Betty Townes. Her aunt, she said."

Chad gave a sigh of relief, heard Jenna echo it. He started toward the door.

"Wait," Jenna told him. "Is she a regular customer?"

"I wouldn't say regular, but she's been in before."

"Recently?"

"I couldn't say," the clerk answered. "I'm only here on weekends."

"Have you sold her roses—say, in the last month?"

The woman considered. "No, I haven't. I could look at our records and see if she bought any from another salesperson."

"Please."

They waited, Jenna drumming her fingers on the counter, while the woman paged through invoices. "No," she said finally. "She bought an arrangement of spring flowers a month ago. No roses."

"Thank you," Jenna said. They left the shop.

Back in the car, Chad leaned his head on the steering wheel. "I thought for sure Sandra was Rose."

"We don't know that she isn't. Maybe she's bought roses somewhere else. Maybe she didn't want a confrontation today. Maybe the 'spirits' are still holding her back."

Chad shivered as he started the engine. "I can't picture Sandra writing those letters. She seems harmless. Still, she acted strange."

"She's shy," Jenna said. "She also has a crush on you, Mr. Foster. Big time."

Chad considered her answer as he steered the car out of the parking lot. "But why? I've never given her any reason to think I'm interested."

Jenna sighed. "Don't you have any idea how you affect women like Sandra?"

"What do you mean?"

"Clerks in stores, waitresses. I noticed it the first day I spent with you. You smile at them, say something nice, make them feel special. For the average woman, you're a pleasant customer she hopes will come back because you brighten her day. For the wrong woman, it's a turn-on."

"Just being nice?"

"Yes, that's enough for a person like Rose," Jenna replied. "A woman who's shy, impressionable, a loner with an active fantasy life. She misreads the signals. Thinks you're interested in her, begins to fantasize about you, starts writing you letters. You might have smiled once or twice at Sandra or someone like her and put the wheels in motion."

"I guess I should work at being reserved," he said thoughtfully.

"Of course not. Don't change your personality. Unfortunately, you crossed paths with the wrong woman, that's all."

"That's all? I smiled at someone and created a monster."

"I'm sorry, Chad. I know this is hell for you." She put her hand on his arm consolingly, then glanced out the window. "Slow down. I want to see if Sandra circled around and followed us." She adjusted the side mirror, checked a cross street. "I don't see her car."

He was relieved at that, but Jenna was right: Sandra or Rose or whatever her name was had made his life a living hell. She intruded on his most private moments, fouled what should have been a tranquil morning.

Jenna stroked his arm. "I'm glad we're getting away from Houston."

He covered her hand with his, squeezed it tightly. "Me, too." They both needed this weekend—now, more than ever.

The drive to Galveston took only an hour. Traffic on the Gulf Freeway was light, and they sped along. Marshy land came into view along with signs for vacation cottages, resorts, and seafood restaurants. They crossed the causeway onto the island and drove past palm trees and Victorian-style homes. The smell of salt and sand hung in the air. They headed west past hotels and condos and finally drew up before the Fosters' blue frame three-story beach house.

"Land's End." Jenna read the sign over the door. "I like the name." Inside she exclaimed over the white wicker furniture and the Gulf view. "It feels like the Caribbean, not that I've ever been there."

They quickly made sandwiches, put swimsuits on under their shorts. Chad took his camera, and they started off on the bicycles.

Late-afternoon sun sparkled on the sand. Salt spray flicked across Chad's cheeks. He enjoyed the view of Jenna's legs as she pedaled—the clear ivory of her skin, the play of her muscles in the smooth up-and-down motion. Everything about her—from her body to her mind and heart—fascinated him.

They found a deserted spot where large rocks separated a small section of beach from the open shore. Spreading their blanket in a sandy space between the rocks, they stripped down to their suits, and ran, hand in hand, into the surf.

They splashed, they swam, they chased each other through the waves. The tension they'd lived under all week seemed to roll away with the tide. They waded back to shore, then Jenna wandered down the beach, picking up shells. Her stride was easy, her laugh freer than he'd heard in days, and her smile put the sun to shame.

He grabbed his camera and snapped a picture of her as she knelt to study something in the sand; another of her coming toward him, her face glowing. "A perfect sand dollar," she said, holding it up for him to see. He took another shot. "It's good luck." She laid it carefully on her T-shirt and sat beside him.

Chad focused the lens on Jenna once more, then clambered up the nearest rock for a wide-angle view of the beach. He wanted to remember everything about this afternoon.

They were alone here. Two joggers had passed by earlier, but now the area was deserted save for a lone woman walking farther up the beach. Pleased with the view, he photographed the woman silhouetted against the expanse of sand. She stopped to look out at the water, and he took another shot before she turned to walk back the way she'd come.

They ate their picnic dinner, watched the setting sun's reflection set the Gulf ablaze with orange flame. The sky darkened; the moon rose, a flickering golden ball suspended over the water, dusting the sand with amber.

Chad lay back on the blanket and stretched his hands over his head, enjoying the endless star-studded sky, the deep roar of the waves. They were in another world here, a velvet-dark world far from cares and fears.

Lazily, he watched Jenna. She picked up a handful of sand, let it sift through her fingers, then leaned over and began to dig. After a few minutes, she abandoned the hole she'd dug and began another a foot away. "What are you doing?"

"Making a tunnel. Why don't you help?"

He sat up and complied, scooping sand from the hole, constructing a path to meet Jenna's. They sat facing each other, inches apart, intent on their feat of beach engineering. Chad brushed away another handful of sand, edged his hand into the opening, and touched Jenna's fingers on the other side. "Success!" He caught her fingertips with his. With his free hand he tugged at her, and she toppled over into his arms. The tunnel collapsed.

"We ruined it," she grumbled, scowling up at him.

"Who cares?"

He wrapped his arms around her, leaned down, and covered her mouth with his. Her arms and chest were damp with salt water, gritty with sand. Her braid, still heavy with moisture, slapped against his shoulder. He didn't care. The only thing that mattered was her body flush against him, her breath mingling with his. He kissed her, driving his tongue deep but wanting more. Their suits were a thin, damp barrier, but even they were too much. He needed to feel her skin.

He rolled them onto their sides and pushed his leg between hers. Her thigh rubbed against him, making him hard, making him burn. He fumbled with her bikini top, but she grabbed his hand. "We're...outside," she panted. "What if someone..."

Throbbing, he managed to sit up and focus on the area around them. "No one can see us."

"I...don't know."

He stroked her thigh, bent to kiss it, trailed his tongue up...up. "I want you, Jenna."

"I...I've never done this before—outside."

He kissed her through the suit, outlining her damp, pulsing center with his tongue. She moaned.

He lifted his head and smiled down at her. "Neither have I."

She studied his face for a moment, then grinned, her eyes gleaming. "Okay."

He grasped her bikini top, peeled it away, then, with a groan, buried his face in the crevice between her breasts. She smelled of the Gulf. He lifted one breast, turned his

ead to kiss its sweet roundness. He held a goddess in his
rms, Venus risen from the sea.

His fingers shook as he dragged away the final scrap of
naterial that covered her, then tore off his own suit. He
rew her beneath him and plunged inside her.

She sheathed him with fire. Her legs and arms wrapped
round him, holding him a willing captive. He began to
nove. Behind them, the waves rolled in relentlessly,
ooming against the sand; his heart and hers echoed their
hunder. Faster, wilder, a final thrust, and he was swept
p in a raging tide, then tossed onto the quiet shore.

He lay, spent, in Jenna's arms. The soft sea breeze
luttered over him, cooling, caressing. A gull called and
nother answered.

Water trickled over his toes. The tide had risen. Jenna
ave a little yelp as the cold water washed over their an-
les. "We're getting wet. We should move."

"Even a tidal wave couldn't make me move now."

Another wave came, higher now. Jenna wriggled be-
eath him. "Up, Foster."

"Keep moving like that and we may stay here and
rown." But he got to his feet and pulled her up with him.
hey struggled back into their damp suits and snatched up
he now wet blanket.

Jenna wrinkled her nose. "We're covered with sand. I
hink it's time to go home and shower."

He grinned and hugged her as they headed for the
ikes.

They pedaled home as fast as their tired legs could carry
hem. When they arrived, Chad immediately headed for
he bathroom and turned on the shower. "Come here."

She walked toward him slowly, seductively, her eyes on
he bulge already swelling under his suit. When she
eached him, she hooked her fingers on the waistband of

his trunks and pulled them down, inch by lingering inch. Her hands stroked along his thighs, down his calves as she bent to her task.

He stepped out of his suit, kicked it aside and reached for her, but she waved him away. Slowly she trailed her lips upward along the path her hands had taken. When she took him into her warm, sweet mouth, he let out a groan. "Jenna!" He grabbed the towel bar and held on; his knees had turned to jelly.

She continued to kiss and caress until he teetered on the verge of climax. Then, with uncanny timing, she backed away, stripped off her suit and nudged him backward into the shower.

The exquisite torment began again. She soaped him slowly, lavishly, working the lather over his skin, then rinsing it off, punctuating her ministrations with long, drugging kisses while he could only lean against the tile, lost in a sensual haze. "Jenna," he croaked. "No more. I...can't...wait."

"Now, then." She stood on tiptoe, wrapped herself around him and guided him home.

Two powerful thrusts, and he exploded.

When he recovered his breath, he whispered, "Now let me." A bottle of bath gel sat on a shelf in the shower. He opened it, poured a generous portion into his palm, then spread it over her. The fragrance of orange blossoms mingled with the scent of her skin. He unfastened her braid, found shampoo and pleasured himself by washing her hair, massaging her scalp, and rinsing until her hair shone.

He urged her to the floor, cradling her in his lap. With his lips and hands, he brought her to a climax that made her cry his name over and over.

While water sluiced over them, they sat on the floor, exhausted. Finally Jenna groaned and struggled to her feet. "I think we need a bed."

He turned off the shower, and they went upstairs. The master bedroom was large and airy, with a king-size bed. While he pulled off the spread, Jenna wandered around the room. She stopped at the dresser where a group of family pictures sat. She picked up an old photo of the Foster siblings. A snaggletoothed Chad crouched on the sand, with Daniel balanced on his back, and a triumphant Ariel kneeling on Daniel's. "Cute."

She reached for another photograph, a family grouping. "Who's this?" She pointed to the woman beside Chad.

"My ex-wife."

"I...didn't know you'd been married." She looked shocked.

"It only lasted a year."

She sat on the edge of the bed, still holding the picture. "What happened?"

Chad sighed. "Our timing was wrong. We fell in love too fast, for all the wrong reasons." At her raised brow, he explained. "Sex. The attraction of opposites. We were different in every way that counted."

She stared at the slim, dark-haired woman beside Chad as if she might discover those differences in the photograph. "What ways?"

"Marina was easygoing—I was intense. She liked to party—I was a workaholic. I'd just taken over as manager of KLTX in Lubbock, my first time to head one of our stations. We were newly married— Marina wanted us to enjoy ourselves. She complained that I didn't delegate responsibilities, but I didn't want to. There I was, the heir apparent to the Foster chain. I wanted to be involved in every aspect of the station, to learn all I could.'' He shook his head, remembering his frustration and Marina's. ''We couldn't find a middle ground.''

''That's too bad.''

''We both realized what we had to do. The divorce was amicable. No recriminations.''

''Where is she now?''

''In California, married to an actor. You may have heard of him—Sean Prather. He's making a name for himself.''

Jenna nodded, got up and put the picture back in its place. ''You didn't marry again.''

Chad laughed. ''No, I'm not looking to set a record for wives.''

She leaned against the dresser and studied him, her brows furrowed. ''But you've been involved.''

''Yes, but I learned something from Marina's and my experience—to proceed with caution.''

Jenna stood, watching him thoughtfully. He went to her. ''Come to bed.'' She let him lead her there, then she lay quietly in his arms.

He could have told her so much more, Chad thought, snuggling against her. That he wanted a woman who understood his need to commit himself to his work...and he thought he'd found her. That he wanted someone whose mind and heart appealed to him as much as her body... and he thought he'd found her.

But he wasn't ready. With Jenna, too, things had happened quickly. Their situation was far from normal—she was his bodyguard and he was a potential victim being stalked by a fanatic, constantly on edge. In addition, now, as when he'd married Marina, work was the focus of his life, constantly challenging him with new responsibilities and new goals.

When Rose was out of their lives, he'd know. For now, he would be silent, waiting for the time when he could be sure of Jenna and of himself.

Long after Chad slept, Jenna lay awake, staring into the darkness. What had she learned tonight? Despite all their lovemaking, Chad wasn't ready for a long-term commitment. Perhaps he never would be. She'd begun to think they could have something lasting. She knew now those dreams might never come true.

Jenna came to a decision. She'd allow herself to have her fantasy. But when she wrote "Closed" on his case, she'd walk away. Rose's behavior indicated that would happen soon. By the Fourth of July, Jenna would probably be back in her own world, at the police officers' picnic, downing barbecue and beer.

WHEN THEY RETURNED from Galveston, Jenna spent two fruitless days following up on tips from viewers who'd seen Nick's and Franklin's pictures on the Foster stations. Someone thought he'd seen them heading for the Mexican border. Another caller had spotted a similar-looking pair in Lafayette, Louisiana.

Then there were the crazies—a man who'd sighted them being lifted into a flying saucer, another who'd received a message through his spirit guide saying they were in Pakistan. A psychic offered her services. A gypsy fortune-teller promised that the purchase of a black candle—from her, of course, for only a hundred dollars—would purge the evil surrounding Nick and bring him safely home. Jenna wouldn't have been too surprised to get a call from Rose. After all, everyone else wanted to get into the act. Even the rational calls led to dead ends.

"Face it, Jenna," Zack said. "This may be one of those cases that's never closed."

She refused to give up. She pinned her hopes on "Police Files." As Chad turned on the TV on Tuesday evening, she asked, "Are you sure they'll show it?"

"Of course, they will. It'll be on at the end of the program."

She sat through the show, fiddling with her braid, swinging her foot until Chad put a hand on her knee. "Relax, honey. Just a few more minutes."

A commercial break, then the narrator appeared again. Solemnly, he began. "Tonight a special bulletin about a missing child. Nicolas Morales, age ten, was last seen outside his Houston home on May third when he left to mail a letter at the mailbox around the corner." The camera cut to a scene of "Nick" heading down the front walk of a house that bore little resemblance to the Morales home. "Sometime within the next few minutes," the narrator continued, "Nicolas disappeared."

Jenna rarely watched the show. She thought the enactments of the featured cases were amateurish, the host melodramatic. But tonight his ominous tone seemed appropriate.

"Police in Houston have only one lead. Franklin Reeves, a substitute teacher who filled in at Nicolas's school the previous week, was seen at his home that evening with a young boy who fit Nicolas's description. A neighbor who visited Reeves saw the youngster asleep on the couch in the living room. Reeves told the neighbor that the boy was his nephew and they were going on an extended vacation." Now they showed a re-creation of Mrs. Kramer's conversation with Franklin Reeves.

"The next morning the neighbor saw them leave. They have not been seen since. If you have information on the whereabouts of Nicolas Morales or Franklin Reeves, call our hotline."

Pictures of Nick and Reeves flashed on the screen along with the hotline number, then faded away.

Jenna let out a breath. "I hope this works."

"We've sent a crew over to the Morales's to film them watching this," Chad told her. "The clip will show on the ten o'clock news on all the Foster channels. That should help, too."

"Thank you." That was all she could manage over the lump in her throat.

The segment at the Morales home was very moving. Anita and her husband Pete sat on the couch in their small living room, flanked by their older children, the two youngest on their laps. Father John, their parish priest, and a group of neighbors crowded around them. They were shown watching the broadcast, then Anita held up Nick's picture and made a tearful plea for information as she fingered the cross at her neck. "We are praying for our son's safe return. Please help us," she concluded.

Jenna's cheeks were wet when Chad turned off the television and drew her close. "You've done everything you can," he said.

She nodded. All she could do now was wait.

On Wednesday, calls started coming in. Dozens. Hundreds by the end of the day. Jenna and Zack sorted through the messages, divided them by state, then within states, looking for a pattern.

At first all they could see was a jumble of random tips—three calls from various spots in California, several from the East Coast, even one from Anchorage, Alaska.

Then Jenna flipped through the Texas calls. "Zack, look at this!" she cried excitedly. "We have a call from north of Houston, another one from Nacogdoches, two from Longview. It looks like a trail. I'm going to check these out first."

She got on the phone, asked questions and made notes. The first caller had seen a man and a young boy in a green pickup stopped at a roadside park a few miles outside the Houston city limits. "I remember them because I tried to make conversation with the child and the man hurried him away. The little boy looked like he was in a daze. I thought maybe he was sick."

"Do you remember what he was wearing?"

"Jeans and a T-shirt. An Astros shirt."

Nick had worn an Astros shirt the day he disappeared!

Next she reached a motel employee in Longview. A man answering Franklin Reeves's description had checked in early on the afternoon of May fourth. "The room I gave him was near the office, so I was able see him when he parked in front. He opened the door of his truck and lifted out a boy, carried him into the room. A few minutes later the guy came out to the lobby to buy a newspaper. I asked him if everything was all right, and he said his kid was tired from the trip, that's all."

The motel clerk confirmed that the man drove a green pickup. He'd registered as Harry McClanahan.

Jenna made another call, this one to the small town of Linden. "Mrs. Lewis, this is Jenna Wakefield, Houston police. You called the 'Police Files' hotline this morning."

"Yes, I did." The voice was pleasant, grandmotherly. "I'm sure I saw the people you're looking for. There's a little country grocery a ways out of town. My husband and I stopped there for a drink on our way to Texarkana a week ago. The man and the little boy were shopping for groceries, and I noticed them because the way he handled the child seemed peculiar. He had hold of the boy's arm, wouldn't let him go, wouldn't let him talk to anyone. Pops Landry, who owns the store, is as friendly as they come, loves children, and he offered the boy some candy. But the man just pulled the little boy away, paid his money and got out of there.

"Afterward I asked Pops who they were. He said someone had rented the old Claiberg place out in the woods, and it might be them. Said they'd come in once before and the man acted the same way. Pops thought the little boy wanted to say something, but he seemed frightened. I could give you Pops's number if you like."

"Yes, ma'am."

She called the store and Pops confirmed what Mrs. Lewis had said. "That man's a strange one, all right. He don't let the kid outta his sight, not even to go to the bathroom."

"I understand he's renting a house that belongs to a family named Claiberg."

"Yes, ma'am. Bill Claiberg. Lives in Texarkana. I'll give you his number."

She called Mr. Claiberg, and he verified that he'd rented his cabin to a Harry McClanahan, beginning May fifth.

When Jenna hung up, she was euphoric. She flew down to Zack's office. "We've hit pay dirt!"

Zack read over her notes. "Sure seems like it."

"Okay. I'm calling the county sheriff's office up there. And as soon as I can make arrangements for someone to stay with Foster, I'm out of here."

"Great. Take Corey Phillips and Wendell Blair with you. If everything works out, they can bring Reeves back and you can fly in with the kid."

She made arrangements for Wendell to meet her at Chad's, told Corey they'd pick him up on their way out of town, then left her office. Chad would be ready to go home soon, but she had a stop to make first.

The Morales home looked the same as ever—Nick's baseball equipment still sitting on the porch, a yellow ribbon around the tree—but when Anita answered the door, Jenna immediately sensed a difference. Hope gleamed in Anita's eyes, brightened her voice. "Come in, Sergeant Wakefield."

The two women looked at each other. Anita grabbed Jenna's hand. "I can see by your face you have news."

"Yes. Let's sit down."

Veronica came out of the kitchen as they sat on the couch. "Manuel," she called, "the police officer's here." Her brother appeared in the doorway, and the two stood waiting.

"We've had several calls about sightings of a boy who fits Nick's description and a man who fits Reeves's in east Texas."

"Oh, God be praised!" Anita cried out and clutched her breast. Her face went pale and she slumped against the cushions.

"Mama! Quick, get her some water," Veronica called. She ran to Anita, put her arms around her mother's neck. "Don't cry, Mama. He's alive!"

"Alive!" Anita echoed, tears coursing down her cheeks.

"Here, Mama. Drink this."

Manuel pressed a cup into her hands. Concepción wandered in from the hall. "Mama! Mama, don't cry." She climbed into Anita's lap and patted her cheek.

Anita hugged the little girl. "I'm fine, *hijita*. Better than I've been in a long time." She turned to Jenna. "Tell me everything you know."

Jenna dreaded what she had to say next. "You mustn't get your hopes too high. We haven't made a positive identification yet."

"But you will. You will! I know it."

"I hope so." She'd never hoped harder. "I'm going up there tonight. We'll go out to where they're staying early in the morning. I'll call you the minute I know."

"Thank you. And the man from the television station, thank him, too."

Oh, yes, she'd thank the man from the television station. With all her heart.

He was waiting for her in his office when she arrived. She shoved the door shut behind her and ran into his arms. "I think we've found Nicolas."

"So soon? This is wonderful news."

She covered his face with kisses. "Thank you for what you've done."

He held her away. "Don't thank me. That's the station's purpose—to help the community."

She ran her fingers over his cheek, through his hair, loving the feel of him. "You've said that before...."

"And now you finally believe me."

"Yes. Are you ready to go? I have to leave tonight. I'm going up there to make the arrest."

He frowned. "Will it be dangerous?"

Jenna shook her head. "Police work is never entirely safe, but on a scale of one to ten, this one's about a two."

"I...guess that makes me feel better," Chad said.

"I've made arrangements for Buck to stay with you while I'm gone."

"Buck? The guy who was with you on the stakeout? He's not my type."

"Chad!"

"I was thinking about a female officer. About five-foot-six, nice curves—" He drew a shape in the air.

Jenna punched him. "Don't even think it, Foster."

Buck was waiting for them in the parking lot outside. He got into his car and followed them home.

As they drove, Jenna asked, "Any mail from Rose?"

"Another letter warning me to get rid of the seductress in my house. She says she's losing patience."

"We need to do something more to draw her out, maybe have you send another message on TV. We'll talk about it when I get back."

The rest of the way home, she told him about the tips they'd gotten from "Police Files" and the calls she'd made. When they drew up before Chad's town house, she jumped out of the car, eager to be on her way. She hurried to the front door, then stopped so abruptly that Chad bumped into her from behind. "Oh, my God!"

On the doorstep lay the remains of a blood-red rose, its petals scattered and torn to shreds.

CHAPTER THIRTEEN

"I DON'T BELIEVE THIS. Can't that damn woman leave me alone?" Chad grabbed a handful of petals and crushed them between his fingers, surrounding the two of them with the heavy fragrance. Forevermore, Jenna would associate the scent of roses with evil.

"Go inside," she ordered and swung around to face the street. Buck's car pulled up behind hers. She glanced back at Chad. He stood, his eyes glazed, running the ravaged petals through his fingers. "Inside, Foster. Now. Stay put. I'll be right back." He opened the door, but paused on the threshold. "And shut the damn door."

She ran down the walk to meet Buck. Out of breath from nerves, she leaned against the car door. "The stalker's over the edge. She tore up a rose and threw it on the porch. Check the street—circle the block, then look in the garage. I'll take the house."

As she dashed back to the house, she heard Buck's motor start. Weapon drawn, she opened the door. "Chad!"

"Right here." His voice came from the living room.

"Stay there. I'm going to search the house." She opened the hall closet.

"I already have. No one's here."

She slammed the closet shut and marched into the living room. Half out of breath again, she shouted, "Damn it, I told you to stay put."

"It's my house," he said mildly.

"What if she'd been here? What if she'd had a knife or a gun?" Tears welled in her throat. "What if she'd—" She couldn't finish. She swung around so he wouldn't see the moisture on her cheeks. She stared at the books in the bookcase without seeing them, ran her fingers over the shelf. Swallowing the rest of her tears, she murmured, "I'll call Corey and tell him to go after Reeves without me."

"Why?"

Because I can't leave you. Because you aren't a case anymore. Because, regardless of how you feel about me, you're my life. "Rose is about to blow up. I'm assigned to your case. It's my responsibility."

"Jenna." He came up behind her and took her by the shoulders. "The Morales case is yours, too. I know how important it is to you. You need to go."

Her fingers tightened on the shelf. "No."

He turned her in his arms. "I want you to go."

She put her arms around him and held him with all her strength. "Come with me, then."

"On a police raid? What would I do? I'd be in your way."

"You'd be out of Rose's reach."

He kissed her forehead. "I'll be safe here. Buck will be with me."

That wasn't enough. She wanted him where she could see him, touch him. "Buck doesn't know enough about Rose. You'll be safer with me."

"Jenna." He tipped her chin up. His hand smelled of roses. "I can't leave. The 'Soapbox' airs in a couple of days. I have to fire Nabors. I can't let Rose dictate my life. I need to do my work."

"Then I'll stay."

"And you need to do yours."

At an impasse, she stared at him.

His eyes darkened; he pulled her closer. "Kiss me."

She did, communicating with her lips what she couldn't
yet put into words: *I love you.*

Footsteps sounded outside. The doorbell chimed.

Chad drew away. "Answer it, then go and get ready."

Buck stood at the door. "Street's clear. Garage is, too."

"Good. So's the house. Wendell will be here in a few
minutes to pick me up. I'll get my things, then I'll brief
you."

She ran upstairs to change into her uniform. As she
glanced around the room, her eyes lit on the sand dollar
she'd found at the beach. She put it carefully in her purse.
A lucky charm couldn't hurt.

When she returned to the living room, Wendell Blair
had arrived. Jenna greeted him, then gave Buck his instructions. "And don't let Foster out of your sight. If he
disobeys an order, handcuff him to a chair."

"Got it."

"Okay, let's go."

Chad walked them to the door. She wanted to hold him,
to feel his body pressed against hers. Instead she said, with
a break in her voice, "Take care."

"You too, Sarge. Good luck."

IN THE DARK HOURS of the night, Chad dreamed.

He was toiling in his office. "Soapbox" plans. A new
afternoon show. A more dynamic news team.

The phone rang. Rose's voice. "I'm coming for you.
Coming for *her.*"

"Wait! Not her. We're just pretending—"

"You're not pretending . . . not pretending. . . ."

"Wait! Please!"

The line went dead.

The door opened. Mitchell Nabors stepped into the room.

"You can't be here. I fired you. Yesterday."

"No, you didn't." Nabors sneered, teeth showing. "You were just pretending." He moved closer, pace by pace, lips curled back, like a tiger stalking its prey.

He reached the desk, a knife in his hand. Where had it come from? The blade... the blade crimson. Rose petals dripping from gleaming steel. Nabors raised the knife—

"No!"

Suddenly Jenna was there, her face white. "Run!"

Chad leaped from his chair, grabbed a heavy statue, heaved it. Nabors staggered to his knees, raised the knife.

Chad slammed the door, heard the blade strike wood, heard Nabors's voice. "I'll get you, Foster."

Together he and Jenna ran. Down a passageway he'd never seen. Dark, twisting.

They rounded a corner. A shadowy form loomed ahead.

A light flashed on, illuminated the form. Lynn O'Donnell. A rose in her hand. "I've come for you." Rose's voice.

He whirled around, grabbed Jenna's hand. They ran back, turned down another passage, then another. Ran past a window. Saw Nabors's face behind the glass, the knife in his hand.

"Run!"

He couldn't get his breath, but he ran. His feet pounded on the floor, his heartbeat echoed in his ears. Down a ramp, into a cavern. Musty, damp, quiet.

He reached for Jenna. She'd disappeared. He swung around, whirled back again. She was gone.

"Jenna!" he shouted. Shouted again.

The walls of the cave closed in, then vanished. He was in the doorway of an office, empty except for a desk across the room. Sandra Townes stood, smiled at him. She reached behind her, held out three long-stemmed roses, wrapped in green wax paper. "Mr. Foster, I've brought you some roses."

"No!"

"Yes. I'm not pretending...not pretending. See, I have more...more...more...." She held a dozen now, their petals falling like bloody raindrops.

"No!" he shouted. "No!"

"Mr. Foster, Mr. Foster—"

He lunged for the door, grabbed for the knob, missed. His hand closed over something soft—

His pillow.

He sat up, heart pounding, sweat running down his back.

The voice from his dream called his name again. "Mr. Foster, are you all right?"

Buck.

"I'm okay. Just a dream."

A nightmare!

As his heartbeat slowed, anger replaced fear. He'd find a way to deal with Rose, get her out of his dreams, out of his life.

JENNA LEANED AGAINST the squad car. Beneath the trees along the country road night lingered, but in the east the sky lightened to a murky dawn. A bird twittered, then another. Almost time.

A few feet away Wendell Blair and the two sheriff's deputies stood smoking. From their squad car came the sound of country-western music. Corey sprawled on the front seat of the HPD patrol car, mouth open, snoring. Wendell came over, opened the door, and shook him.

Corey came awake with a start, rubbed his eyes, and reached for the thermos he'd brought along. He leaned out the window. "Want some coffee?" he asked Jenna. She nodded, took the disposable cup he handed her, and sipped gratefully.

By rights she should have slept in the car coming up here, but she'd been unable to. As they'd sped through the night, her thoughts had focused on Chad, the scattered rose petals, Rose's eerie voice on the phone. She prayed Chad would be all right until she returned.

Now she cleared her mind, breathed deeply, and prepared herself for the morning to come.

One of the deputies ambled over. "Ready?"

"Ready."

He tossed his cigarette in the dewy grass. "Let's go."

Corey slid over behind the wheel, Jenna and Wendell got in. Their car fell into line behind the deputies'.

They turned onto a narrow gravel road, and Jenna leaned forward. A house came into sight, a two-story white frame with a wraparound porch. Ahead of them the squad car came to a stop. One of the men got out, came back and leaned in the window. "We'll walk from here. Surprise 'em."

They got out and headed up the drive without speaking. Their feet crunched on the gravel. Somewhere far away, a dog barked. The house before them was quiet. Franklin Reeves would be asleep. They'd have the advantage.

When they reached the yard, Jenna paused, deferring to the deputies. One of them motioned her forward, but she shook her head. "It's your jurisdiction."

"Your case."

"Right."

She climbed the porch steps, pounded on the door and peered through the window. A man shuffled into the living room, struggling into a robe. She recognized him immediately. Her heart hammered. Franklin Reeves!

He called through the door. "Who is it?"

"Police. Open up."

He came to the window and looked out. She held up her badge and pointed to it.

The door stayed shut. "What do you want?"

"We want to talk to you."

"You must be at the wrong house," he said. "Or maybe you want the owner. I'm just renting."

"Franklin Reeves?"

"Harry McClanahan," he answered.

Jenna motioned to the men, waiting on the steps. "There are five of us here. You have ten seconds to open the door before we—"

The door swung open. Weapon drawn, Jenna shouldered her way inside. Corey came in behind her. The others crowded onto the porch.

"This is an outrage." The man's voice shook. "You have no right to barge in here."

"Search warrant." One of the deputies strode forward, shoved a piece of paper at Reeves. He stared at it, then silently let it slip from his hands.

Corey caught Jenna's arm. "The kid," he whispered.

A dark-haired boy wearing a pair of baseball pajamas stood in the hallway, terror-filled eyes darting from Franklin Reeves to the police, then back. "Nicolas," Jenna breathed.

Reeves turned. "Go back to bed, Jonathan. They've come to the wrong place." The boy took a step backward. "Go!"

"No," Jenna said. Lowering her gun, she left the man to Corey and hurried to the child's side. She knelt down. "Nicolas, I'm Sergeant Wakefield. I've come to take you home."

His mouth opened, but he said nothing. His eyes swiveled to the man.

"You're frightening him. His name is Jonathan. Go back to your room, son."

The child froze.

Jenna put her hands on his shoulders. "Nicolas, look at me. You don't have to be afraid."

The boy's eyes measured her. She waited. "He calls me Jonathan," he whispered.

Reeves lurched toward the boy, but Corey shoved him back. "You have some identification, mister?"

"Of course, I do. My name is Harry McClanahan. I—"

"His name is Mr. Reeves." The childish voice was high, frightened. "He was my teacher."

"Tell me your name," Jenna said to the child.

"My name is Nicolas Morales."

Jenna rose, put her arm around Nicolas. "All right, Mr. Reeves. You're under arrest for kidnapping. You have the right to remain silent—"

Reeves covered his face and began to sob. "No, no! I'm not a kidnapper. The boy's my son. He's been lost for five years, and I found him. Don't take him away." Shaking his head, Corey took out a pair of handcuffs, pulled Reeves's hands away from his face and locked the cuffs in place.

"Jonathan," Reeves whimpered. "I'm your father. Tell them. Don't let them do this to me."

Nicolas stood, eyes wide and terrified. "Will they hurt him?"

Jenna stepped in front of the child, shielding him from the sight of the sobbing Reeves. "No. Now, let's go and get your clothes. Your family's waiting. I'm going to take you home."

She followed Nicolas into the bedroom, waited while he donned the jeans and Astros T-shirt he'd worn when Reeves had taken him. Then she took his hand. "Let's go."

The child hung back, his hand clutching Jenna's as they walked toward the living room. "I'm going to make a couple of phone calls," she explained. "Then we're going to ride to the airport in Texarkana—"

"And him—Mr. Reeves? Is he going with us?" Fear shone in the boy's eyes.

"No, we'll go in another car."

"Y-you won't let him take me away again?"

Jenna knelt and looked into his eyes. "Never."

He trailed after her while she made her calls, one to the airlines, the next to "Police Files." They'd arrange for a crew to film Nick's arrival. Then the final and most important call: to Anita Morales. "This is Sergeant Wakefield. Nicolas is coming home."

"Gracias a Dios," Anita said between sobs. "Thank God, thank God."

Jenna handed Nick the phone. "Want to say hi to your mom?"

The child took the receiver. "Mama?" He listened for a moment, then handed the phone to Jenna. "She's crying."

"He's all right, Anita," she said. "You'll see him in a few hours."

During the ride into Texarkana, she sat beside Nicolas in the back seat of the county patrol car. Every few minutes the child looked fearfully over his shoulder out the back window as if to reassure himself that Reeves wasn't following. "He won't find me again, will he?"

"No. Did he hurt you when you stayed with him?" Jenna asked.

Nick shook his head. "But he scared me. He told me I was his boy, but I knew I wasn't. Then I started to think maybe I was."

"Can you tell me what happened, how he got you to go with him?"

"I went to mail a letter, and he drove up to the mailbox and asked how school was goin'. I told him we had a science test and I thought it was gonna be pretty hard. He said he could help me because he was a teacher. I could come over to his house and he'd explain the stuff. He said he'd call my mom and tell her." He broke off and stared at the floor. "I know I'm not supposed to go anywhere with strangers," he mumbled, "but he wasn't a stranger. I guess my dad's gonna be mad."

Poor kid. Feeling guilty on top of everything. She'd let someone else talk to him about caution later. For now, he needed reassurance. "No, he won't." Nicolas looked uncertain. "I promise," she said. "Tell me what happened after you got in Mr. Reeves's car."

"We went to his house. We went inside, and he gave me some lemonade and said he'd go call Mama. And then I got awful sleepy and I woke up in the car. I was real scared. I told him I wanted to go home, but he said I was going to live with him."

Nick sniffled, and Jenna handed him a tissue. "You'll be home soon."

The flight to Houston was short. As soon as they landed, Zack came on board to take Nick into the airport and allow Jenna to avoid the cameras. But she stood off

o the side and watched Pete Morales run to Nicolas and
ift him up, then set him down beside Anita. Tears
treaming down her cheeks, Anita wrapped her arms
round the child.

"Mama, he called me Jonathan," were the child's first
vords.

Cameras from Channel 6 recorded the event. A news
eporter asked a few questions, then hurried away.

Zack waited until the television crew disappeared, then
ignaled Jenna to join him and the family. "We'll have a
loctor check Nick over tomorrow... just to be sure ev-
rything's all right."

Anita hugged the boy close. "Of course. Where?"

"Memorial Hospital. Nine-thirty."

"Yes, we'll be there." She turned to Jenna, her eyes
gain full of tears. "God bless you, Sergeant. We'll never
orget what you've done for us."

Her own heart full, Jenna hugged Anita.

As they watched the family walk away, Zack said,
'Good job, Wakefield. This is one that turned out right.
Where can I drop you?"

"At h— At Chad Foster's." She'd almost said, "At
1ome." Funny, she'd begun to think of Chad's house as
1ome. She'd have to watch that.

CHAD AND JENNA had dinner at Vargo's that night. The
arge, airy dining room looked out on a stream and gar-
lens where peacocks strolled. They shared chateaubri-
1nd and a bottle of red wine. Jenna recounted the capture
of Franklin Reeves and the reunion of Nicolas with his
amily. "What about you?" she asked. "Anything more
rom Rose?"

"One letter. She's still struggling against the bonds that
1re holding her back. She'll come to me when she can.

Meanwhile she's watching. The woman's beginning to sound like a broken record.''

"I know. I'm sorry."

"You're doing your best. On a more positive note, the final plans are in place for 'The Public Soapbox.' We've had an incredible response. Requests for tickets to Sunday's show are coming in like crazy. We've moved from a small studio to a medium-size one, and now to the biggest one we have."

"That's wonderful."

"Yeah. I'll start off the show welcoming the audience—"

"Wait a minute." She dropped her fork. "*You're* not going on the show?"

"I just said I was. Why?"

"You can't."

"Hey, it's my station's show. I can do whatever I want." He sipped his wine calmly, but his eyes dared her to disagree.

"Chad," she argued fervently, "don't you see? Rose could show up in the studio with a gun."

"Look." He set his wineglass down with a clatter. Liquid sloshed over the sides. "I'm not going to let this nut case run my life *or* dictate station policy."

"But—"

"But nothing. You heard what she said in her last letter. 'They're' still holding her back. They can do it awhile longer."

She wanted to shake him. "Chad, be sensible."

"No, *you* be sensible. If I don't appear on that show, I'll be giving Rose exactly what she wants—control over my existence. I've had enough. I won't do it anymore. Life has to go on, Rose or no Rose."

Nothing she could say or do would change his stubborn mind, she realized. "All right. I'll talk to Nate. We'll station plainclothes officers in the audience. We'll set up metal detectors—"

"Whoa! You're not going to make Channel 6 into an armed camp. No metal detectors."

"Chad—"

"Send one plainclothesman, but you're not going to subject my audience to metal detectors. That's my final word."

Jenna glared at him but said nothing except, "God, you're bullheaded." She shoved her plate away. The chateaubriand, which had melted in her mouth minutes ago, now had the appeal of an old shoe.

THE NEXT MORNING she knocked on Nate's door. "Congratulations, Wakefield," he said. "I hear you did a bang-up job on the Morales case."

"Yeah, I wrote 'Closed' on it this morning."

"And now you can put Avery Sullivan to rest."

"I'll never be able to wipe the slate entirely clean," Jenna said, "but this one helps."

"Good. What's the latest with Foster?"

"The pigheaded fool's airing a new show Sunday in front of a studio audience, and he's planning to appear. I tried to talk him out of it, but the man is stubborn enough to put a mule to shame."

"We can plant someone in the audience," Nate said, making a note.

"I told him that, and he agreed to it. What he wouldn't go along with was metal detectors. Said he wouldn't subject his audience to that."

"Hmm, I can see his point," Nate said.

"I can't. Rose could come in with a gun, take a shot at him before we could stop her—" She choked at the thought.

Nate stared at the wall for a moment, brushed a speck of lint from his sleeve, then said, "You sound like you're overreacting to this situation."

Could he read her so easily? She forced a laugh. "You know me, Nate. I always get involved with my cases."

She must have convinced him because he made no further comment, only okayed her request for a plainclothes officer.

Gracie, however, was not so easily misled. She fixed Jenna with a too-knowing gaze as they sat across from one another at lunch. "Aren't you getting . . . emotionally involved in this case?"

"I—" Jenna broke off, fiddled with a button on her uniform, then, to her own surprise, blurted, "I'm in love with him."

"Jenna, no!"

"I'm afraid so." She propped her elbow on the table, set her chin in her hand, and gazed dejectedly at her friend. "Pretty stupid, huh?"

"Have you told him?"

She snorted. "No, I'm not that stupid."

"How does he feel about you?"

She tried to shrug it off, failing miserably. "He's attracted. I'm there, after all. But he's not into long-term stuff."

"Damn! Those jerks should never have sent you over there."

"It's not anyone's fault. I fell in love with him all by myself. But," she added with a false smile, "one day soon we'll nab Rose, and I'll be outta there. It'll all be forgotten."

Gracie regarded Jenna thoughtfully. "Is that what you want?"

Jenna sighed and shook her head. "No, but it's what I'm going to get." She dropped some bills on the table and stood. "I have to get back to my office."

"Yeah." Gracie put her hand on Jenna's arm. "If you need a shoulder to lean on, you know I'm here."

"Thanks, Gracie." Together they left the restaurant and walked back to headquarters.

SUNDAY AFTERNOON Jenna paced Chad's office. He was off doing whatever last-minute things television executives did before a new show. Jenna wasn't pleased with the security. She would have liked a dozen cops here, even one for every row in the studio, a bulletproof vest for Chad, a couple of attack dogs, and someone to frisk everyone who came through the door. Instead, she had herself and one other officer.

Unable to wait any longer, she left the office and went down the hall. She stopped at the door of the accounting office. Closed. She didn't have to worry about Sandra Townes. Or did she? Sandra could always wander in and join the crowd.

Jenna headed for the studio, glancing around corners and into other offices along the way. She went in, found a spot—on the side of the room out of camera range, where she could see both the audience and the set—and leaned against a wall. She felt for the pistol tucked in the shoulder holster beneath her jacket. She was ready.

Cameramen milled around, bantering with one another. A production associate—thank goodness, not Lynn O'Donnell—checked the set.

Even though the room was cool, a trickle of sweat seeped into Jenna's blouse. A muscle twitched in her cheek. Her nerves stretched tighter by the second. If only the show were over.

At five-fifteen members of the studio audience began wandering in. Jenna shut her eyes, took a breath, and prayed.

CHAPTER FOURTEEN

JENNA OPENED HER EYES and scanned the crowd. They were excited, eager, but was any of them Rose? That blond woman wearing a bulky jacket? The exotic-looking woman with waist-length black hair and an intense gaze that made Jenna nervous? Was it fervor she saw or madness? She spotted Buck Monroe in the throng, saw him take a seat near the back.

Chad strode in, a broad smile on his face. *He's really pumped up,* she thought, and could see why a woman would fixate on him. His navy suit didn't conceal his broad shoulders and muscular body, he had a sexy, I'm-all-male grin, and his blue eyes sparkled. He drew the attention of every woman in the audience.

The crew made final preparations. Hugh McIver, the show's host, took his place on the set along with the three guests for the evening, a city council member, an official from the Texas Department of Corrections, and the president of the Montrose Area Homeowners' Association. The last seconds ticked away. The director gave the signal, and the program credits appeared on the two screens at the front of the auditorium. The announcer introduced the show.

When the credits had run, the camera focused on Chad. "Good evening, ladies and gentlemen, and welcome to the first 'Public Soapbox.' Each week we will focus on an issue of importance to the people of Houston. Our guests will be experts who present their insights on the issue to you, the audience. But we conceived this as *your* show, a forum for you as citizens to ask questions, express your views, and ultimately influence public policy. This week we will discuss the proposed halfway house for newly released prisoners in the Montrose area. In future weeks, we'll focus on zoning, juvenile crime, tourism, and public transportation. Channel 6 is excited about 'The Public Soapbox.' I think you will be, too. And now, your moderator, Hugh McIver.''

Chad acknowledged the enthusiastic round of applause, then took a seat near the front of the auditorium, facing the audience and out of camera range. But not out of pistol range.

Eyes narrowed, muscles taut, Jenna ignored the presentations and watched the audience, searching for that one person whose attention wasn't on the discussion but on Chad. If she had to, she could reach him in three seconds, knock him to the floor or shield him. But everyone in the room seemed intent on the program.

The experts' presentations ended. The moderator announced that the rest of the time would be devoted to questions and answers. Hands waved from the crowd. It was harder to watch now, with all that movement. Damn, she needed a few more sets of eyes. She regretted settling for only one officer.

A man got up and moved into the aisle. As he headed for the exit, he said something to the usher at the door, then slipped out. Jenna wiped sweat off her brow.

Five more minutes, four, three. McIver brought the program to a close. Music came up, credits rolled up the screen, and the cameras pulled back.

Before the audience left, Chad again took center stage and thanked the guests for coming. Good grief, wasn't that intro enough? Did he have to set himself up again?

When she got him alone, Jenna decided, she'd put an end to the case—she'd murder him herself.

When he finished, he beckoned to Jenna and she hurried to his side. He put his arm around her waist as they joined a group of people exiting through the side door. As they strolled out, he accepted congratulations from some of the guests.

"Great, huh?" he murmured to Jenna. "Show went off without a hitch. We're on a roll, Sarge."

"You're right. It went beautifully. And," she muttered, "I aged ten years." But it was over now. She could relax.

They went into the corridor. Members of the audience filed out after them. Others coming out the back door of the studio filled the hallway ahead of them. Everyone moved in orderly fashion toward the exit.

Jenna stood on tiptoe to check the corridor behind them. She saw someone rounding the corner, coming their way. Silhouetted by the light, the figure was only a dark shape. One of the technicians carrying equipment? Jenna strained to see. No, the figure was slight. A woman.

A woman holding a bouquet of flowers!

She shoved Chad sideways. "Get to your office. Lock the door!"

"Wha—"

Before he could finish the question, Jenna swung around. "Hold it!" she yelled. The woman turned and ran.

People blocked her path; she elbowed her way past them. "Hey, watch it!" a woman grumbled. Jenna kept moving. She didn't want to take out her gun—too many people around. Past the crowd, she began to run.

At the end of the hall, she slowed. Which way? She made a choice, tore down a corridor. Damn, she should have insisted on more security. She tripped over something, but kept running along the hall, toward the exit, into the parking lot.

People were getting into their cars and pulling out, obstructing her view. Grabbing for her weapon, she raced through the lot, dodging cars, ignoring shocked stares.

She heard a woman's shrill voice. "Look, she has a gun!"

"Probably a security guard."

She reached the back of the lot. It was shadowy here. She turned in a slow circle but saw nothing, then glanced downward. At her feet lay a long-stemmed rose. A few inches away she saw another, half crushed. Others were scattered nearby. And over there, a crumpled card. But where was Rose?

Jenna dashed back inside the station, rounded up Buck, and together the two of them searched the lot and the building. They found no one. Finally she went back to Chad's office and knocked. "It's me."

He opened the door. "What in hell happened? Was it Rose?"

"It was Rose. She was here, but she got away. We found a dozen roses in the parking lot. She was so close. Too close." Jenna realized her knees were shaking. She put her arms around Chad and held him tightly, needing to reassure herself that he was safe. They stood in silence, holding one another.

Finally Jenna said, "We'd better check with the security guard at the door. You ask the questions. I may have already blown my cover, but—"

They hurried down the hall. At the door the guard, a burly gray-haired man, sat reading a car magazine.

"Did you let in a woman carrying roses earlier?" Chad asked.

"Yes, sir."

"Was it someone you know, someone who works
re?"

"No, sir. I never saw her before. I guess she was from
lorist's."

"Can you describe her?"

The guard shrugged. "Medium height, brown hair, just
average person. She was wearing a . . . um, blue dress.
eally didn't pay much attention."

Before Chad could answer, Jenna drew him aside. "I
nt this guy down at headquarters tomorrow. We'll get
artist to come up with a drawing. Nate will take care of

"Okay." He walked back to the table. "Norman, I'd
e for you to talk to Lieutenant Nate Harris at the po-
e department tomorrow, help him come up with a pic-
re of the woman."

The guard's eyes widened. "Is something wrong?"

"We've been getting some threatening letters," Chad
id. "I just want to be on the safe side."

"Gee, Mr. Foster, I'm sorry I let her in. She looked
ay to me."

"It's all right, Norman. See you tomorrow."

As she and Chad left the building, Jenna thought she'd
en wrong earlier. She hadn't aged ten years; she'd aged
hundred. In the car, she slipped Rose's card from her
cket and strained to read.

"What does it say?" Chad asked.

She swallowed. " 'Flowers for our first and last night
gether. Love, Rose.' " Jenna held the card out to Chad.
low the signature was the penciled drawing of a dag-
r.

HE NEXT MORNING Chad sat in the control booth beside
e director of "Houston A.M.," the station's morning
lk show. The host was interviewing a local psycholo-

gist, Dr. David Frommer, who'd published a book
personality types.

"Do certain types of personalities go together bett
than others?" the talk show host asked.

"Definitely. For example, the Leader and the Icon
clast are a lethal combination. Now, the Caregiver cou
go perfectly with either."

"Why don't we take some calls?" suggested the host

Chad half dozed through several questions and a
swers. He didn't think Frommer had anything new to sa

"We have time for one more call. Go ahead, you're
the air."

"Doctor," the voice was muffled as if the caller had
mouthful of cotton, "my name is Rose."

Good God! Chad sat forward. "Are you getting that
tape?" he asked.

"Always do," the director answered around a stick
gum.

"Doctor, I have a question," the caller continued. "
two people love each other and they're both the same, li
they know everything the other is thinking or feeling
wanting, are they both the same personality type?"

"Well, I'd have to know more, but it's a distinct po
sibility. Of course, it's highly unusual for two people to t
so much alike."

"But they are. Their auras are the same, their though
are the same, and they want to be together so much they'
walk through the Valley of the Shadow of Death to get
each other."

The psychologist was clearly shaken by the conversa
tion. "Well, um, do you have another question?"

"My question is, Doctor, what if something or som
one is standing in their way? Shouldn't they do every
thing to cut that person down, even if it's unpleasant
bloody or, um, you know, fatal?"

"Miss—"

"And shouldn't *he* be the one to do it? I mean, isn't it responsibility? The man is the leader in the family. He s the God-given responsibility to cut away the weeds in e family garden—"

"I'm sorry," the host interrupted. "We're out of time."

"Commercial," the director said. He leaned back in his air and turned to Chad. "Lord, that last phone call was zarre, wasn't it?"

"Yeah," Chad muttered. Valley of the Shadow of eath? He felt like he'd been punched in the gut. "Get me at tape ASAP."

On the set, he saw that David Frommer and the host re conferring. When the commercial break was over, e host said, "One last word from our guest."

"Yes. This is a message to our last caller. Rose, I'd like talk to you again. We don't have time on the show, but re's my office number. Please give me a call and let's k some more." The number flashed on the screen, and e host brought the show to a close.

Chad hurried down to the set, shook the psycholo-st's hand. "Thanks for asking that caller to contact you. ink she will?"

"Hard to say. People like that tend to act impul-vely."

"What did you think of her question?"

"Clearly out of touch with reality."

"Could she do something violent—say, try to elimi-te her rival?"

"Possibly, or the man—if any of this is true. It could be ntasy."

Chad didn't want to tell Dr. Frommer too much, so he ttled for, "We've had similar calls recently. Sounds like e same person. I'd appreciate your letting me know if e contacts you."

"Of course. If she does, I'll do everything I can to g
her into treatment somewhere."

"Thanks. Come back again soon."

Chad went back to his office and called Jenna. She li
tened to his description of the call. "We'll watch the ta
together this evening. Be careful, Chad. Don't leave t
building."

"I have a tentative meeting at—"

"No! Cancel it!"

"Who's the plainclothes officer today? Harv? He c:
drive me."

"No! Promise me, Chad."

Reluctantly, he gave in. "All right."

Catherine came in later to hand him the day's ma
"Your fan club's growing," she remarked, handing hi
two envelopes marked "Personal."

They were, of course, from Rose. He struggled to d
cipher the almost-illegible handwriting. Both letters a
luded to "the woman."

She's a witch. She's a sorceress. She's put a spell on
you, but we'll break her power. There are ways, secret ways. I can get magic that will destroy her, but
you must be patient, my love. I must go through the
labyrinth to find it, follow the path to the place of
power. They will help me. And they will watch over
you. Then we will have the magic, and you will be the
one to use it. I will come to you. Soon.

                                        Rose, your phantom lover

Cold terror clutched at his stomach. Break her power
Destroy... Jenna? He wouldn't let that happen.

Every time the phone rang, every time he heard a knoc
on his door, his breath stopped and his heart jerked in a
uneven rhythm. He wished to hell Jenna were here. H

ısn't as concerned now about what Rose might do to
ım as he was about what might happen to Jenna.

She arrived early. Not bothering with a greeting, she
ok a chair and said, "Do you have the tape?"

"Right here, but read this first." He handed her Rose's
test letter.

Jenna scanned the sheet quickly, then switched on the
pe. She listened with complete absorption, stopping the
pe, replaying Rose's words over and over. Every time he
ard Rose's voice, thought what she might do to Jenna,
had's anxiety increased notch by notch until his nerves
ere screaming.

"Enough," Jenna said finally. "It's clearly Rose, and
e's clearly over the edge. She'll break soon."

He rewound the tape, then said, "That's what I want to
lk to you about. I want you off the case."

She flinched as if he'd slapped her. "Why?"

"Do you even have to ask? The woman's making
reats against you. She's seen us together. She wants you
stroyed, cut down." He got up and paced to the win-
w. "I didn't think of this when we started our charade.
didn't realize how dangerous this could be for you."

"I live with danger every day. Every cop does," she re-
onded coldly.

"I know that, but I sure as hell don't like thinking
out it. And *I* don't have to add to the danger. You can
t out before it's too late."

Jenna jumped up. "Forget it, Foster. I'm already com-
itted to this case. I'll see it through. Besides, Rose al-
ady knows about me. Taking me off the case won't
ange a damn thing."

He ignored her remark. "Don't you have some vaca-
on time coming? You can use it and get out of town for
while."

"No way."

Exasperated, he took her by the shoulders. "I'll talk the chief, get him to relieve you—"

She thrust his hands away. "The hell you will. This my case, Foster, and nobody—not you, not anybod else—is taking me off it." She poked at his chest. "Ur derstand?"

"Jenna—"

"Shut up, Foster. Get your briefcase. We're goin home."

They didn't speak on the way. *Okay,* Chad thought. *S she's mad. Tough.* What mattered was to protect her. it wasn't too late.

Jenna pulled into the garage, got out and slammed th car door. She stomped off, leaving Chad to shut the ga rage. As he came around the corner, he heard her voice– high, shocked. "Chad!"

He raced toward her, fists clenched, ready to defend he against Rose or anyone else. Instead, he found Jenn staring at a note taped to the front door.

Scrawled in lipstick were the words, "Get rid of her o you both will die."

"Don't touch it!" Carefully, she peeled the tape awa and slipped the paper from the door.

"That's it!" Chad jammed his key into the lock an shoved the door open.

He strode into the house, Jenna at his heels. "What ar you going to do?"

He grabbed the phone. "Call the chief."

"No, damn it—"

He pushed her away and punched in a number. "Chie Macauley. Chad Foster calling."

He waited, glowering at her while she glared back "Buster, this is Chad. This Rose business has gone too far What? No, I'm fine, but I think we need some changes i our approach. I want a meeting with you and Harris to

orrow morning. Ten-thirty? Fine. I'll see you then."
nna's mouth opened as he slammed down the receiver.
Don't say anything," he warned.

"All right, I won't. I'll save it for tomorrow. If you
ink that meeting's going to be a summit for the three of
u, you can forget it. I'm coming, too."

"Of course," he said, calmer now. He went to her and
ok her hand, holding tightly when she tried to jerk away.
Can't you understand how I feel, with Rose threatening
u?"

"How do you think I've felt from the very beginning,
owing she might go off the deep end any minute,
owing she might hurt you?"

"Not good, I suppose." He pulled her into his arms and
ried his face in her hair. "Don't make this hard for
e."

She took him by the shoulders and pushed him away.
We'll talk about it tomorrow."

They said little else to each other that evening. Jenna
nt upstairs, Chad watched television. When he went up,
s bed was empty. The door to the guest bedroom was
osed. He stood before it, hesitated, then turned the
ob. The door was locked.

Too bad, he thought. Let her be angry. No matter what,
'd keep her safe.

NNA'S ALARM WENT OFF at six. Barely awake, she
ached out and slapped the button. She rolled over to
ddle against Chad and remembered. She was in the
est room. Alone.

All that had happened yesterday came flooding back—
aad's anger, his insistence that she quit his case. Well,
ey'd see about that. She got up and went into the bath-
om to shower and dress.

Chad was at the breakfast table when she came down. She said nothing. Neither did he. She poured herself a cup of coffee. This morning she needed to be alert.

She wouldn't sit at the table with him. Instead, she stood staring out the window, listening to the ticking of the kitchen clock. She heard the rustle of the newspaper as he folded it and set it aside. "Time to leave," Chad said. "I have to stop by my office first." He picked up his briefcase from the bar.

The phone rang.

Chad answered, listened, then hung up, frowning. "Rose."

No matter what happened at the meeting this morning, Jenna was still in charge. "What did she say?"

"'You betrayed me. I saw you with her at the beach. She's shameless. She was half undressed. You will pay, and so will she.' Then she hung up." He shuddered.

"How could she have seen us at the beach?" Jenna asked. "Pictures again?"

Chad shook his head. "I picked up the snapshots one day last week, but I've been so busy with 'Soapbox' I didn't even look at them myself, much less show them to anyone." He shut his eyes and thought for a moment. "Wait. When we were by the rocks, I saw a woman walking nearby." His face paled. "God, she must have been Rose."

Jenna frowned. "I don't remember a woman."

"She was there when I took a couple of wide-angle shots. She's in them."

"Get them."

He was already on his way upstairs. He returned with an envelope containing a set of prints. He thumbed through them quickly and found several of the woman— too far away to be seen clearly, just a figure strolling along the shore.

Jenna squinted at the tiny figure. "We need these blown up."

"Yeah. We can stop at the lab on the way downtown. The office can wait." He dropped the envelope in his briefcase.

In the car they lapsed into silence. Jenna stared out the window, planning what she'd say when they met with the chief. She hadn't argued when he'd assigned her to this case, but she'd damn sure argue now. No one could protect Chad like she could.

He pulled up before the photo shop. "Wait for me in the car."

"I'm still on duty *and* still in charge." She got out and slammed her door.

Chad strode ahead of her, but she caught up. He shoved the door open and shot her an angry look as she pushed in beside him.

No one was at the counter. Chad punched the small bell that sat on one end, and a woman came in. "May I help—" She stopped and stared at them from behind a pair of glasses that magnified her pale blue eyes. Her gaze darted from Chad to Jenna and back to Chad. "You're here again," she said.

"Yeah. Back again. Listen, Martha Jean, I need some pictures blown up as large as you can make them. Could you ask the guys in the lab how long it'll take?"

The clerk nodded, then pointed at Jenna. "And you—"

"I'm with him," Jenna said.

"Yes, of course. I'll be right back." She took the pictures and went into the back of the shop.

Chad glanced at his watch. "If they can get the pictures done right away, we'll wait. If not, we'll come back later." Clearly on edge, he paced from one side of the small customer area to the other.

Jenna leaned her elbows on the counter and eyed the desk behind it. Pens, pencils, a battered typewriter. A notepad and a pad of stationery. White paper...with a red rose.

"Chad!"

"Hmm?"

"Get back. That woman—she's Rose." She grabbed for the pistol tucked in her waistband.

"What!" Chad took a step toward her, and she motioned him back, then turned, weapon in hand.

Too late. He'd distracted her for two crucial seconds.

She heard the shot, felt the impact as the bullet rammed into her shoulder, and stumbled backward. Another shot hit her arm. She sank to the floor.

Gun in hand, Rose darted around the counter. Her voice high-pitched and strong, she waved the gun at Jenna. "Whore of Babylon! He brought you here to die. Now!"

"No!" With a feral roar, Chad lunged across the tiny space, grabbed Rose around the waist and knocked her down. The gun dropped from her hands and slid out of reach.

Jenna heard voices, the sound of running feet. "Shots!" a man's voice called. "What happened?"

"Call 911," Chad shouted. "Police and ambulance. Tell them an officer's down."

"Not...down," Jenna muttered and struggled to a sitting position. She was on duty. She still had a job to do, and no matter what, she'd do it right.

A loud, keening cry pressed against her eardrums. For an instant, she thought it was her own. No, she realized, the wail came from Rose. Kicking and thrashing, the woman flailed against Chad's hold. "Traitor! You chose her—how could you? You were mine...."

Chad's grip faltered.

Jenna realized she was still holding her pistol. She released the safety and trained the gun on Rose. "Freeze! You're under arrest."

For an instant the woman stared at her, wide-eyed, dazed. Then she turned back to Chad. Face contorted, she screamed at him. "Let me go. I hate you." She kicked him again and he gasped but held on.

Jenna kicked her purse over to Chad. "Handcuffs...inside."

She fought against the pain, watched Chad fish out the handcuffs and fumble with them.

Rose tried to wriggle away. She stretched a hand toward her gun.

"Don't move," Jenna shouted, then breathed a sigh as Chad grabbed Rose's arm, pulled it back and fastened the cuffs around her wrists. Rose lay still now, whimpering quietly.

Jenna lowered the gun to her side. The room swam before her eyes. Blood soaked her sleeve and pooled around her on the floor.

Chad came and knelt beside her, his face white. "Hold on, honey. The ambulance will be here in just a minute." He lifted her slightly, sat and cradled her in his arms, then pulled a handkerchief from his pocket and tried to stop the bleeding.

"Rose..." she mumbled. "I need to...read her rights."

"Hush. Someone else will do it."

"No, I have to... wrap it up." She was getting weaker, her vision blurring, but she had to hold on. "You have...the right..." she began.

The sound of a siren outside drowned out her words. The door flew open. Two officers rushed in, pistols drawn. Seeing the situation was under control, they holstered their guns. One of them knelt by Jenna. "Wakefield!" His voice cracked. "What happened?"

"Suspect's subdued," she muttered. "Under arrest . . . assaulting a police officer. I was reading her rights—"

"Shut up, Wakefield. We'll take care of it." He rose and gestured to his partner. "Get her out of here."

Rose was hauled none too gently to her feet and hustled out the door. As Jenna watched, other squad cars pulled up outside. Within minutes the room was crowded with police. They all seemed to swarm toward her.

The room spun around. Jenna shut her eyes. Noise and confusion swirled over her. Voices, questions. "Who shot her?" "Is she okay?"

And Chad's voice, "Get back, all of you. Give her some space. Damn it, she's bleeding. Where the hell is the ambulance?" He touched her cheek. "Just a little longer, honey."

His voice sounded desperate, so she opened her eyes and made an effort to focus, to reassure him. "I'm okay."

Another siren came closer. Then footsteps. Two men with a stretcher rushed into the store. "What happened?"

Chad's voice again. "She was shot."

One paramedic knelt beside her and applied pressure to the wound. Jenna clenched her teeth against the pain. She didn't want Chad to see how much she hurt.

"Okay, ma'am. We're going to lift you onto the stretcher. It'll hurt, but just for a minute."

Jenna bit the inside of her lip. Pain surged through her entire body. The medics carried her out, through a sea of blue uniforms, past curious spectators.

When she was settled in the ambulance, Chad climbed in. He sat beside her, holding her uninjured hand.

"We . . . got her," she mumbled. "I . . . I was scared . . . to death."

"You? My fearless cop? I thought you were never afraid."

"Always," she whispered.

"So was I," Chad confided. "When I saw her coming toward you with that gun, I was terrified."

"You . . . saved my life."

"You saved mine, too."

"I—"

"Shh, honey. We'll talk later."

"Yeah." Through the haze of pain she felt Chad's hand holding hers, heard his voice murmuring things she couldn't quite catch. The wail of the siren reverberated in her head. She stared upward. The white of the ceiling seemed to blaze into her brain, so white, so dazzling she could hardly stand it. Chad's voice began to fade away. A swarm of black dots circled before her eyes. Then there was nothing but darkness.

CHAPTER FIFTEEN

JENNA OPENED HER EYES. The first thing she felt was the pain in her shoulder. The first thing she saw was Graciela's face. "Gracie," she said weakly.

"Hi. Welcome to the land of the living." She reached for Jenna's good hand. "How do you feel?"

"Like I've been shot."

"Yeah, we were all pretty worried about you. They had you in surgery for a long time." She brushed at a tear that trickled down her cheek.

"Hey, I didn't die."

Gracie sniffled. "I know, but you're the first good friend I've had who's been wounded. I guess I'm entitled to a few tears." She blew her nose. "Can I get you anything?"

"Uh-uh."

Gracie sat quietly for a while, then rose. "I'd better go. The nurse said not to tire you. Besides, I know Chad wants to talk to you."

"Is...is he here?"

"Here? Sweet pea, he hasn't left since they brought you in. He just went down to get a cup of coffee."

"Oh." Jenna fingered the sheet with her good hand. "It was nice of him to stay."

"I don't think so. He didn't act like a man who was just being nice. I got here while you were in surgery, and he looked frantic." She grinned. "When the doctor came out, Chad grabbed the poor guy's arm so hard, he almost broke it. Nope, I'd say Foster was concerned.''

"Well, that's natural," Jenna said. "He's been through a frightening experience."

"Sure." The door opened and Chad came in. "She's awake," Gracie told him and turned to Jenna. "I'm gonna run. See you tomorrow."

Chad came to the side of the bed and stood looking down at her, his expression unreadable. "Jenna." His voice cracked.

Jenna gaped at him in surprise. She'd never seen him like this. His hair was mussed, the beginnings of a beard showed on his face, his eyes were red-rimmed. His shirt was wrinkled and stained with blood. Her blood. "Sit down," she said. "You look tired."

"A little." He sat and took her good hand, holding it gently in both of his. "How do you feel?"

"I'm hurting a little."

"Shall I call the nurse?"

"Uh-uh. I imagine it's supposed to hurt some after what happened this morning." She turned her head, trying to read the clock on the night table. "What time is it?"

"One-thirty."

"But it's dark."

"One-thirty in the morning," he said. "You were in surgery a long time. The doctor says you're going to be fine, though." He lifted her hand and brought it to his lips.

The door opened and a nurse came in. "Good, you're awake." She slipped a thermometer in Jenna's mouth and took the hand Chad had been holding to check her pulse. "See," she said to Chad. "I told you she'd wake up soon. Now *you* need to get out of here and get some sleep."

"Yeah, I'll do that." He waited while the woman checked the reading on the thermometer and took Jenna's blood pressure. When she left the room, he bent and kissed Jenna's cheek. "I'm going to go sack out. I'll see you."

When? she wondered as she watched him go. *Someday?* Now that he knew she was all right, he didn't have to come back to the hospital. He could get on with his life, free of Rose. Maybe he'd think once in a while about the cop who'd been his pretend love interest, maybe not.

She'd get on with her life, too. The memories would be enough. They'd have to be. She would hear his laugh, remember the way he slept with his cheek pillowed on his hand, the way he kissed....

She shut her eyes. For the rest of the night she slept off and on. The doctor came early in the morning and checked her shoulder, said she'd come through the surgery very well. A nurse's aide gave her a sponge bath. A young man delivered flowers—thankfully not roses—from the Juvenile Division. The nurse gave her something for pain that made her sleep again.

By lunchtime she felt better. When Gracie came in, Jenna had the bed raised and was eating a pasta salad. They talked for a while, then Gracie said, "I have something to show you. I thought I'd wait until you were awake enough to be properly surprised." She lifted her hand and flashed an engagement ring.

"Jorge," Jenna said.

"Who else? We're getting married Labor Day weekend."

Jenna reached for her friend's hand. "This is wonderful news." They talked about wedding dresses until Gracie had to leave.

Shortly after, Nate came to see her, looking big and uncomfortable in the hospital room. "You did good, Wakefield," he told her. "The chief's pleased."

Jenna nodded. "Big case solved. Good for his image."

"Yeah. You've been in on two big ones. He won't for-
t." He paused a minute, frowning at her. "How are you
ing, really?"

"Fine. I'm fine."

"They booked Rose—Martha Jean Backus is her real
me. She'll end up in a psychiatric ward, I imagine."

"That's good. She needs help."

"From what we could piece together she was pretty in-
herent—Chad was a regular customer. He'd talk to her,
d her when he came in, and she misinterpreted it."

"Easy to do," Jenna said in a tone that had Nate
owning again. "Anyway, I'm glad it's over." She *was*
ad, for Chad's sake.

After Nate left, she turned on the television and
atched a couple of soap operas. Then she slept again,
d woke late in the afternoon when Chad came in. She
as surprised to see him. And happy.

"Feeling better today?" he asked.

"Yeah, but I want to get out of here. Another day and
l be stir-crazy."

He grinned. "I talked to the doctor this afternoon. He
id you can go home day after tomorrow."

She was about to ask what else the doctor had said
hen a knock sounded on the door. "Come in," she
lled.

Corey Phillips walked into the room. He stopped at the
ot of the bed. "Hi, Jenna. How're you feeling?"

"Okay." She introduced him to Chad.

"You're the guy from the stalker case."

"Yeah. Here, why don't you sit down?" Chad relin-
ished his chair and went to the window. He leaned a hip
gainst the sill and listened as Corey caught Jenna up on
vision news.

After a while, Corey stood. "I'd better go and let you
t some rest." He bent to kiss her cheek.

Chad pushed himself away from the window an
moved toward the bed.

"When you're on your feet again, I'll call you," Core
said.

Chad took another step, planted himself beside the be
and put a proprietary hand on Jenna's uninjured shou
der.

Corey continued. "Maybe we can take in a movie...."

Chad shot Corey a lethal look that had him steppin
back.

Jenna stared from Chad to Corey as the two me
measured one another. "Give me a call, Corey."

"Yeah." He backed away another step. "See you." H
turned and hurried out of the room.

Jenna glared at Chad. "What was that about?"

"What?"

"You know what I'm talking about. Whatever was go
ing on between you two." She gave a disgusted snort
"*You* looked like a lion with a piece of meat."

Chad shook his head. "Like a man with the woman h
loves."

Her mouth opened. "Wh-what?"

He sat beside the bed, took her hand, and brought it t
his lips. "You heard me, Sarge."

"I'm not sure. Maybe you should say it again."

"All right. I love you. Have for a long time."

"You never said—"

"I was afraid. The situation we were in—you have t
admit it wasn't normal. I wanted to wait until it was over
until I could be sure of myself. But when I saw you lyin
there in a pool of blood, when I saw Martha Jean wit
that gun, I knew what you meant to me. If you'
been—" His voice broke.

Jenna squeezed his hand. "Chad."

"I want you to come home with me to stay. Forever.
an and wife. Till death do us part."

She couldn't seem to get her breath. "Chad, I . . ."

He dug in his pocket, pulled out a box. "I brought you
mething. Actually, I bought it a long time ago."

She opened the box. The ring they'd seen at The Gal-
ria. He slipped it on her finger. "It'll do for now as an
gagement ring, until we can get the real thing."

She stared at the ring sparkling on her finger, then
oked into eyes that were filled with love. "I don't know
hat to say."

He grinned. "Say yes, you love me. And yes, you'll
arry me."

Suddenly her breath returned. "Yes," she said. "And
s." She reached up, put her good arm around his neck,
d pulled him down to her for a long, sweet kiss.

HARLEQUIN®

Deceit, betrayal, murder

Join Harlequin's intrepid heroines, India Leigh and Mary Hadfield, as they ferret out the truth behind the mysterious goings-on in their neighborhood. These two women are no milk-and-water misses. In fact, they thrive on

MISCHIEF & MAYHEM

Watch for their incredible adventures in this special two-book collection. Available in March, wherever Harlequin books are sold.

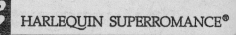

HARLEQUIN SUPERROMANCE®

The Wrong Twin
by Rebecca Winters

Abby Clarke is unmarried, unemployed and pregnant—but she's not *really* on her own. Not while she's got her twin sister, Kellie.

Kellie insists that Abby go to her husband's ranch in Montana for a few weeks' rest—but she insists that Abby go *in Kellie's place.* Despite Abby's reluctance, Kellie manages to convince her.

Then Kellie disappears. And Abby is left trying to explain to Max Sutherland why he's come home to find the wrong twin in his bed—a woman who looks exactly like his estranged wife. A woman who's pregnant with another man's child...

Rebecca Winters is an award-winning romance author known for her dramatic and highly emotional stories. The Wrong Twin will be available in March, wherever Harlequin books are sold.

HARLEQUIN SUPERROMANCE®

ADAM THEN AND NOW
by
Vicki Lewis Thompson

It's been twenty years since Loren Montgomery last saw Adam Riordan, and a lot has happened since. For one thing, Adam now has an eighteen-year-old daughter named Daphne—the name Adam and she once dreamed would belong to *their* daughter. And Loren has a son, Joshua—the name they'd chosen for the son they'd hoped to have.

Is history about to repeat itself? There's no doubt that the kids are attracted to each other—a development Loren isn't entirely happy about. There's also no doubt that the chemistry between Adam and Loren is just as strong as it was when *they* were teens. All Adam has to do is convince Loren that sometimes dreams are simply put on hold....

REUNITED!
First Love...Last Love

Available in March, wherever Harlequin books are sold.

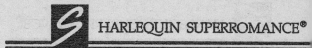